"Striker to Eagle One, do it!"

Mack Bolan dived for cover behind the guard shack just seconds before the front gate erupted in intense flame, the blast from the LAW rocket tearing the heavy gates from their hinges.

The Executioner got to his feet and sprinted unchallenged through the gap. A few guards sniped at him on his approach to the hacienda, but no one came close. He reached his vantage point and decided to generate some heat of his own.

Up until now he'd been forced to take the actions of others into consideration. Not anymore.

The gloves were off. Now the enemy would have to play by *his* rules.

Don Pendleton's Mack Bolan®

Ultimate Stakes

A GOLD EAGLE BOOK FROM

WORLDWIDE®

TORONTO • NEW YORK • LONDON
AMSTERDAM • PARIS • SYDNEY • HAMBURG
STOCKHOLM • ATHENS • TOKYO • MILAN
MADRID • WARSAW • BUDAPEST • AUCKLAND

First edition September 2006

ISBN-13: 978-0-373-61513-1
ISBN-10:   0-373-61513-2

Special thanks and acknowledgment to
Jon Guenther for his contribution to this work.

ULTIMATE STAKES

Printed in U.S.A.

There are a thousand hacking at the branches of evil to one who is striking at the root.
> —Henry David Thoreau

I will strike at the root of those who prey on the innocent. If others choose to stand idly by and do nothing, it makes little difference. The job will be done.
> —Mack Bolan

To the men and women of the
Drug Enforcement Administration

PROLOGUE

Quito, Republic of Ecuador

The day had started as any other for Senator Mario Esposito; awake by 5:30 a.m.; shower and shave; two poached eggs, half a grapefruit and decaf coffee. The only thing that made this day special was his meeting with President Reynaldo Gustavo and his advisory cabinet. Esposito dressed in his best suit and proceeded to the suite's foyer to meet four big men. Esposito knew each of the bodyguards personally. He'd handpicked them from a team of semiretired agents he'd known from his days riding the South American desk as a CIA analyst.

Of course the young, well-dressed man who greeted him as he stepped off the elevator had quite a number of his own escorts; there were no choirboys in that crew. In fact, their five-hundred-dollar suits, dark sunglasses and slicked hairdos made them look more like a gang of hired thugs than executive security. Then again, it occurred to him that maybe this was exactly the kind of look they were going for.

Hernando Gustavo's appearance was certainly more debonair than that of his bodyguards. Gustavo was a little taller than his father, maybe five-foot-ten, with soft brown eyes and short, neat hair. Esposito had met the man once before, although it had been a few years, and as they shook he noted the soft, manicured hand that weakly clamped his own.

"Senator Esposito, it's certainly nice to see you again," Gustavo said with a plastic smile.

"Likewise, sir," Esposito replied. More formally he added, "May I extend my compliments on behalf of the President and the United States of America."

"You're too kind," Gustavo replied in a tone that said he thought anything but that. He gestured in the direction of the waiting limousine, visible through the revolving glass doors of the hotel. "My father waits. Shall we go?"

While Esposito didn't like the younger man's attitude, he could understand it. Before the Proctor Initiative—the rather extensive trade agreement he was here to negotiate with President Gustavo—terms between the two countries hadn't been friendly. There were those who preferred the U.S. stay out of Ecuadorian affairs entirely, and Hernando Gustavo had certainly not hidden his past support of this position. Still, his father had a tremendous influence over him and had convinced his impressionable offspring to offer to escort Esposito to the talks being held at the presidential estate.

"You understand the reason for my staying here at a hotel and not having you pick me up at the U.S. Embassy?" Esposito asked as they walked toward the exit.

Gustavo nodded. "My father was very clear on the importance of security. That's why I brought so many men. And of course, our limousine is equipped with all the latest in protective measures."

Esposito nodded and said, "Well, it sounds as if you've thought of everything."

"Your safety is our number-one concern, Senator," Gustavo said.

Two guards from each crew pushed through the revolving door first and took positions on the street before allowing their charge to emerge from the hotel. That's when it all became a blur for Esposito. The first thing he felt was something hard and forceful strike his briefcase. A moment after that he felt his knee give out. At almost the same moment he watched as the heads of the two bodyguards who'd taken point exploded. Then he collapsed as his right leg burned and seemed no longer able to support his weight.

In the next second, as he realized he'd been shot, Esposito watched as both of Gustavo's bodyguards met the same fate as his own. The CIA-analyst-turned-diplomat had enough sense through the pain to reach out and yank on Gustavo's pant leg, upending him from his stiff-legged stance and dumping him to the pavement. At least the sidewalk in front of the armored limo offered cover over standing upright and petrified.

The bodyguards who brought up the rear nearly

jammed themselves inside the revolving door to reach their clients. Once outside they reacted with the speed and timing of solid professionals, working in concert with each other to take their clients out of harm's way. One of Gustavo's men ripped open the limo door. Esposito suddenly felt strong hands slide between his armpits and lift him quickly but carefully off the ground. He moaned at the stabbing pains that ran through his leg, but he knew the alternative was death.

The bodyguards tossed him headlong into the rear seat of the limo, one following to lie on top of him as a shield. Moments later Esposito felt tugging and bumping and yelling and general hysteria as Gustavo followed. Only after the driver put the limousine in gear and roared away from the scene did Esposito hear the back door close.

"Get off me," he said, barely able to get the words out as the weight of the bodyguard nearly suffocated him.

"Shut up and stay still," Warren Travis replied.

Esposito held his tongue. Travis was actually the best of the four men and knew what the hell he was talking about. If he chose to stay in that position, then Esposito was confident he had a damned good reason for it. They could argue the what-fors and where-nows later.

"What the hell is going on?" Gustavo asked in Spanish.

Esposito finally noticed Gustavo's face directly across from him, pressed into the opposite seat in much the same way as his own. One of Gustavo's men was covering the young man like Travis covered Esposito.

Unfortunately that cover didn't last because the limousine suddenly lurched to a stop. Brakes squealed. The force threw Travis off Esposito and onto the floor between the seats.

"What—?"

Travis never completed the outburst. The window of the limousine separating the driver's compartment lowered and a passenger in the front seat shot him through the head with a short burst from a machine pistol. Gustavo's bodyguard reared back, clawing for hardware beneath his jacket, but he never even cleared it from shoulder leather. The assassin shot him point-blank in the forehead. The man's head exploded with the unforgiving muzzle force, dousing the limousine's clean and stark interior with blood and brain matter.

Esposito tried to twist into a sitting position, but the passenger directed the machine pistol in his direction. Smoke still wisped from its muzzle as the ironlike odor of blood mingled with spent gunpowder permeated the interior. Esposito realized his ears were ringing with the reports.

"Ah-ah," the gunman warned. In Spanish he continued, "Don't move from that spot. I know all about the little piece you carry beneath your pant leg. My orders are not to kill either of you, but I need only one of you alive. And since Señor Gustavo is not wounded prey, that would make you the prime candidate."

"Orders from whom?" Gustavo asked.

The man's smile chilled Esposito. "You will know soon enough."

Their captor's knowledge of Esposito's personal habits stunned him. On most occasions he did carry a Hungarian-made PA-63 in an ankle holster. He'd opted to leave it at the hotel on this trip so as not to alarm security at the presidential estate. It wouldn't smack of good diplomatic relations to set off the metal detectors in the home of the president of Ecuador any more than it would to come armed to the signing table. Well, his captors would eventually search him and discover he was unarmed.

At some point in the last minute Esposito realized the limo had started to move again, this time traveling at a frenetic but unimpeded pace as the driver weaved through morning traffic. From his position, he could no longer discern in which direction they were headed. Not that it mattered. He wasn't going anywhere fast, particularly not with a bullet hole in his leg. Esposito calmly reached back and felt for an exit hole. He found one and breathed a sigh of relief through clenched teeth. At least that lessened the chance of dying from infection.

"You aren't going to get away with this," Gustavo said.

"On the contrary," the gunman replied. "I believe we already have."

Gustavo snorted. "You think you can hide? This is a presidential limousine. They're probably tracking it as we speak."

"Oh, I'm sure they're tracking a limousine, but I can assure you it's not this one. The limousine they're tracking is presently bound for the nearest hospital, which is of course where our man told us it was headed." The man expressed faux sorrow and in a mocking tone added, "After all, they have a wounded VIP from the United States on their hands. We wouldn't want to create an international incident."

Esposito believed their captor, although he couldn't figure at that point how they had managed such a ruse. They had probably switched the vehicles using an inside contact. The CIA had never classified security within the Ecuadorian government as first-rate by any stretch of the imagination, but to pull off something of this magnitude would have required the devices of a traitor high up within the government.

"My country will never cooperate with terrorists," Esposito said. He attempted to keep the accusation out of his voice, so as not to agitate the man.

Despite the cautionary approach, a look of resolute wickedness shadowed the man's countenance. "My people are not terrorists. Our aims are not so self-indulgent. We have a much greater mission than terrorism."

"I trust you don't plan to use that at your trial when they charge you with kidnapping and murder."

"What makes you think there shall be a trial?" The man snorted. "Even if the Ecuadorians were to take us alive, which I can assure you is only a remote possibility, there will be no trial. They would simply hang us."

Perhaps the man hadn't realized it, but he'd betrayed a telltale clue as to his identity. He had mentioned "the Ecuadorians" and that belied the fact he wasn't from Ecuador. Based on that fact, plus the dialect he used and his features, Esposito made him as Colombian. That meant either political insurgents or drug-runners. The former CIA analyst wouldn't be able to make a firm decision until he heard more.

He tried to keep the gunman talking, but the guy ignored him, shaking his head to indicate he wouldn't speak further. His glare told Esposito he'd be wise to do the same. In any case it didn't matter. He had enough to go on right now, and since he couldn't do anything about the current situation he figured it was better to gather as much information as possible. Perhaps the leadership would be more amenable to discussing their motivations. At least it would provide a necessary distraction.

He could only hope his country would send someone to rescue him.

CHAPTER ONE

Mack Bolan divided his attention between dual LCD computer monitors as he tuned out the drone of the Learjet 36A engines.

One monitor displayed the picture of a young, dark-haired man alongside a complete CIA dossier on him. The other monitor showed split-screen images of Harold Brognola and Barbara Price as taken by real-time cameras in the Communications Room of the Annex at Stony Man Farm. Bolan knew all of those images were being sent via a secure-satellite carrier wave, one small demonstration of the advanced technology at the disposal of the Stony Man cybernetics capabilities helmed by Aaron "The Bear" Kurtzman and his crack team of high-tech cyberwizards.

"The guy you're looking at is Senator Mario Esposito, head of the oversight committee to the White House for South American affairs," Brognola said.

"Says he used to be CIA," Bolan said as he probed the dossier.

"Yes," Brognola replied. "He worked a desk in Ecuador for three years as an analyst, which is ultimately how he came to his present position."

Bolan shook his head. "CIA to high-profile politics isn't a switch you see often."

"It's definitely less frequent than it used to be," Brognola added.

No doubt there. The face of America's political infrastructure had changed since Father Time rolled her into the twenty-first century. The increased number of terrorist acts against the U.S. had left many in clandestine operations wanting out of the game entirely. Retirement to the quiet life rather than a romp in the political hotbed held a lot more appeal. It said a lot when guys like Esposito moved up with the hope they could make things better for America and her allies.

"In either case," Brognola continued, "I appreciate your letting us get you on short notice."

"You said the Man brought this down," the Executioner replied. "He doesn't pull my chain often, so I figured it's important. What's the angle?"

Barbara Price answered. "Pretty straightforward, Striker. About twelve hours ago, Esposito and the guy you see on the other screen now were kidnapped from outside a hotel in downtown Quito."

"Inside job?"

Price nodded. "They somehow switched out one of the presidential limousines with a knockoff," she continued. "All the vehicles in the presidential fleet are well-armored and tracked by GPS with backups that are a lot like the antitheft systems you see today."

"Any idea how they did it?"

"Unfortunately not," Brognola said. "We're having a lot of trouble getting President Gustavo to talk. He's concerned that if he permits outside involvement it will mean goodbye Hernando."

"That's the party line anyway," Price added. "Only problem with that theory is it's been quite a while now and neither a ransom demand nor a set of terms have been sent."

Bolan scratched his jaw and considered that for a moment. "They could be sweating him out, but that seems weak. Whoever snatched these two went to the trouble of using insiders. That usually carries big risks and a high price tag. If this were about money or politics, my guess is they'd have already made their demands. There's obviously something bigger going on."

"You could be more right than you know," Brognola replied. "You want to give him the details, Barb?"

"As you may know," Price said, "Ecuador has a significant petroleum resource at its disposal, and in recent years this has accounted for nearly half its export earnings. Since gas prices here have continued to rise and the American public is screaming for help, the diplomats have been asking the Saudis to moderate negotiations with OPEC in the hope of soliciting some relief sanctions. Unfortunately the Arab world at large isn't budging, given America's foreign policy on terror."

"So prices stay up until we let up off terrorist necks," Bolan said with a nod. "Typical."

"Right. About six months ago, the Oval Office opened a dialogue with Ambassador Lucio Fuertes at his Washington chancery. A good number of the general consulates at offices throughout the U.S. have been begging for American intervention. Much of Ecuador's economy started destabilizing back in the late nineties, and at the suggestion of some very bright people, implementing the U.S. dollar as recognized currency restored stability and resulted in one of the first truly legit presidential elections in years.

"Since Reynaldo Gustavo took office, he's abated many of the economic and foreign relations crises in Ecuador. What he's been unable to do is weed out the corruption within his own government, even among his cabinet officials. It's believed that much of what's decided with regards to internal politics is driven by the hand of crime syndicates, particularly the money-laundering operations."

"So you think whoever kidnapped Esposito and Gustavo is politically motivated by organized crime factions," Bolan concluded.

"It's the strongest theory we have going for us, and it just happens to fit a number of the facts."

"What kind of deal was Esposito supposed to broker?"

"No bargaining was going to be necessary. Ecuador jumped at the chance. They were going to sign it that day after review. It was a trade agreement called the Proctor Initiative," Brognola replied. "It's the brainchild of a popular congressman from Texas named Frederick Proctor."

Bolan nodded. "I know the name. He fits into some pretty big circles with the Texas Oil Barons Association."

"That's probably an understatement," Brognola said, chuckling. "TOBA is the big circle as far as any native Texan is concerned. When we first got wind all this was going down, I had Aaron and Barbara start digging through everything about them we could get our hands on. Just so we were prepared. TOBA stands to make a lot of money from this deal."

"So that rules them out as the culprits, anyway."

"Right. I was so concerned about the risks here, I contacted the Man and offered to send Able Team along as Esposito's security detail."

"He passed," Bolan said.

"He didn't want to risk exposing them to media scrutiny. It was a fairly high-profile thing once the word got out, but they chose for security reasons not to announce it until just a few hours before the meet was to take place. I guess they figured that would be sufficient."

"Which is just another fact that says inside job," Price said.

"I suppose it's safe to assume we dangled some big carrots in this deal."

"Of course," Brognola said. "Cheaper petroleum and rights of first refusal will always come with a hefty price tag. That and the fact that the tap was supposed to start flowing within forty-eight hours after the agreement was signed. In return, we provide long-term advisers to help them improve their refining techniques, and all the latest gadgets and high-tech equipment to sweeten the pot. That was our major card."

"We're also sending political consultants to assist with their infrastructure, maybe help clean up some of the corruption," Price said. "Oh, and there's a small team of antinarcotics specialists out of Miami-Dade's DEA branch who were to spend a few months in Quito helping local police better manage the illegal flow of drugs from Colombia and Peru."

"Okay, for the moment let's just say your theory is right, and this is some major money-laundering group behind this," Bolan said. "That means we'd have to assume the target was Gustavo's son. Why bring Esposito into it?"

"We think they saw an opening and figured to kill two birds with one stone," Brognola said with a shrug. "Maybe they wanted to increase their bargaining power."

"No dice," Bolan said. "We've already agreed there are no monetary or political motivations since the kidnappers haven't contacted anyone. You can also rule out a terrorist group for many of the same reasons."

"Not to mention that terrorists know American policy on negotiations," Price added. She winked at the Executioner. "Are you thinking what I think you're thinking?"

"If you realize this whole time everyone's assumed the target was Hernando Gustavo, then yes," Bolan said.

"You think it's Esposito they were after?" Brognola asked incredulously.

"Yeah," Bolan said. "We probably have it backward. I think they wanted to make sure Esposito didn't make his appointment, and Gustavo was the bonus."

"But why?" Price asked. "It doesn't make any sense."

"Not to mention we have a truckload of intelligence on Mario Esposito," Brognola added. "We combed through every scrap of information on his affiliations in South America, both during his time as an analyst and those things that led up to his present post. There's nothing we can find that suggests even a remote impropriety."

"And you're probably right," Bolan countered. "I'm sure Esposito's clean. Look, I won't argue money-laundering's not a big racket in Ecuador. But let's think about who else might benefit from insuring something like this trade agreement doesn't happen."

"Such as?" Price asked.

"Drug-runners. It's always been easy for Colombians to use Ecuador as crime central because of corruption among government officials and the inefficiencies of law enforcement. Now you're talking about major U.S. involvement in a number of operations that are very tightly linked. That's bound to get a lot of people mad, but especially the drug-runners. Many times these various elements are at least in bed with each other."

"Which could explain why possibly our original theory still has some merit," Brognola concluded.

"Precisely," Bolan said. "Now if you've already got a cover worked up for me, then I'll go with it. But I may need some running room on the other side, which means freedom to call the ball or to change the game at my discretion."

"We can accommodate whatever you have in mind," Price said. "We decided not to let President Gustavo or any other officials know that you're in-country. You'll be using the Colonel Brandon Stone cover, but retired and now working as a private security consultant. You should be able to move throughout the area with autonomy. There's not exactly a shortage of white faces in Ecuador, not to mention that a few American greenbacks can take you a long way."

"Sounds good," Bolan said. "I'll go with it and get back to you as soon as I know something."

"Understood," Brognola replied.

MARIO ESPOSITO WOKE to a dark and dank world. A fog of pain swirled inside his head. As his eyes adjusted, he noticed the light that spilled through the small barred window set into a wall far above his head. Beyond that window he could hear the music and drunken laughter of men. Occasionally he detected the playful outcry of a woman, but all of it boiled down to little more than a mishmash of riotous noise for Esposito.

"Hernando?" he called, hearing the hoarseness in his own voice. He licked dry lips with a sandpaper tongue.

After sitting in silence for a time, he realized he wasn't feeling much pain from his bullet wounds. He reached down and felt something thick and heavy wrapped around his leg. Bandages, perhaps? He couldn't really tell, because something that felt like leather restraints bound his hands and feet and permitted very little movement. The thirst, nausea and lack of pain told him that his captors had probably drugged him. The last thing he could recall was the dangerous limousine passenger watching, keeping his gun trained on him and Gustavo.

What happened beyond that he couldn't know; he might never know. How many hours had he been out? He looked at his left wrist but his watch was gone. He saw that his suit jacket had been removed, which had held his wallet and credentials. In fact, he noticed his captors had stripped his clothes and replaced them with a khaki shirt and pants. Something covered his feet that felt like slippers or those thin booties they issued in hospitals.

Esposito figured he was strapped to some sort of restraint device in a dungeon of sorts. Over the noises of partying, he heard the occasional sounds of birds and soft, steady rainfall. He knew those sounds well. They were the sounds of the jungle. So he was probably destined to rot away in this godforsaken jungle prison at the hands of a brutal and merciless enemy. It might have been a fate he expected while working for the CIA but not while acting as a foreign-relations diplomat. Yet, he cursed himself for not having been prepared for this kind of action. He definitely had enemies.

Esposito turned his head at the sound of a heavy door scraping on the floor. Near the window a new light source poured through the doorway and illuminated concrete steps descending into the bowels of his dungeonlike prison. It was then that Esposito realized the window was actually set into the wall just above the steps. Four men came through the doorway and headed down the stairwell. Three of them were dressed in jungle camouflage fatigues, black berets and boots. Submachine guns dangled from straps slung across their shoulders. Two men carried what appeared to be small camping lanterns.

The fourth man was dressed in slacks, a white silk shirt and leather shoes. His hair was dark and wavy, molded to perfection against a chiseled, tanned complexion. As they reached the bottom of the steps and approached, Esposito could see that expensive rings adorned his fingers. He wore a gold watch and as the bobbing lights danced across his face Esposito noticed a diamond stud in the left ear. When the man came close enough, Esposito couldn't conceal his shock at the sight of that face.

"My God," he whispered. "Adriano Rivas."

The man smiled. Under other circumstances it would have been ingratiating. Rivas had a reputation as a lady-killer, although his sexual appetite for young boys was no secret. He was said to be gregarious and charming, kind to guests and strictly well-mannered. He was also one of Colombia's largest drug dealers and believed to have been responsible for the deaths of at least fifty people: lawyers, doctors, women, children, competitors and law-enforcement officials were just some of those who could be numbered as victims of Adriano Rivas.

"You know me," Rivas said. "How nice. It would seem formal introductions are unnecessary."

"Of course I know you," Esposito replied, expressing horror. "Anybody who's somebody in Ecuador should know you. But you're…alive."

"Oh, yes, Mr. Esposito," Rivas said. "Or I guess it's Senator now, is it not?"

"But that's impossible. I saw the pictures of your dead body. I read the reports from the medical examiner that confirmed it was your DNA found at that processing lab."

"Ah, yes, you're referring to the photographs I arranged for circulation." Rivas looked toward the ceiling, making an exaggerated show of recollection. "The DNA was a bit trickier, of course, but we managed to pull it off. Do you realize how severely underpaid doctors are in Ecuador? That entire setup cost me quite a bit of money. I had to either bribe or to eliminate a good number of people to fake my death. It was a most traumatic time for me."

He looked at his guards, slapping one on the shoulder. The men laughed in unison as if someone held up a cue card.

"I had such a sense of loss when I read of my death in the papers," Rivas continued. "In fact, I experienced an identity crisis. I thought perhaps I would have to seek therapy, but then I realized I couldn't do that. I was dead."

More laughter.

"And those poor, unfortunate souls to whom I paid all that money had to die. I could not have loose ends."

Rivas shook his head in mock regret. "What a terrible waste, but at least the widows were taken care of."

"Yes. I can see you're all torn up about it." Rivas didn't hide his amusement at Esposito's glib remark. "What the fuck do you want with me, Rivas? And why all the deception?"

"I have my reasons for wanting the rest of the world to think me dead," Rivas said. "I let too many people get close to me. The police had all but managed to convince my siblings to turn on me, and I'd made a number of enemies among U.S. military units. I had to let things quiet down some."

Esposito knew about that. The local authorities in Quito had used a number of pressure tactics, many less than legal, to get Rivas's brother and sister to turn on him. The pair had been living and working together, running the family hotel business actually owned by Adriano Rivas and funded by his illegal drug trade. At the time of his "death," Rivas had all but cornered the market on the coca product smuggled out of Colombia and through the port city of San Lorenzo on the northwest border.

Esposito had to admit that Rivas had done an excellent job. Most of those within the interior ministries of Ecuador and Colombia had considered the death of Rivas a major blow to the drug market. They had then turned their focus to other avenues, figuring Rivas's fall would stem the tide of drug exports and convince any competitors to go for more legitimate business aims. In fact, many of them did go legit or got out of the game entirely.

Rumor had recently cropped up that some new power

lurked, but it was little more than rumor, and local authorities swore there was no indication of a larger drug network starting up again. They complained more about problems with drugs internally circulated among the population than drug exports. Obviously, Rivas had somehow maintained his income, which meant he was still exporting the white death to other countries.

Esposito was betting America was still number one on Rivas's list of top customers.

"You can't stay dead forever," Esposito said, scoffing at Rivas's bravado attitude. "Sooner or later someone's going to figure out you're still alive and then they're going to come find you and do the real job."

"Tough words for a man who probably won't live to see the end of this week."

Esposito swallowed hard but tried to conceal his fear. "If you're going to kill me, then I'd advise you just do it now and get it over with. I'm not going to talk and I'm not going to help you, so you're wasting your time."

Rivas burst into an uncontrolled fit of laughter. His men stood by and smiled dutifully. After he regained control, Rivas said, "You think too much of yourself, Senator. I have no intention of interrogating you. And to torture you would only be out of whimsy or for the purpose of entertainment. No, you're important to me but not in the way you might think."

"Sure I am," Esposito said. He knew he risked insulting or angering Rivas, but he needed to keep the guy talking. The first rule the CIA had taught him when escape wasn't possible was to get as much information as possible. All of that intelligence might prove useful if the opportunity for escape did arise.

"You don't believe me?" Rivas asked. "You are no good dead to me, I can assure you, Senator. That's why I ordered my men to take you alive. That's why I went to such trouble to insure we could take you alive. The wound you suffered to your leg was an unfortunate accident. Totally unintentional. I can assure you that the man who shot you has been dealt with."

"Really," Esposito deadpanned.

"Yes." Rivas winked at one of his men. "Lunch for the alligators, eh, Chico?"

The man called Chico smiled with a snappy nod and knowing expression.

Rivas looked at Esposito with intense brown eyes. "Who do you think took care of your leg? My own personal physician patched you up. Yes, you are valuable to me alive for now, my friend. But don't think you can't outlive your usefulness. If you try to escape, my men have orders to kill you. Now, get some rest."

"Wait a minute."

Rivas had started to turn but stopped and looked back. "Yes?"

"Where's Hernando Gustavo? If you do anything to him, his father will hunt you down and destroy you."

"Your friend is fine. You will join him again soon. For now I want to keep you separated. You are each valuable to me in your own way."

"Why? You still haven't told me why you're doing this, Rivas."

"All in good time, Senator, all in good time," Rivas replied as he crossed to the stairs and ascended them, his men fore and aft. Fortunately they had left one of the lanterns behind so Esposito wouldn't have to sit in utter darkness. "I will have food and water brought to you. Good evening, Senator."

The door clanged shut.

Esposito's mind still reeled from the complications surfacing with this latest discovery. The thought that Rivas was behind this kidnapping didn't make a bit of sense to him. He couldn't see what the drug dealer had to gain, except maybe using them as a bargaining tool with the Ecuadorian government. Still, he'd gone to great lengths to fake his death and now he'd risk revealing himself? Didn't make sense.

Esposito considered his situation, which on the surface seemed absolutely hopeless. He imagined they were somewhere in the Colombian jungle, probably near the border of Ecuador. The chance of anyone finding him out here was slim. For now, he would eat and regain his strength, and decide the best way to escape his bonds. Even if he could get out of his restraints and manage to slip past security, he wouldn't go far on a bum leg. If he managed to find young Gustavo, he stood a better chance of escape. Maybe they could steal some transportation. Best he could do now was watch for openings and seize an advantage if the opportunity presented itself.

Until then, he had plenty to think about: like the fact Adriano Rivas was alive!

CHAPTER TWO

Jack Grimaldi, ace pilot for Stony Man Farm, studied the Executioner with a wry grin. He'd known his friend for so long he could damn near predict his every move to the letter.

Sure, Bolan was methodical, but there was much more to him than that. He had an aura of command authority and a mental and physical discipline unlike any other man Grimaldi had ever known. He watched as Bolan mechanically shrugged into a leather shoulder holster and then checked the action on his Beretta 93-R before nesting it beneath his left armpit. Twin clips of subsonic 9 mm Parabellum rounds rode in specially designed quick-release straps under the opposite arm. Some additional tools of the trade were spread across the bed in their hotel room, but for now Bolan had elected to go solo with the Beretta on this first step of his mission.

Grimaldi felt big-time empathy for the soldier. Bolan

was operating off scant information. He was about to wade through the scum of the city in hopes of getting a lead on the whereabouts of Esposito and Gustavo, but even worse, he had to do it without raising the attention of local authorities. As Grimaldi understood it, the government of Ecuador didn't even know they were in-country. They had to keep a low profile, and that wasn't easy for a gringo in this part of the world, even one where a white face wasn't uncommon.

"From what you told me, it doesn't sound like you have much to go on, Sarge," Grimaldi said. "Where do you plan to start looking?"

Bolan fixed Grimaldi with ice-blue eyes as he cinched the straps on the shoulder rigging. "Esposito built a number of contacts here in Quito from his days with the Company. One of them caught my eye when looking through Stony Man's files, a guy named Erasmo Cabeza. He's a money launderer gone legit, and allegedly he helped Esposito cut out some of this city's cancer."

Grimaldi furrowed his eyebrows. "You think he'll help you?"

"With a little luck and the right persuasion, yeah," Bolan replied.

"How can I help?"

"Stay low-profile for now but be ready to go on a moment's notice. I need you to play liaison between me and the Farm. It'll be easier for me to funnel info through you when I'm on the move than to try to contact Hal directly."

As Bolan finished dressing, tossing a lightweight

sports coat over the Beretta to conceal it, Grimaldi said, "Understood. Watch your back out there."

THE EXECUTIONER HAD to take Jack Grimaldi's advice as soon as he stepped outside the Hotel Othello.

Bustling foot traffic jammed the sidewalks, while cars and cabs crowded the twin one-way lanes of Amazonas Avenue. Bolan picked out the tail immediately, despite the crowd. Across the street, a tall, lanky native leaned against a lamp pole and read a newspaper. There was no reason for him to be there with so many café tables nearby, and that wasn't a bus stop. Bolan saw the guy look up once, and when he met his gaze the man quickly returned his attention to the paper.

An amateur.

Bolan turned and headed toward the central north part of town. This area had the busiest nightlife and things were already in full swing. A quick check of his watch told him it was 7:45 p.m. None of the heat of the day had dissipated, and it felt to Bolan like his hair and clothes were pasted onto his skin.

The Executioner continued toward El Encontrar on Calle Calama, a posh club that served grilled delights and played Latin rock music. He had good reason for heading there. According to his intelligence, Cabeza had owned and operated El Encontrar since his "conversion" to legitimacy. Frankly, Bolan wasn't buying that Cabeza had gone truly straight and narrow. According to Stony Man's intelligence, Esposito had Cabeza dead to rights on a number of charges that would

have put him behind bars for good if convicted under
Ecuador's laws. For some reason Esposito had decided
it better to keep his hold on Cabeza's short hairs. With
Esposito out of the picture—and perhaps he was out of
it permanently—Bolan had no reason to doubt Cabeza
would quickly find his way back to his former life. Still,
the Executioner knew he'd have to give Cabeza the benefit of the doubt if he wanted his cooperation.

As soon as Bolan rounded the corner at Calle Calama, he jogged across the street and wove between vehicle traffic that was at a standstill. The neon sign
marking El Encontrar stood out prominently against
those of the lesser establishments around it. Bolan
hoped his beeline for the club would give him enough
distance advantage that he could lose himself in the interior. He risked a glance back long enough to insure the
tail turned the corner and then continued to the front entrance of the club.

A pair of hard cases stood watch at the entrance. These
were professionals, as they didn't carry themselves like
general-purpose thugs who were armed and knew it. Bolan
couldn't determine positively if they were carrying or not,
so he assumed they were and decided to play a cool hand.

"How's it going?" he asked with a cheery grin and
half wave. Neither man spoke, although the shorter of
the two acknowledge him with something that passed
for a nod. "I'm here to see Erasmo."

"Mr. Cabeza doesn't take visitors unannounced," the
bigger guy said in a heavy, native accent. "Afraid you'll
have to make an appointment."

"Would it make a difference if I said Mario Esposito sent me?"

Something not perceptible to the untrained eye but obvious to Bolan's expert study changed in the man's expression. It didn't change for the better. The man turned to his partner and jerked his head to indicate he should go inside and check on it. While they waited, Bolan put his hands in the pockets of his designer jeans and whistled, studying the area around him as if he didn't have a care in the world. Less than two minutes passed before the little man returned.

"He'll see you," he told Bolan.

The Executioner nodded and grinned at the bigger thug before following the man's cohort into the club. The conga rhythms of the Latin music bopped inside Bolan's head as his guide pushed through the dancing and drinking throng. Disco-style lighting charged air that stank of cigarettes and alcohol, and the many stale perfumes oozing from both males and females. Their winding journey eventually ended at a solitary table that stretched across a small dais overlooking the rest of the club.

Bolan couldn't make out the features well in the dim red lighting above the table, but he knew the man had to be Cabeza. A blocky head sat atop a body as round as a doughnut and massive rings adorned pudgy fingers. Sweat stains were visible at the shirt collar and armpits of Cabeza's thousand-dollar suit, and for some strange reason he wore dark glasses. Cabeza studied Bolan with a toothy smile, which included one gold incisor, and then gestured to a chair across from him.

The Executioner sat and noticed the escort had taken a position behind him. He told Cabeza, "Lose the ape."

Bolan couldn't see the man's eyes, but he got the message from Cabeza's lack of response. He casually reached beneath his jacket and produced the Beretta. Bolan kept it under the table until the muzzle found some fleshy part of Cabeza's lower torso. "Please?"

Cabeza visibly stiffened but quickly waved the man away. Bolan turned to make sure he was gone, then returned the Beretta to its place.

"Who are you?"

"I'm asking the questions," Bolan replied coolly. "You're answering them."

Cabeza produced a carefree laugh and leaned back in the booth, which groaned with a noise audible even above the music. "Well, you sure as hell can't be from Mario because he's no longer among the living."

"You know that for sure?" Bolan asked.

"I haven't seen a body, if that's what you're asking. But you can be sure that whoever took him has fed him to the alligators by now. Mario wasn't exactly a popular guy among the natives."

"It's interesting you say that, Cabeza, because that's why I'm here," Bolan replied with a frosty smile. "I want to know who these 'natives' are."

"You with the *federales?*" The toothy smile remained, as if it were chiseled into Cabeza's face.

Bolan stared hard at him. "We've been through this. I ask, you answer."

"Okay, fine," Cabeza said, splaying his hands.

"I want names of anybody who'd like Mario Esposito out of the way, and don't even think about jerking me around."

"Couldn't we talk more privately? I have an office in back."

Bolan considered the request. It seemed a bit out of the ordinary. This was Cabeza's club and he probably had a private office, which meant they wouldn't have to shout over the music or din from the crowd. That also meant Cabeza could have an office with a dozen goons hiding behind the door leading to it. Better to stay put. At least he could keep one eye on the doors, and if it went hard then the area was open enough he would see it coming and have time to react.

"We'll stay here," Bolan said.

Cabeza shrugged. "Okay, so you want to know who wanted Mario out of the way. It would take me less time to tell you who didn't want him gone."

Bolan's gaze shifted from Cabeza to the club activities and then back as he asked, "He made lots of enemies?"

Cabeza nodded. "From his days with the CIA. Personally, I always liked Mario. I owe him my life, but it looks like now I may never get a chance to repay that debt. But not everyone in Ecuador can say they owe him the same, and particularly not here in Quito."

"What do you mean?"

"This is a city of action," Cabeza said with a smile. "The kind of action you cannot find in the smaller towns, if you take my meaning, señor. Mario did a lot to destroy that action, and there were many people angry at him when he left."

"You still haven't told me who," Bolan said.

"That's because I am no longer in this business. I run a club now." Cabeza gestured dramatically around him. "This is my business, and she's been good to me. I own her outright."

"Look, I don't know who you're used to dealing with but I'm not falling for this legitimate businessman game," Bolan said.

Something hardened in Cabeza's expression, but it had no effect on the Executioner except to note that Cabeza looked more like a fat clown now than he had a moment earlier.

"Even if you have gone straight," Bolan continued, "you still know people. I imagine you still get offers regularly to go back to the way it used to be."

"Of course," Cabeza said, his smug expression returning. "I was very good at what I did."

"I'll bet," Bolan said. "So that means you know who's in charge of things these days."

"There is only one man I know who has the resources and the balls to pull off this kind of job successfully. The only trouble is—" Cabeza leaned forward conspiratorially "—he's dead."

Bolan's expression went flat. "A dead man doesn't help me, Cabeza."

The former criminal held up a finger and said, "That's not all. I have heard some disturbing news recently. News so disturbing that it almost pains me to utter it."

"Try to get past your grief and spill it," Bolan said.

"The man I speak of is now called a spirit of the dead."

Bolan cocked an eyebrow. The expression in Cabeza's eyes told him the guy was telling the truth. The soldier didn't know exactly what this meant, but he understood the impact. Most South Americans were very superstitious; myth and legend filled nearly every corner of their culture, including education, literature and even fine arts. In some ways, their beliefs rivaled even those of the Rastafarians or Polynesians. In fact, such folklore was the part of every culture and what might have seemed ridiculous to some might be quite real to others. The Executioner understood that concept all too well.

"What are you talking about?" Bolan pressed.

"I speak of Adriano Rivas," Cabeza replied.

Bolan needed no introduction. Rivas had been a well-known drug lord and money-laundering kingpin in the heydays of Ecuador's financial troubles. Nothing came into or out of Colombia without a stamp of approval from the Rivas family. However, Bolan had heard of Rivas's death and the subsequent collapse of drug-running operations between Colombia and Ecuador. Allegedly the battle between the drug lords of lower South America had been reduced to little more than petty squabbles that had most in Washington confident the local authorities could take it from there.

"Maybe everything is not as you thought it here in our little part of paradise, eh, *señor?*" Cabeza asked.

"You believe the story about Rivas?"

Cabeza shrugged. "I don't know. It could be true. I think, however, that this sounds more like something his brother would cook up in the wake of Mario's disappearance. The news travels through the underworld first and there are no two people I can think of that would hate Mario more than Rivas's brother and sister."

"Where can I find them?"

Cabeza reached beneath his suit coat and Bolan's hand went to his pistol. Cabeza noticed the warrior's reaction and inclined his head to indicate he wasn't reaching for hardware. The man carefully proceeded on a nod from Bolan, and seconds later he withdrew a business card. He passed it over to the Executioner who studied the writing carefully while keeping one hand near the pistol butt.

"What's this?" he asked.

"It's a card for the Rivas family business," Cabeza replied.

Bolan fixed Cabeza with that gunmetal stare. "You just happened to be holding one of their business cards?"

"As you pointed out before, I still know a lot of people in my former line of work. It doesn't mean that I'm working with them…or even for them."

Bolan nodded and looked back at the card. "Says here they're in San Lorenzo."

Cabeza nodded. "It is the perfect place for them to run their operation. It's a port city with easy access in and out of the country, and Rivas's family has enough money that they can buy whatever security is needed.

As far as I know, they're still working deals even with
Adriano gone. If anybody has the ability to take out
Mario, it's these people."

"You wouldn't have an ax of your own to grind with
them, would you?" Bolan asked. "If this is some personal vendetta, I won't come back in a good mood."

"I have told you everything I know," Cabeza said. "If
you don't want to believe me, that's your problem. Now
get out of my club. I'm tired of talking to you."

Bolan thought about squeezing Cabeza but quickly
dismissed it. It wouldn't serve any purpose. The guy
seemed to be leveling with him, and the Executioner figured he was going to make enough enemies in the area
once word got out he was asking questions about Esposito and Gustavo. It was possible he might just need
some people on his side.

As Bolan rose, Cabeza asked, "Who are you anyway,
friend? Why are you so interested in this? Are you from
the CIA?"

"Something like that," Bolan said. "Let's just say I
have a personal interest in getting Esposito back in one
piece."

"Ah, so it's the Proctor Initiative that has you most
concerned," Cabeza said. "I think you are from the
American government. That's fine, it's no business of
mine. I just run my club."

"How do you know about that?"

"Are you that naive, *señor?*" Cabeza let out another
bowlful-of-jelly laugh. "This is Quito. Everybody
knows about everything here. There are no secrets, so I

wouldn't break my neck trying to keep any. I could find out who you really are if I wanted to know badly enough."

"I'm sure you could," Bolan deadpanned.

"But as I said, I owe Mario my life. Now if this information pays off for you and you get him back alive, you tell him we're square."

"I'm not a messenger boy." Bolan turned to go, then added, "By the way, someone followed me here from the hotel. I haven't been in the country long and you didn't look like you were expecting me. I figure the guy's not one of yours."

"You would be correct," Cabeza said. "I had no one follow you."

"Good," Bolan said. "I didn't want to risk killing the wrong guy."

The Executioner didn't wait to see Cabeza's reaction as he walked down the dais steps and headed for the exit of the club. He'd come across his first hard piece of intelligence, although he wasn't sure he could believe it.

Cabeza's story seemed far-fetched. Drug lords rising from the dead? Even after all he'd seen and experienced, the Executioner found that a bit hard to swallow. Rivas had been dead for at least three years, and that was a long time to stay out of things and still survive in the business of drug trafficking. Someone else would have already muscled into his territory—even if only a small-timer looking to make a name—which would have left Adriano Rivas out in the cold. Unless there was something to Cabeza's belief that Rivas's brother or sister might have something to do with these kidnappings. From the sounds of it, either of them probably had the contacts and the kind of money it would take to pull off a gig like this. Chances were good the pair might even be operating together. Well, Bolan would find out soon enough. He'd go to San Lorenzo and see what was what.

Outside the sweltering heat had turned muggier. The nightlife was now in full swing. Traffic clogged the streets and was practically at a standstill. Bolan spotted his tail directly across from the club entrance.

Time to ask some questions.

The Executioner crossed the street, dodging the honking traffic. The watcher was a little surprised to see Bolan on a direct intercept course. For just a moment uncertainty flashed in the guy's eyes before he turned and began to run away. Bolan decided to pursue, launching his body into high gear. Muscular legs propelled him along the edge of the sidewalk. He opted to take the area between the sidewalk and street since the traffic was moving slow, and it would have been more difficult to pursue his wiry prey if he had to fight the people crowding the sidewalks. The genius Bolan chased hadn't obviously considered this as he knocked a number of people down in an effort to escape.

Bolan caught the guy quickly enough, grabbing a handful of the back of his shirt collar and hauling him into a nearby grocery store. The Executioner slammed the guy roughly against a nearby display and the man toppled to the ground amid a rack of magazines. The grocer began to shout and hold up his hands, shaking a fist at Bolan who turned and gestured for the man to calm down a bit. He then returned his attention to his quarry. He reached down and hauled the guy to his feet before half dragging him toward an exit that opened onto an alleyway. Once outside, Bolan tossed the lithe native against a stucco wall.

"Why are you following me?" the Executioner asked in menacing tone.

"No comprende," the man stammered.

"You understand perfectly," Bolan replied. He produced the Beretta 93-R and pressed it against the man's forehead. "I'm only going to ask once more. Who sent you?"

Before the man could reply, his eyes went wide and a look of shock mixed with horror crossed his expression. This happened about the same moment the Executioner watched the guy's chest get ripped open by an unseen force in a spray of pink froth. Some of it doused the front of the Executioner's sports coat. The guy's mouth opened in what would have probably been a scream but no sound escaped. He just slid down the wall and died.

Bolan twisted and knelt, the Beretta tracking for a new threat. He never saw one. People just passed slowly at the entrance of the alleyway, and none was even looking in his direction. Bolan looked above them and then he spotted it: an open window on the second floor of the building. Someone had sniped Bolan's tail from there, probably using a sound-suppressed rifle so as not to reveal position.

The Executioner waited another few seconds before rising and holstering his pistol. He looked back at the dead man and shook his head. He should have expected something like this. It was just as Cabeza had said: there were no secrets in Quito, Ecuador. Everybody knew what was going on, and there wasn't a damn thing Bolan could do about it. In fact, the best thing he could do was to use that fact to his advantage.

And that was exactly what Mack Bolan planned to do.

CHAPTER THREE

Houston, Texas

The hour was late when Congressman Frederick Proctor entered Gentry Tower. The aged politician mumbled with a casual wave at the four security officers ranged around the front desk as he proceeded past them to a reserved elevator. Once inside, he passed a special badge in front of a reader, then watched absentmindedly as the numbers climbed toward the penthouse of the thirty-story building.

The double kidnapping weighed him down to the point he felt as though someone had strapped a half-ton truck to his back. Points of pain like hot needles poked incessantly behind his eyes. The migraines were back, impervious to the prescription medication he took; the doctor would again give him hell about blood pressure at his next physical. Well, that was too damn bad. The doctor didn't have his job.

The doors opened onto a spacious suite of rooms that circumvented the conference room at its center. A burnished table with wheeled leather executive chairs occupied the majority of that space. A good number of the chairs were already occupied and the eyes of every man in the room turned toward him expectantly. He even heard a few sighs of relief. This room meant safety for all who came. These men were his trusted allies and business associates. Most of them had helped finance his bid for political office and supported him either financially or by forging allegiances to the most powerful special interest groups in Washington, D.C.

Yes, this was a room of gentlemen with power, the sanctuary of the Texas Oil Barons Association. Four generations before Proctor had been members of this elite crew. They represented the finest oil companies in the country, and they had the power and money to back them. They were a law unto themselves and yet they didn't abuse that position. They had served as consultants to many of the most influential people in the country, past and present, and what they said went in the Lone Star State. Nothing about the petroleum industry at large escaped their notice. TOBA had its finger on the pulse of every oil-producing country in the world, but right now the focus was Ecuador.

Every man started to rise but Proctor quickly dismissed the gesture. Secretly he enjoyed such attentions, but the motto here was every man equal for the benefit of all.

"Good evening, gents," Proctor said as he took his

seat next to the head of the table. That spot was reserved for the association chairman, Hoover Weygand. "Apologies for being late."

"Not at all, Fred," Weygand said. "We're sorry to drag you back here at such short notice."

"No trouble," Proctor replied. He nodded at the rest of the entourage and added, "It's good to see all of you again."

"Been too long, Fred," one board member commented, and a few others parroted his sentiment.

Weygand waited a respectful amount of time before clearing his throat. "This emergency meeting of the TOBA is called to order. Motion to waive reading of the minutes and proceed to the immediate subject at hand." After a second from a couple of members, Weygand continued. "The situation is grim, as I'm sure you all agree. Let's cut to the chase. Fred, I'd like you to start us off as I think your opinion's the most important one."

Proctor nodded, trying to collect his thoughts through the incessant throbbing pain of his migraine. "I was in telephone contact with President Gustavo on the plane from Washington. He is very concerned with the fact the White House doesn't plan to take any action. At least… not immediately."

"Excuse me for interrupting, Fred," one of the men cut in. "Are you suggesting our own country plans to just stand by and do nothing while Senator Esposito and President Gustavo's son are missing? Because if that's the case then I for one say we do something about this right now."

Proctor showed his colleague a half-smile and waved his hands in way of placation.

"Why don't we all just calm down and listen to what Fred has to say first," Weygand said.

The room fell quiet.

"I don't know what the President plans to do about this yet," Proctor went on. "What I do know is that he's been in practically endless conferences with every adviser from here to there, and cleared his schedule for the next day to decide what to do."

"I'm not sure we have that kind of time, Fred," Benjamin Samson said.

Samson was a broker and financial consultant to TOBA, and doubled as TOBA's attorney. He knew Wall Street like nobody else, and when he made an observation on a fiscal point he was usually right. He'd made every one of them a lot more wealthy and successful over the years with his prudent investment advice. However, this wasn't a matter of money. If any sort of ransom demand had been made already, TOBA would have put up the cash instantly to get Esposito and Gustavo returned safely.

What everyone else outside that room didn't realize was TOBA's significant investment in the Proctor Initiative. These men represented the power base controlling approximately ninety percent of American oil reserves. It was significantly cheaper to help the U.S. government finance the agreement with Ecuador—thereby keeping oil reserves off the market—than to start shelling out the kind of money required to distribute petroleum products. Reserves meant an even higher gas crunch. It would lower prices in the short term but in the long run it would mean TOBA's fiscal ruin, not to mention inventory dropping to dangerously low levels.

"The market won't hold out much longer without relief," Samson continued. "Americans are screaming their asses off, and the ears of a good number of your people in D.C. are growing weary."

"First off, the good folks in Washington are not my people," Proctor replied, raising the volume a notch. "They're our people, and they were bought with our hard-earned cash. Now listen, we stand a good chance of watching this problem spiral out of our control very quickly. We need to act and quickly. There are a number of competitors, the Saudis included, who would like nothing better than to see us cave under this new crisis. People aren't going to pay these kinds of prices forever. When they start tightening the screws they'll start with us, and we won't have any choice but to dole out our product reserves and prevent price gouging. The government has full authority to regulate prices if we try any funny business."

"I won't let any of you be blackmailed by political policy," Samson said.

Proctor produced a derisive snort and studied each man in the room. "You won't have any choice in the matter. None of us will, let me assure you. This isn't about oil, gentlemen, it's about the unwillingness of Congressional representatives to back off our policies toward Arab terrorism. It just so happens that right now they hold all of the cards. Why do you think I pushed so hard on my initiative to dramatically improve relations with Ecuador?"

Proctor leaned forward. "I can guarantee you if we

have to wrestle for control over our investments every last one of us will come to ruination. You think we ran into hard times in the gas crunches before, you haven't seen anything yet. The economy's more unstable than it's ever been in the area of all natural resources, oil included.

"Now, I won't try to take the reins on this thing alone. I'm a team player like the rest of you. So out of respect I'll defer to the majority rule." He looked at Weygand—a man who had always been his strongest supporter and greatest friend—and added, "As usual. But there's very little I can do in my position. I'm under too much public scrutiny. I agree that we have to do something, but what we do is going to have to come from this room and nowhere else."

There was some throat-clearing and muttering, and Weygand waited for that to sink in. Finally one of the members motioned for them to go to a closed session and it was quickly seconded.

Weygand turned to the secretary who was there taking minutes and said, "That will be all for now, Gwendolyn. You may take the rest of the evening off."

The woman nodded in perfect understanding. This wasn't the first time this prestigious board had gone into closed session and it sure wouldn't be the last. There were just some things that TOBA reserved as sacrosanct and therefore best left for discussion behind closed doors. When the secretary had left, Weygand passed a box of cigars as a few others rose to get drinks from the bar.

"Okay, gentlemen, nobody hesitate to speak his mind."

Rutherford Emerson cleared his throat. The eldest and wealthiest member of the group, Emerson was an oil baron's baron. Harvard-educated and old school all the way, Emerson's great-grandfather had been one of the first East Coast hopefuls to come west and make his fortune in Southern California. Emerson had some paralysis from a stroke suffered a few years earlier. In spite of all that—or maybe because of it—he still possessed enough spunk to spit in the eye of the youngest business hotshot in America and not miss a wink of sleep over it.

"Seems to me we're making much ado about nothing," Emerson said. "There's nothing says we have to release our reserves if we don't want to, and I don't give a good goddamn if those whelps on the Hill start yammering at us or not."

"Mr. Emerson," Proctor began, addressing Emerson formally as every man did, and forcing a smile. "I'm afraid you don't understand. We—"

"Don't you tell me I don't understand, you puppy," Emerson scolded with a waggling finger to assist. "I was doing this kind of thing when you were still wearing rubber underwear. I vote we do things the old-fashioned way by going down to this backwoods country and kicking some Latin American ass."

A few of the board members fell silent and the remainder tried to act appalled. Unfortunately nobody was buying the reaction either from themselves or their colleagues. They all knew Emerson had hit the nail on the head. They couldn't afford to wait on government action. Even Proctor realized that while Emerson might have been a kook in some respects, he still had enough piss and vinegar in him to understand how to deal with things.

"Okay," Weygand said slowly. "Well, I think we all understand where Mr. Emerson stands. Any other suggestions or opinions?"

Silence.

"Anybody."

More silence.

"Well, I for one happen to like Mr. Emerson's suggestion," Weygand said. "I'd like to make a motion we go forward with this and consult our PMC. Would somebody like to second?"

"I'll second," Proctor muttered.

"All in favor?"

Everybody belted out a "yea" except Samson, who decided to abstain. He was a money guy and realized that at this point he was somewhat out of his element. Proctor wished he hadn't opened his mouth to begin with. He didn't particularly like Samson, and he never really had. The rest of the men in this room deserved his respect because they had earned it. Sure, Samson had made him some decent money and done some good investments on his behalf, but he'd been well compensated for his services. The guy demanded a whopping twenty-five percent from any successful deal. He'd robbed them all blind and had done it in a perfectly legal fashion.

Proctor was beginning to feel a new headache coming on. "You want to use our own people on this?"

"Why not?" Weygand replied with a shrug. "We pay

them well and we rarely require their services. I'm sure Kenney's chomping at the bit by now for some action. The only question remaining is, can you square this with President Gustavo?"

"Reynaldo will listen to me," Proctor said, rubbing at his temples.

"On a first-name basis now, are we?" Weygand sat back in his deep chair with a self-satisfied grin.

Proctor just shrugged and waved it away.

Weygand looked at the others and said, "With your permission, gentlemen, I shall contact the Quail Group immediately."

Nods of assent cinched the deal.

Mound Bayou, Mississippi

CURTIS KENNEY FELT the blood course through his veins as he crept through the dusky, variegated flora of the jungle.

He could feel the sweat drip down his back and soak those points on his body where the jungle fatigues were snug. He was in excellent physical condition—had gained only a few pounds since leaving the military—and could still hold his own against guys half his age.

His career had changed in a very sudden and dramatic way. After twelve years in the Army, the latter nine being a Delta Force commando and team leader, Kenney had opted to trade reenlistment for a job in the civilian sector. It hadn't taken much for a buddy to convince him of the money a skilled soldier could make with some of the larger government contractors who often required "special services" to maintain security. In these modern-age, big-dollar companies, autonomous entities who were backed by the American government and basically answered to no authority but their own, Curtis Kenney had found his destiny.

He'd also found his fortune.

Companies paid Kenney and his band top dollar for their unique brand of services. Kenney was very particular about his associations, and he wouldn't work for any employer who viewed him as a "mercenary." In fact, he despised the very term because it meant that a prospective employer didn't give a tinker's damn about his professionalism or ethics and, what's more, didn't understand them. Kenney wasn't leading some band of amoral cutthroats here; the Quail Group was composed of pros all the way.

Kenney turned at the sound of movement on his left, brought his M-16 A-3 into target acquisition and stroked the trigger twice. The reports cracked through the humid air as the weapon recoiled slightly against his shoulder. Twin splotches of red spread across the shirtfront of his aggressor. The man jerked spasmodically in throes of death and collapsed. Kenney grinned. Lady Luck had no hand there; he'd taken his target strictly with skill and cunning.

The radio mike attached to the shoulder strap of his Kevlar vest squawked for attention. Kenney frowned as he snatched the receiver and barked into it. "What?"

"Boss, you got a call from our friends in Houston. Said they need you to call back right away."

"Goddamn it, Jonesey, if I've told you once I've told you a hundred times not to interrupt me during training."

The microphone keyed twice before Buford Jones answered. "I know, I know. But they said it was important. They said it's a job, sir."

Kenney took just a moment to flash a wicked grin at the rising "dead" man in front of him and then replied, "Understood. We'll be there in ten. Out here."

Kenney clicked off and looked at his second in command. "You should've been an actor instead of a professional soldier, Pete. That was damn fine acting, damn fine."

"Up yours," Peter Morristown said as he slapped with irritation at a mosquito that had welded itself to his neck. He drew a mixture of blood and sweat away in his palm. "I'll just be glad to get the hell out of here. I don't know why you insisted on buying this worthless piece of rotted land in the middle of Nowheresville, anyway, especially when we could've just as well had a fine training camp up in Montana or South Dakota or somewhere like that."

"Aw, what are you complaining about?" Kenney said as the men retrieved their rucksacks for the eight-minute hike back to their firebase. "I paid for the place out of my own pocket, didn't I?"

"Yeah, well, that's because you insisted on doing all of our training operations here and didn't give the rest of us much to say about it."

"Look, at least nobody in their right mind would think to mess with us out here."

"Nobody in their right mind would think to mess with us, period," Morristown shot back.

"Heh, you know it, buddy," Kenney said as they traded high-fives.

It took Curtis Kenney only a moment to think about the job presented to him by the Texas Oil Barons Association before he agreed to it.

The mission was simple. Fly to Ecuador and talk with President Gustavo. They could expect the full cooperation and authority of the Ecuadorian government, not only in locating Gustavo's son, Hernando, but also in getting back Mario Esposito. And the money was right, too. Two million in cold hard cash would be theirs if they got the job done, and Kenney was able to get one-quarter of it wired to the Quail Group's private account up front to cover their expenses, including any bribes that might be required.

Kenney had only been to one previous mission in Colombia, and he'd never gone into Ecuador, but he did know one thing. If there was something that didn't come cheap in South America, it was information. Even what TOBA had on their two missing men was scant, and Kenney was hard-pressed to find any information in the thin files on Esposito and the Gustavo family. They would have to play the rest of it by ear. Still, he was happy to be getting the cooperation of the government on this one.

Discretion would still be a major requirement, of course. Weygand had tried to explain all the political ramifications to him if they attracted attention to themselves or stepped on the wrong feet. He'd also started to expound upon the complete deniability angle if they got caught or caused an international incident and all that rot, but Kenney had pared that conversation to the bare minimum.

"All due respect, Mr. Weygand, I don't need a pep talk," Kenney had told him. "Just give me the basic parameters and we'll do the rest."

Now looking at the files faxed over to him, Kenney was wishing he had another chance to talk to Weygand, but these were the rules. One contact, then it was communications silence until there was something worthwhile to report. Which meant the Quail Group would call with either a mission success or mission fail report. Kenney had never been much for suits, most of who had never known a hard day's work in their lives, breathing down his neck during an operation. He didn't care how much it paid.

Morristown plopped down in the seat across from Kenney. "So what did you get from those files?"

Kenney clucked his tongue as he tossed them lazily at his long-time friend. "I'm getting that I should have asked old man Weygand a few more questions before letting him off the phone."

Kenney had first met Pete Morristown in the Army. They'd served together in Afghanistan and later during the latter part of Operation Iraqi Freedom. They had fought together in some of the worst hellholes on Earth—saved each other's lives countless times—so it hadn't been hard for Kenney to consider recruiting his old buddy. This kind of soldiering in missions where they were allowed to succeed and make a whole lot of money doing it at the same time appealed immediately to Morristown. He'd joined up before Kenney barely finished pitching it to him.

"You don't even want to think about it?" Kenney had asked him.

"Nope," Morristown had replied. "Count me in, bro."

Three years had passed and Morristown had never looked back.

Morristown looked up from the files with a sardonic laugh. "You're putting me on. This is it? This is all they've got?"

Kenney nodded. "Pretty thin, I know."

"We're going to need every dime of that bribe money."

"I'm hoping it doesn't come to that," Kenney said, looking out the small port window at the darkness. "The natives aren't known for their hospitality or cooperation with outsiders. But Mr. Weygand assured me we'll get President Gustavo's cooperation."

"We're going to need it," Morristown said with a snort. "You have any ideas where to start looking?"

"No, and I won't waste time theorizing. We'll just shake things up a little." Kenney smiled. "I'm quite sure a solution will present itself."

CHAPTER FOUR

Night had fallen and Mack Bolan was rigged for war.

He had changed from his night-on-the-town attire into one more comfortable and familiar. His formfitting blacksuit had gone through a number of modifications over the years but the basic premise remained the same: blend with shadows but present a grim sight when blitzing the opposition. The big soldier took on the aura of the angel of Death any time he donned the blacksuit, and even after all these years that look still managed to strike terror in the hearts of his enemies.

The .44 Magnum Desert Eagle rode in a hip holster on his right side and a Belgian-made FN-FNC Para carbine was slung across his back. Four German-made Diehl DM-51 hand grenades hung from his black web belt, as did pouches that stored an assortment of other equipment, including a multipurpose tool, Colt Combat Knife and a garrote. Originally he'd considered a soft probe but he was wise to the fact that within this den was a pack of killers. Not to mention the place was apparently a major nerve center for drug trafficking in Quito.

Once he'd returned to the hotel and contacted Stony Man about his chat with Cabeza, Price and Kurtzman ran down the history on Adriano Rivas. The intelligence proved interesting. Drugs still went through Quito in volumes equal to those at the time of Rivas's death.

"Either the operation there wasn't Rivas's to begin with or Cabeza's giving you the straight story on it," Price had told him. "I'd check it out, Striker."

Bolan did that now as he looked through the monocular NVD and studied the grounds. The mansion sat on land occupying a prominent spot on the northern outskirts of the city. According to Stony Man's info, it had proven extremely difficult for the Ecuadorian government to shut down the place. Informants had told stories of a processing and distribution center as big as a warehouse beneath the grounds, but that alone never constituted enough evidence for the judicial system to sanction a search by law-enforcement authorities. Especially considering it was owned by trust of Pascual Santos, leader of the Roldosist Party, which just happened to hold the second largest number of seats in Ecuador's national congress.

The Executioner opted to go hard all the way. If he couldn't get his information the easy way, then he'd shake the tree to see who fell out. He'd put a bunch of drug-runners out of business even if it didn't get him closer to finding Esposito and Gustavo, although somehow Bolan figured Cabeza was right, and this had everything to do with the Rivas family's control over drugs in Ecuador and subsequently abroad.

Bolan studied the lay of the land carefully to determine his best angle of approach. No doubt there were electronic security measures in addition to the guards roaming the grounds with dogs and submachine guns. The Executioner withdrew an illuminated stopwatch and timed the rounds. Two minutes between guards. Not enough time to cross the grounds and reach the house before rotations intersected. He lowered the night-vision device and gave it some thought, pressing his lips tightly together as he looked things over once more. He'd have to take his chances crossing the grounds as quickly as possible and hit the enemy before they could respond. The other problem would be the interior layout of the place. He hadn't been able to get any information on it, since standards were very lax in Ecuador at the time it was built. He'd have to feel his way through.

It was all or nothing once he put the ball in play.

Bolan checked the action of the FN-FNC Para and breathed deeply. He studied his flanking positions to make sure the enemy didn't have a card up its sleeve, then burst from the line of trees on the edge of the massive grounds. The soldier easily scaled the ten-foot fence, vaulted over and hit the ground running. He scanned the area as he moved toward the house while the numbers ticked off in his head. When he got within fifty yards, it went hard.

A guard rounded the corner and spotted him. The

man reached for the subgun slung at his side, but Bolan already had his 93-R out and tracking. He squeezed the trigger twice. The first round punched through the man's chest before he could acquire Bolan as a target and the second round ripped away his throat. The body flipped backward and collapsed on the flagstone that bordered a colorful garden.

A second guard appeared, obviously alerted by the reports from the pistol. Like his comrade in arms the sentry waited a bit too long and Bolan made good use of the hesitation. He triggered a single round that struck the man in the face and blew out a large part of his left cheek, his eye exploding from the pressure created by the bullet's path. The man tumbled forward and sprawled onto the slippery grass.

The unmistakable bark of a dog commanded Bolan's attention. He turned in time to see a guard approaching his flank and a big, dark Rottweiler snarling and snapping on a lead, yanking at his master's hand and begging to be released. The guard obliged, and Bolan felt a pang of regret even as he whipped the Colt Combat Knife from its sheath. Simultaneously the warrior aimed his pistol at the guard who had to have thought Bolan would be too panic-stricken at the sight of the charging dog to worry about him. He was wrong, and it cost him his life as a 9 mm bullet ripped through his heart.

The Executioner barely had enough time to react as he watched the giant, aggressive beast leave the ground on a direct collision course with him. The animal's jaws snapped within inches of his throat. Bolan dropped and let the dog's body pass over him. As the exposed belly moved past his face Bolan clenched his teeth and jammed the hilt of the knife against it. The animal sailed past him with a yelp but managed to land on its feet as Bolan jumped to his own. The dog emitted some more hurtful yelping as it charged once more. This time Bolan was ready, his Beretta 93-R out and tracking the injured animal. He had no wish to prolong the battle or the dog's suffering. A single 9 mm Parabellum round drilled through the dog's skull. It backflipped, then lay still.

Bolan holstered his pistol as he walked to the dead animal and quickly retrieved his knife. It was a sad thing that the dog had to die doing what it was trained to do, but he let the thought pass quickly. He'd done the most humane thing he could, and that was that. No point in dwelling on something he couldn't control.

The Executioner turned and continued unchallenged toward the mansion. He could hear shouts from inside the house as he reached the main entrance. Bolan put his two-hundred-plus pounds to the heavy door and kicked it in, the FNC assault rifle in battery and set to full-auto. Trouble appeared in the form of a pair of guards descending a large, curved staircase to his left. They were still trying to bring their weapons to bear when Bolan triggered the FNC. The weapon chattered loudly within the cavernous interior as a hail of 5.56 mm NATO rounds cut through the pair of gunman. The impact tumbled the first man down the stairs, the subgun he was carrying clattering immediately after him. Bolan's sustained burst slammed the second against a wall, the force pitching him forward and causing him to flip over the ornate banister of the grand staircase. The hard-guy's body hit the floor below with the sound of cracking bones.

As the echo of weapon's reports died, several men emerged from a doorway on the far side of the massive entrance hall. They were obviously the day crew because they were attired in various modes of dress, everything from loosely buttoned shirts and pants to nothing but muscle shirts and boxers. The commonality lay in the assorted weaponry they carried. Bolan went to one knee as he palmed one of the Diehl DM-51s. These grenades had both an offensive and defensive capability. While the round bomb was capable of delivering a tremendous blast, Bolan found them most effective for defensive use when the sheath packed with 2 mm steel balls covered the exterior of the body.

Bolan yanked the pin and lobbed the grenade in a quick underhand toss designed to bring it in low. This would more effectively attract the enemy's attention, distracting them while allowing Bolan the spare time he needed to find cover. The last thing the men were obviously expecting was this big man in commando black to toss something in their direction in the middle of a firefight. Their surprise and hesitation cost all four of them their lives. The grenade rolled to within inches of one of the guard's bare feet and before any of them could react it exploded. More than six thousand super-heated steel balls engulfed the quartet, ripping through their flesh like hot knives. Shouts of surprise died in their throats, replaced by the sounds of agony that preceded such death and destruction.

The Executioner didn't wait to watch them die, instead ascending the winding steps three at a time. The idea of trapping himself on the upper level didn't appeal to him, but he didn't surmise he'd find anything useful on the main floor. The master of the house, assuming he was home, would be on the second story and probably hiding from the sudden and violent assault being launched on his domain. That was fine with Bolan—it would make it easier to find the man. If Pascual Santos was involved with Rivas's family, or had associations with other known drug lords, he would prove an invaluable source of information. For all Bolan knew, Santos was himself a drug lord although somehow the soldier couldn't picture a politician of his stature being cut out for that kind of work. Santos didn't strike him as someone who would risk dirtying his own hands when he could pay someone else to do it and still make a profit.

Bolan began a room-by-room search, starting with suites down the first hall off the main second-floor walkway. He found a library and a couple of spare bedrooms, but no sign of Santos. Bolan continued to the second hallway and as he did he heard the slap of boots on the stairway. It looked like reinforcements were arriving.

The Executioner pushed through the first door he came to and moved inside the darkened room. Light spilled from the hallway and illuminated the interior enough for Bolan to see it was a spare bedroom. He closed the door behind him and quickly changed out magazines on the FNC Para. He could hear doors begin to open and the shouts of men. He couldn't tell exactly how many from the voices, but he estimated at least half a dozen. Bolan checked his watch and shook his head. Already almost five minutes into the operation and things were falling apart.

Well, he'd planned for this one to go hard from the beginning, so he would have to play the cards as they were dealt to him.

Bolan chambered a round, set the selector to 3-round-burst mode, then left the room and entered the hallway with the muzzle level and the stock pressed to his shoulder. He took his first pair of targets as soon as they rounded the corner, triggering the weapon. Three rounds ventilated one guard's chest, punching him off his feet and dumping him on the burgundy carpet. Two of the slugs from Bolan's second volley caught the remaining gunner in the head and sent him stumbling backward. The man's lifeless body continued in that backward motion, arms reeling wildly and propelling him faster—even though he was technically dead his body hadn't obviously caught up with his brain on the matter—and inevitably he reached the banister lining the second-floor landing. The corpse toppled over and disappeared from view.

Bolan could still hear the others searching the upstairs wings, obviously unaware he was reducing their ranks. He continued searching the other rooms, as well, hoping to reach the master of the house before his men did. With a bit of luck, Bolan found the master bedroom.

As light from the hallway illuminated the scene, the soldier grinned. The covers were rumpled on the bed, as if someone had left it in a hurry. Bolan quickly swept the room with the muzzle of his weapon, then closed the door and locked it. He walked to the bed and felt the sheets with the back of his hand: warm.

The Executioner turned a moment before he heard the movement to his rear. A lone figure burst suddenly from a bathroom door and charged at him, something long and big raised over its head.

Bolan raised his carbine in a two-handed block in time to avoid having his skull caved in by the attacker. The object hit the center part of the receiver with a dull clang that sounded like wood. As the soldier took a moment to better view the object, he realized his attacker was wielding a toilet plunger. Bolan immediately countered by ramming the butt of his rifle against his opponent's chin. The impact crunched bone, and he felt the warm, wet spray of blood on his hands.

The man yelped in pain, dropping his plunger-club and bringing his hands to his face. Bolan reached out and grabbed the man's collar, swung him around onto the bed and pressed the muzzle of his assault rifle to the man's head.

"Pascual Santos?" Bolan inquired.

"Who are you?" the man asked, groaning.

Bolan pressed the weapon harder against his prey's forehead. "Are you Santos or not?"

"If I'm not, will I live?"

"Whether you live or die is up to you," Bolan said. "I'm not here to murder anyone. I'm looking for information."

"About what?"

"About who," Bolan corrected him. The noises of hardmen busying themselves on the upper floor got louder. Time was almost up. "I hear rumors you're manufacturing dope in your basement. True?"

Santos hesitated but Bolan's prodding with the weapon reminded him who had the upper hand. "Yes."

"Where?" Bolan asked.

Santos quickly muttered how to access the processing lab at the basement level.

"Good," Bolan said. "Now, who's financing your operation? I hear the Rivas cartel is behind it, and that Adriano Rivas may still be alive."

"I have heard the same rumors," Santos replied. "I don't know if this is true. But we do pay money to someone."

"And that someone represents the Rivas family?"

"I have been told not to ask, but my own people tell me this is true."

There was a heavy beating at the door and the sound of a man speaking rapidly in Spanish. Bolan looked at Santos a moment and then swung the assault rifle in the direction of the door and triggered a sustained burst. The Executioner kept his finger on the trigger as he approached the door, the hail of bullets chopping the wooden double doors of the bedroom to shreds. They continued onward through the door and took out the cluster of men waiting on the other side.

Bolan reached the splintered door and put his foot against it in the hope of distracting anyone still standing. As he came through the jagged frame, he saw there wasn't anyone standing. The heavy dose of firepower had sealed their collective fates, killing all four of the unsuspecting men who had stood in front of Santos's door.

As Bolan stepped over the carnage, he cast a backward glance at the bleeding, broken man who watched him with half interest, half fear. "Get out of this business, Santos. In fact, get out of politics." He dropped the magazine and slammed a fresh one home, for emphasis adding, "Ecuador has enough problems without men like you at the helm."

Bolan didn't wait for a reply, instead descending the stairs and heading in the direction Santos had told him to go. He found the concealed entrance in the large library at the back of the house and took the elevator to the lower level. The doors opened on to a small, deserted anteroom. The warrior was surprised there were no sentries present. He paused to listen for evidence of an ambush awaiting him on the other side of the swinging double doors, but only silence greeted him. Perhaps the junk makers felt themselves safe enough with the concealed entrance.

Or...

Bolan sensed a trap. He'd learned that survival was best achieved by doing the last thing the enemy expected: taking the offensive. Bolan yanked two of the DM-51 grenades from his web belt, pulled their pins and let the spoons fly away. He edged to the doors as the twin hand bombs cooked off, then kicked them open simultaneously and unloaded the grenades. Bolan hit the ground—mouth open and hands over ears—as the twin explosions rocked the small room. Balls of red-orange flame erupted from the doors seconds before the massive concussion ripped them from their hinges.

Bolan didn't wait for the debris to stop falling before bringing his weapon up and stepping through the doors. He spotted several bodies, flesh burned from bones and limbs grossly angulated. One man writhed on the ground and moaned in pain. Blistering burns covered his upper torso, and a good part of the left side of his face was missing. Bolan put a 3-round mercy burst in the unfortunate sentry to end his suffering.

The Executioner pressed onward, storming through the hallway beyond the doors that opened onto the laboratory. Several of the men in lab coats who had been working on the coke had ceased activity and were now studying Bolan with fearful looks. Bolan jerked his head toward the elevator and the lab techs immediately rose and rushed toward it.

So much for dedication, he thought.

He moved quickly through the laboratory, even checking the bathrooms and the sparse office in the back for any clues that would bring him closer to finding out who was heading up the trafficking in the area, which he also believed would bring him closer to finding out who had taken Esposito and Gustavo. Bolan found some computer disks inside the desk, as well as one still inside the computer in the office, so he pocketed them before returning to the main part of the lab.

Bolan had seen places like this many times before, and if he knew anything about them it was the flammability of the chemicals used to process cocaine. The crystal-blue liquids in beakers interspersed across the massive table topped with processed and refined coca powder, a good part of it bundled and ready for distribution, looked particularly volatile. Bolan suspected his one remaining grenade would do the trick nicely. He pulled free a grenade, primed it, left it near the beaker, then raced out of the lab.

The doors to the elevator opened just as the explosion ripped through the lab. Bolan stepped calmly through them as the flames began to cast a shimmering yellow glow against the slick metal before being obscured by grayish smoke. But by then the doors had obscured the view of his handiwork.

Bolan stepped off the elevator in time to encounter a trio of guards carrying heavy-duty assault rifles. He knelt and took the first one with a short burst to the abdomen. It drove the man into one of his companions, and before either could recover Bolan took out the second of his opponents with a head shot.

The remaining gunman was a bit more nimble and dived to the side, escaping Bolan's initial shots while trying to draw a bead on him. The Executioner rolled away from a heavy blast of sustained fire and came to a crouch on the man's flank. There was a brief look between them, just a heartbeat's worth of expressions, before Bolan triggered his weapon. The man opened his mouth to scream but nothing came forth as the bullets ripped through his chest and drove the wind from his lungs. The scream turned into more of a gurgling squeak, then the gunner pitched forward and landed on his face.

Bolan rose and made for the exit of the house. He had probably encountered the last of the resistance. So the rumors had been true about Santos running a drug lab in his mansion, and Bolan was confident enough the local authorities could collect enough evidence to put the bastard behind bars.

With any luck, the disks Bolan had collected would have some useful information on them. For certain, the Rivas name had now come from two different people. Something was cooking in Ecuador and it was more than just drug labs. No, there was a bigger game afoot now, and the Executioner believed he knew where it started.

Yeah, it was time to pay San Lorenzo a visit.

CHAPTER FIVE

Colombia

"We may have a problem, boss," Chico Arauca said as he entered the private veranda off the master bedroom of Adriano Rivas's hideaway

Rivas turned from where he'd been watching dawn break. He had come to love his jungle compound. He'd arranged for it to be built in the heart of the mountainous Colombian terrain bordering Ecuador in anticipation of his impending "death." Three commercial-size generators buried deep in the jungle floor provided power, and the house and four outbuildings were constructed with special composite materials that prevented detection from airborne infrared surveillance.

Rivas ground the remains of his Cuban cigar beneath his booted foot and snickered. "I believe it's you who has the problem. I pay you to make sure there are no problems."

"I earn my money," Arauca replied evenly.

Nobody else would have ever dared to speak to Rivas like that, but Arauca was one of the few who could get away with it. The two had known each other since childhood and grown up in the same tough neighborhood of a small Latin American town. Arauca had served as chief enforcer and loyal bodyguard since Rivas's first foray into the world of drug-running.

"True," Rivas said. "But you know I have my hands full with other matters, and little time to worry about trivialities. So what exactly is this great crisis?"

"The worst kind," Arauca replied. "One of my men in Quito just advised that the entire operation we had going out at Pascual Santos's place was completely destroyed."

Rivas could feel the rage begin to swell within his chest. He had assigned his sister to look after those holdings, which were particularly important to the fiscal stability of his little empire. Well, it probably wasn't Carmita's fault. His younger sister had never had a great sense for this kind of thing; even if she had, the time would have eventually come for Rivas to retake control. It sounded as if that time was now.

"Okay," Rivas said with a nod. "This means our timetable must move forward. We'll have to accelerate operations. Do we have any idea who was behind the attack?"

Arauca shook his head. "I'm still working on getting that information. It could be some time before we have a definitive answer. We do know that it was one man. An American."

"One man?" Rivas echoed. "Santos let one man destroy our entire processing operation there? You realize that's unacceptable to me. Santos has become a liability. You need to take care of that liability."

"Consider it done," Arauca said with a grim smile.

Rivas considered his loyal follower. Arauca loved killing and always had. He was unusually strong for his rather diminutive size, and something bloodthirsty lurked behind his dark brown eyes. While Rivas rarely ordered the elimination of someone—and then only for the purpose of discouraging competition—Arauca was always ready and able to oblige. The man had a high sense of duty, but there was no mistaking the devil inside of him. Arauca was reputed in most circles as a cold, methodical killer, and that kept others in line.

"I must think on exactly how we can accelerate our efforts," Rivas said. "I would guess our first step would be to locate this American. If he's operating in Ecuador, do you think he has the approval of the government?"

"I doubt it," Arauca replied. "I don't think Gustavo would risk losing his son by recruiting an outside troubleshooter."

"Agreed. That means either he's here on his own or the American government sent him to locate Esposito. I would start with our contacts at the airports and hotels. See if we can determine who he is and when he arrived in country. If he managed to locate and shut down our Quito operation that quickly, it's probable he might now be on to Manuel and Carmita. I think it's best you send some of our men to protect them until I can get to San Lorenzo."

"Adriano, I don't think it would be a good idea to show your face there," Arauca said quietly.

Rivas scowled. "It doesn't matter. We no longer have the luxury of waiting. If we don't take this chance now we'll lose it. The Americans are in a serious energy crisis, and I think we should seize that advantage. If everything goes as planned, we'll have them eating out of our hands within a month."

"What about our guests?"

"For now they can remain here. Nobody outside of this camp knows anything about it or its location. Even if this American can get someone to talk to him, it would take time to find us and attempt a rescue operation. We're self-sufficient enough to hold off any assault for months." Rivas waved toward the jungle. "We know any sort of air assault is out of the question. Ground travel is the only way in or out of this compound, and there are miles upon miles of rugged terrain in every direction. We would know of anyone approaching long before they arrived."

"So you plan to go to Quito before San Lorenzo?" Arauca inquired.

"I must," Rivas replied. "There are important people there I must contact, especially since Santos and his people are out of the picture."

"Then I will accompany you."

Rivas lent him a half-smile. "Not this time, my friend. I need you to go straight to San Lorenzo and protect my family until we can determine who this American is and what his plans are. But you may send whomever you choose to accompany me. I will be fine. I am still quite adept at taking care of myself if need be."

That seemed to satisfy Arauca although Rivas knew the man didn't like it. It wasn't customary for him to ever let his employer out of his sight. Despite the fact he didn't like it himself, he had to show strength and leadership. That was more important now than it had ever been. Manuel and Carmita were tough, yes, but they didn't possess the physical or mental constitution to resist an effective troubleshooter like this American—and he definitely sounded effective.

Rivas hoped his business in Quito could be conducted quickly and efficiently. Only then could he go to San Lorenzo with peace of mind. The export of crude or processed oil to America would significantly enhance his distribution. Since they had started their war on terrorism, American security had become almost impenetrable. The DEA now had the backing of the other U.S. federal agencies, something they hadn't really had in the past, at least not to the degree they did now. This opportunity was too good to pass up, and Rivas planned to exploit it to maximum benefit in every way possible.

It was the perfect plan. With Americans spending less for gasoline, there was more money in their pockets for drugs. And the beauty of it was that they could get both products at the same time. Adriano Rivas couldn't see how his plan could go wrong as long as they could keep the competition in line. The Rivas empire was about to be resurrected once more.

Quito, Ecuador

CURTIS KENNEY ARRIVED at the palatial estate of President Reynaldo Gustavo and security immediately ushered him to the Ecuadorian leader's private study. The place was magnificent. Rows of books lined shelves floor-to-ceiling on every wall. Expensive throw rugs covered the hardwood floors. Polished furniture of cedar, cherry and mahogany shone with an oily gleam under the low lights of lamps hanging from the high ceiling. Certificates, letters and other gifts from foreign dignitaries adorned the walls between the bookshelves, arranged in vertical fashion. The place represented security and warmth while also exuding an air of authority.

At that moment as he sat in front of a massive desk, waiting for Gustavo and studying his surroundings, Curtis Kenney realized just how much larger this was than the Quail Group. He probably should have doubled Weygand's price.

As he considered this with an appreciative smile, the door opened and admitted five men. Four of them were big and dressed in suits. Kenney immediately tagged them as presidential security. The man who entered between them was much less imposing. He was short and older, but good-looking in his three-piece suit and patent leather shoes. Salt-and-pepper sideburns and thick mustache gave him a distinguished look but belied an age much greater than his actual forty-two years.

Two of the bodyguards posted at the door and a third stationed himself near Kenney's chair. The fourth accompanied Gustavo to his seat and then stepped forward in front of Kenney and gestured for him to stand. Kenney stood and put his arms to his sides; he knew this drill. It was the fourth time he'd been frisked. To save time—and knowing since the kidnapping that security would be especially tight—Kenney had elected to leave the rest of his team at the dignitaries' estate a few miles from the presidential home.

Kenney took his seat when the bodyguard cleared him, and Gustavo dismissed the security team with a wave. At first, it appeared the leader of the team was going to argue but one sharp look from the president seemed to deter any such notion. The quartet filed out and left the two alone in the study. Kenney surmised a whole legion of armed men were waiting in the wings and would flood the room at the first sign of trouble.

"I apologize for that," Gustavo said in his heavily accented and gravelly voice. "But I'm sure you understand we're at a heightened security alert. I hope you've been treated with respect and dignity."

Kenney attempted an ingratiating smile. "I would have been worried at anything less than their diligence, sir. And, yes, they have treated me well."

Gustavo nodded curtly. "Excellent, then we should move on to business. As I'm sure you're aware, we have received no ransom demands for either Senator Esposito or my son. This concerns me."

"Naturally," Kenney said. "It concerns my employer, too. That's why they've sent us."

Gustavo sat back in his chair as he reached into a top

desk drawer and withdrew a pipe. He tamped it with to-
bacco and lit it, and then reached into the drawer once
more and withdrew a box of cigars. "I forget my man-
ners. Would you like one?"

Kenney shook his head. "I gave up such luxuries
years ago, Mr. President, but thank you for the offer."

Gustavo replaced the box with a nod and continued.
"My advisers tell me that no ransom demand means
very little at this early stage. This could be a tactic to
sweat me out, or perhaps this is strictly about prevent-
ing us moving forward with the Proctor Initiative. We're
not sure at this point whether this is politically or financially motivated since we've had no contact with the
kidnappers."

Kenney crossed his legs, relaxing a bit now. "It's
been my experience that no immediate ransom demand
spells an alternative agenda. My employer doesn't think
this is about money at all. We believe this holdout is
more likely a way to gain some type of leverage."

"You mean blackmail."

"No disrespect intended, President Gustavo, but I
mean what I mean," Kenney said. He cleared his throat
and quickly added, "Look, there can be many reasons
why someone would kidnap Esposito, but it's obvious
there's more going on here than anyone cares to admit.
There's something the kidnappers are hoping to gain by
taking Esposito and your son. There's an old expression
that a bird in the hand is worth two in the bush, but in
this case two birds in the hand are even better. They
could have grabbed either of them at just about any

time and yet they waited until they were together. That tells me they had a good reason for it."

"That was the assessment of my team, as well," Gustavo said. "So what do you think is the reason?"

"If I understand the intelligence from my employer, both Ecuador and the United States stand to gain something of considerable value in the Proctor Initiative. Correct?"

Gustavo nodded agreement.

"That means whoever took these men is looking to gain something by it, as well, but wasn't planning for things to happen so soon. Under normal circumstances, this process would have taken much longer, but pressure is on my government to act quickly."

"So what," Gustavo interjected, "are you saying, that this kidnapping is a stall tactic?"

"That's exactly what I'm saying," Kenney replied. "As long as they hold cards on both sides, the kidnappers have bought themselves time. And obviously that time is a precious commodity to them. This means we have a little time to find Esposito and your son, but not a lot. The hand of this group will be forced and because they have to bump up their timetable that leaves them open to a mistake. The best we can do is to keep the pressure on."

"What are you proposing?"

"Well, the first thing I propose is that we find out who's behind the kidnapping. Once we have that information, my group will know better how to proceed. The information I have on Senator Esposito and your son is scant. Can you tell me anything else about either one of them that might be useful?"

Gustavo furrowed his eyebrows. "Like what, for example?"

"Like any trouble your son's had, sir," Kenney said, staring Gustavo in the eyes. "People he's associated with that might be reputed to have certain questionable affiliations. People at school or within his social circles who could shed some light on things in his past…things that even you might not be aware of."

"Hernando has lived a pretty sheltered life," the president said with a shrug, leaning back in his chair. "I'm not sure I could help you with any of that."

Kenney showed him a skeptical smile. "If there's anything I've learned, Mr. President, it's that boys will be boys. Although I'm sure you'd like to believe he's been a perfect angel all his life, I'd bet your son has gotten into trouble now and again."

Gustavo didn't reply immediately. Kenney could see the man was uncomfortable with the turn this conversation had taken. He was digging for dirt, plain and simple, and it was obvious no father would like that. Frankly, Kenney didn't give a damn. He didn't have time to play games. He needed to get to the heart of this thing and understand the people he was searching for. The information on Esposito's past was an open book, but there was very little intelligence on Hernando Gustavo and with good reason. The campaign reps for Gustavo during the election would have insured they hushed up any potential information leaks that could have led to public scrutiny to such a degree they could serve as points of attack by Gustavo's opponent in the last election. They had to have done a pretty good job because the president had won a landslide election.

Something in Gustavo's expression fell as he finally said, "Hernando did have a problem gambling, but I can assure you that was resolved long ago."

"Who knew about it?" Kenney asked.

"Only me and his mother, may she rest in peace."

"Okay, then I doubt there's a reason to look deeper there," Kenney said. "Anything else?"

"Nothing," Gustavo replied evenly.

"Several of our intelligence leads tell me they think this was an inside job because the vehicle used wasn't actually a presidential vehicle, but a very good likeness. That means somebody who knew quite a bit about how he traveled and when, and that suggests a leak inside your security teams."

"We're looking at that," Gustavo replied.

"I'd like to do my own looking," Kenney said with a forced smile.

"I'd prefer my people made those inquiries, Mr. Kenney."

"And I'd prefer they didn't," Kenney said. "You've already drawn enough attention, and it wouldn't do for identifiable people within your organization to go poking about and asking questions. That's only going to attract more unwanted heat from the press. My team, on the other hand, can approach this in a much more subtle fashion without drawing unneeded attention."

Gustavo appeared to consider that for a time and finally said, "Okay, but you will understand if I keep you on a very short leash."

Kenney shrugged as it was a small victory but a decisive one. "I would expect that. But you must also realize I'm a free agent. I can drop this at any time and walk away."

"Perhaps," Gustavo said, "but I don't think you will. Your reputation precedes you."

"Fair enough."

Gustavo stood and began to pace behind his desk. "There is one other issue I think I should make you aware of."

"Okay."

"Just before you arrived I received a brief from my people that someone attacked the home of Pascual Santos. Mr. Santos apparently escaped unharmed but has since gone missing. His home was burned to the ground. Allegedly, drugs were being manufactured on his estate and distributed to the populace of this city."

"You think this is somehow related to the kidnapping."

Gustavo stopped pacing. "I'm considering that possibility."

Kenney sighed. That wasn't good news at all. It meant that someone else was already working on the case. It could be chalked up to coincidence, but somehow Kenney wasn't buying that. There was more than a remote possibility that persons unknown had information about the kidnappers and was applying the thumbscrews. What Kenney couldn't tie up were the loose ends, such as where the hell drugs could possibly fit into the grand scheme of things.

"As it stands right now," Gustavo continued, almost as if he could read Kenney's thoughts, "we're treating Santos's disappearance as a clear indication he might have something to do with the kidnapping. The authorities in Quito have labeled him a fugitive, since there's no evidence to the contrary and no sign he was kidnapped or injured. All bodies have been accounted for and none of them Santos."

"Seems odd," Kenney admitted.

"Yes. We do know from witnesses we've questioned that the operation was conducted by a single man, an American. Strangely enough, he killed a large number of Pascual's personal security team, but he let the chemists and staff escape unharmed before blowing this drug lab to kingdom come."

"Sounds like the work of a professional."

"My intelligence people are still studying this, but the profilers believe just as you do. What we don't know is what it means."

"So why tell me this, Mr. President?" Kenney asked.

"I wanted you to be aware, just in case these incidents are related and you run into this man. We had his description passed to security and customs agents at all of the airports. Being he was American, I believed someone from Washington sent him to look into the disappearance of Senator Esposito. He was identified shortly thereafter. Came in yesterday afternoon on a private charter, and listed his business in Ecuador as a private military consultant. His paperwork identified him as Brandon Stone, a retired U.S. Army colonel."

"An alias," Kenney said.

"Undoubtedly. We also have information that he was seen questioning Erasmo Cabeza, a local business owner that used to have ties to money-laundering operations. Our intelligence says Cabeza knew Mario Esposito quite well. Bystanders also reported Stone was seen chasing a man just after his meeting with Cabeza, and that man was later found shot to death. We haven't identified the victim yet, but the police in Quito are working on it. This may have nothing to do with the kidnapping, but we're looking at every possibility."

"It's not unlikely this Colonel Stone was sent for the same reasons we were," Kenney said absently. "The timing is certainly interesting, and Cabeza's connection with Senator Esposito."

"Well, if your government did send Stone, I can tell you I don't like it," Gustavo said, taking his seat and madly puffing at his pipe. Clouds of gray, aromatic smoke curled around him. "I'm not keen on men like this being dispatched to my country without my knowledge. Just before you arrived, we were informed that he and his pilot flew up to San Lorenzo. I have arranged transportation for you immediately."

"Any assistance you can provide is appreciated," Kenney said.

Gustavo pulled the pipe from between his teeth, sat forward and pointed a finger at Kenney. "Let me be very clear on something, Mr. Kenney. Do not dispense random violence in my country of a nature similar to that of this American, or I'll boot you out of here so fast you won't know what hit you. I was not elected to start a bloodbath. If you find my son and return him safely, I will forever be in your debt. But despite any outcome, I will not allow you to kill indiscriminately."

"We will take all precautions to insure nobody gets hurt, Mr. President," Kenney said. He stood and added, "But we will defend ourselves if it becomes necessary. After all, we're taking a considerable risk."

Gustavo sat back with a deprecating expression and said, "And you're being well paid for it."

"We'll find your son, sir, and we'll bring him back here in one piece with minimal losses."

Gustavo stood and offered Kenney a hand. "You do that, Mr. Kenney, and I'll personally see to it you never want for anything again."

CHAPTER SIX

San Lorenzo, Ecuador

Mack Bolan maneuvered his rented Chevy convertible through the San Lorenzo midmorning traffic. He'd committed to memory the address of the oceanfront condominium properties alleged to be owned and operated by the Rivas family. Two names in particular filled the Executioner's thoughts: Carmita and Manuel. Intelligence from Stony Man Farm on this pair was thin.

Manuel was the self-made type. He'd been charged with running the business—willed to the three Rivas siblings following the death of their mother—and was reputed as an "upstanding member of the San Lorenzo community." Or so that was the story from the local press and ad agencies. In reality the guy was a worm; he would have turned out to be a nobody were it not for the machinations and protection of his brother.

Carmita Rivas was an entirely different story. She'd

attended one of the finest Catholic schools in Quito until her eighteenth birthday, immediately followed by a college education in Spain. On her return, she opened several boutiques in various large cities that catered to the politically influential and wealthy tourists. She was said to have affluent connections in country and abroad. Stony Man had sent a recent photo along with the dossier. Carmita Rivas was a good-looking woman with long dark hair and caramel-colored skin.

Bolan decided to start with Manuel as the most likely of the pair to be involved in something crooked. He didn't want to involve the woman if he could help it. He'd lean on Carmita only if nothing panned out with Manuel. He knew both of them would know if there was any truth to Cabeza's story about their brother being alive and well, and ready to make a comeback.

Bolan arrived at the condominiums and parked his rental. He double-checked the action of the Beretta, then tucked it beneath his lightweight blazer before going EVA. He found a young woman sunning in a teakwood chaise longue near the swimming pool, and he managed to get directions to the management office. If his luck held out, Manuel would be there and available so they could have a chat.

The Executioner made his way to the counter where a petite native woman sat in attendance. A local radio station droned in the background with native music. The woman was dark-skinned, pretty, with black hair and eyes to match.

"May I help you?" she asked in English, obviously

used to the touristy look Bolan had acquired, and not accidentally.

"Manuel Rivas, please," Bolan replied pleasantly, smiling behind his mirrored sunglasses.

"Mr. Rivas is quite busy today," she said. "Do you have an appointment?"

Bolan looked at his watch. "Actually, I'm just in town for the day and thought I would drop by. We're old friends."

The woman nodded knowingly, as if she somehow recognized Bolan, and without even bothering to ask his name she turned and headed toward a door in the back.

Bolan put his left forearm on the counter and leaned forward to conceal his right hand moving inside his jacket. No point in taking chances. If Manuel Rivas was behind the kidnappings, he'd be more alert than usual and ready for any sudden callers. Bolan watched the door carefully. A minute ticked by, then two. He was about to go around the counter and follow her when the door suddenly swung open and Manuel Rivas appeared. Bolan was a bit surprised by that, but he didn't let on. He was going to play the hand he'd been dealt and hope the cards fell in his favor.

Manuel didn't look all that different from his picture, although now he sported a goatee and what looked like about twenty extra pounds. His manner seemed relaxed enough so Bolan straightened and let his hands drop to his sides in a nonthreatening fashion.

"Manuel!" Bolan exclaimed, grinning. "It's good to see you again!"

The Colombian squinted but approached. He was obviously a bit puzzled, even appearing a little nervous. It was exactly the reaction Bolan hoped for. A man in Manuel's position would have known or met a lot of people in his time, everything from associates in the business to customers and potential customers. He was still trying to place Bolan—looking for any reason to recognize him—and that would keep him off guard long enough for the Executioner to play it out.

"Do I know you, sir?"

"Do you know me?" Bolan echoed. He snorted and made a show of looking exasperated. "I can't believe you'd even ask me that."

"I'm sorry, but I don't think—"

"I come all this way," Bolan said, throwing up his hands, "and then you ask if you know me. I'm disappointed, Manuel. I'm hurt, even."

At this point Manuel was clearly embarrassed. He turned toward the girl, obviously looking for any help she could provide him, but she just shrugged. Manuel turned back and flashed an ingratiating smile. "Wait a minute…you do look a little familiar."

"Well, I should hope so," Bolan said.

Manuel moved to the door leading into the office and opened it. He stepped out as Bolan went around the counter and got out of the view of the girl. As Manuel stepped close, Bolan grabbed his shirt collar and produced the pistol, shoving it into the Colombian's gut.

Bolan whispered, "Play like everything's fine and you might live a little longer."

Manuel nodded, and Bolan put his arm around the guy as he replaced the pistol. He steered the man through the office door and kept chatty, watching Manuel's face carefully for any betrayal. Manuel kept his eyes off the girl and acted as if everything was fine. Good, at least he knew how to follow directions. The two went through the back door and as soon as Bolan had closed it behind them he drew the pistol once more. They were in a small vestibule that connected to a larger sitting area with a set of stairs recessed into a wall on the right.

"Where can we go for privacy?" Bolan asked.

Manuel nodded toward the stairs, and Bolan waved the muzzle of the pistol in that direction. The stairway was a half-flight leading to a loft that had been converted into a functional but cozy office. Bolan ordered Manuel to a sofa against a far wall and to sit on his hands. After Manuel complied, Bolan holstered his pistol but kept a relatively safe distance between them.

"Who the fuck are you?" Manuel asked, his face reddening.

Bolan smiled coldly. "Someone who doesn't scare easily, so kill the tough-guy song and dance."

"You must be an idiot to do this to me," Manuel said. "Either that, or you don't know who you're dealing with."

"I know exactly who I'm dealing with," Bolan replied. "That's why I'm here. Your little operation in Quito is finished."

"I don't know what you're talking about," Manuel said in an even tone.

Bolan shrugged. "Suit yourself. But Pascual Santos won't be supplying any more drugs to the good citizens of Ecuador."

Manuel broke into a long and mocking laugh. "Do you actually think I had something to do with that? I'm not into drug-running. You must have me confused with someone else."

"I don't think so. Two different people gave me your name."

"And so naturally you believed them," Manuel said. "I am afraid to be the one to tell you that you've been deceived. There are many people who hate me, although I have never done anything to harm them. This reputation is undeserved."

"Oh, yeah, I'm sure you're a real saint," Bolan said. "I want to know who kidnapped Mario Esposito and Hernando Gustavo. You're going to tell me."

"What makes you think I know that?"

"Don't be coy. Somebody seems to think you know quite a bit."

"Who?"

Bolan paused a moment, choosing his words carefully. "The same people who say your brother's the real one pulling the strings."

"Adriano?" Something hardened in Manuel's expression. "The joke is on you, *señor*. My brother has been dead for more than three years."

"A few people think otherwise, Manuel. They say Adriano's still alive and that you've been taking care of things in his place."

"I had nothing to do with his...business. When he died, it died with him." Manuel made the sign of the cross. "Our mother never approved of his activities. My family earned its money honestly. Adriano changed all of that with his crimes, and I wanted no part of that. While I was not happy to see Adriano go, I believe he brought his demise upon his own head."

Bolan looked for deception in Manuel's eyes but he saw none. He also hadn't detected any lack of conviction in the man's responses. The Executioner had trained himself over the years to search for telltale signs somebody was lying; he'd almost acquired a sixth sense for it. He didn't see any of those signs in Manuel. He was beginning to believe that perhaps the Colombian was telling the truth.

"I've looked into your background, Rivas," Bolan said. "If your brother's dead, then someone has gone to an awful lot of trouble to point the finger at you. Who do you know would like to see you fall?"

"I have many enemies, *señor*," he replied. "Most of them are my enemies because they were the enemies of my brother, and for no other reason."

"Then it's a wonder you're still breathing."

"I agree with you."

Bolan took a moment longer to study Manuel before he was convinced the guy had told him the truth. So if Manuel Rivas hadn't inherited his brother's criminal legacy, somebody else had to be manipulating the situation. Maybe this guy was into something else crooked and maybe he wasn't, but Bolan was fairly confident Manuel didn't know anything about the disappearance of Gustavo and Esposito beyond what had leaked in the press. The Executioner would have to start looking elsewhere.

Carmita Rivas was next on his list.

"I'll find out who's behind this soon, Manuel," Bolan said, turning to go. "If you're smart, you'll beat feet out of town for a while."

The Executioner descended the stairs and smiled at the girl as he walked through the office and headed for the exit. As he emerged from the portico out front, he spotted a large SUV parking in the lot. Five men climbed from the vehicle and Bolan's senses went into high gear. With the exception of the lithe, front-seat passenger, the remaining men in the crew were big and ominous-looking. All of them moved with the signature gaits of men packing hardware. The smaller man who'd been riding shotgun closed the door behind him and then froze in place when he saw Bolan.

The Executioner saw the others take notice of the reaction and realized he'd stepped right into the middle of trouble.

Bolan went for the Beretta 93-R at the same time as the five hardmen clawed beneath jackets for their own weapons. The soldier was a heartbeat ahead of the rest of the pack and fired his pistol. The first 9 mm Parabellum round caught one of the crewmen in the throat, opening a gaping hole before severing his spine. The guy's head bounced doll-like on his shoulders before his body pitched forward to the pavement.

The Executioner grabbed cover to avoid the maelstrom of autofire that answered his opening play. Glass and wood chips erupted from the front of the office as the remaining quartet of gunners saturated the air with bullets. All but the leader were carrying machine pistols. A cacophony of gunfire drowned all other sounds and blended into a single, thunderous noise storm.

Bolan crawled behind a thick, concrete post and rolled into a seated position with his back against it. He flipped the selector switch to 3-round burst mode and then took a knee. He locked the pistol in a Weaver's grip, left forearm steadied against the pole, and delivered the first of two 3-shot volleys. The men seemed disoriented at first, obviously not prepared to deal with a skilled opponent. They dived for cover, but one gunner was too slow. Bolan's shots cored through the man's stomach and chest. The blast drove him backward and into a hedge growing next to a wrought-iron fence encircling the pool.

Bolan could hear the screams of the young woman who had been sunning herself in peace just a moment earlier. The Executioner looked for her to mark position and to make sure she was clear from his line of fire. Suddenly he spotted her head bobbing up and down as she ran for the gate. A mistake, because as she passed through it she encountered one of the gunners. He reached out and grabbed a handful of the terrified woman's hair. He waved his weapon in Bolan's direction while keeping his human shield in front of him as he shuffled sideways toward cover.

The Executioner gritted his teeth and attempted to

draw a bead on the man, but the woman was moving too erratically. At least she was putting up a spirited fight. Bolan looked to his rear and formulated a plan in seconds. He'd have to go around the back to see if he could flank the guy without being seen. There were still two others to consider, as well, but the life of the captive had to take precedence.

Bolan raced from cover, keeping low. He needed only a minute to circumvent the office building. He ran as fast as his muscular legs could propel him and in less than thirty seconds he had reached the opposite side. He risked a glance around the corner and saw the man now concealed behind a pillar—his back to Bolan—one arm tightly gripping the woman's waist, while he looked frantically around the pole and tried to find a target.

The Executioner couldn't see his two cohorts, but the numbers were running down and he'd just have to risk it. He stepped quickly from the corner of the building and sprinted toward their position. The gunman heard his approach and turned to see his enemy. He couldn't move quickly enough with his hostage pinned to him. The gunner shoved her away as he brought his pistol to bear.

It was all the delay Bolan needed.

He leveled the 93-R and squeezed the trigger. Three rounds struck center mass, one penetrating the diaphragm and the remaining pair through the breastbone. Frothy pink blood sprayed from the man's mouth as his machine pistol flew from numb fingers. He put both hands to his chest as he went down, the air escaping through his fingers with a grotesque hiss as he wheezed for breath. He was dead by the time he hit the ground.

Bolan rushed forward, yanked the sobbing woman to her feet and jerked his head in the direction from which he'd come. "Get over there and stay down."

The woman hesitated a moment, but the penetrating blue eyes quickly snapped her back to reality. She half ran, half staggered for the protection of the building, and Bolan watched her get most of the way before turning his attention to the last of this business. The shooting had stopped, and he couldn't see either of the remaining men. This wasn't the kind of attention he'd wished to attract. He would have preferred to set the time and locale of any engagement with the enemy rather than get pulled into a public gun duel in broad daylight.

Bolan moved toward the pool, since he didn't have much of a vantage point from his current location. He kept the Beretta extended, muzzle sweeping the area, ready for a threat to rear its ugly head. Movement between vehicles caught his attention. He saw the man who'd been driving the SUV dashing from fender to fender in an obvious attempt to flank the point where Bolan had originally taken cover. The Executioner knelt near a tree trunk as he selected single-shot mode and waited patiently for his chance. It came a moment later when the man's head popped up into the Tritium sights of Bolan's pistol.

The Executioner squeezed the trigger. The 9 mm Parabellum round drilled through the man's right temple and blew his brains out the other side. The corpse flipped sideways and disappeared from view behind the car. Bolan traded a tree for one of the thick hedges. Although he had subsonic cartridges chambered, he didn't want to risk letting the little man pinpoint his position.

Bolan had just settled into place when he detected the sound of footfalls on pavement to his right. He turned in time to see Manuel Rivas running for his position, pistol raised. The man was swearing at him in his native tongue. The soldier was only mildly surprised at the sudden assault—especially considering he'd just spared Manuel's life—but he didn't hesitate to react. Hesitation could kill.

Bolan snap-aimed and fired a double-tap, his first round connecting with Manuel's hip and the second punching through his left chest wall and ultimately his heart. The impact spun the man and he toppled to the ground. His body twitched a few times before going still.

More running on pavement caused Bolan to look in the direction of the parking lot once more. To his surprise, the remaining crew member was hoofing it at top speed for the SUV. The Executioner considered pursuit a moment, but the sirens wailing in the distance changed his mind. He leaped from concealment and sprinted for his own vehicle. He had to follow the escapee. With Manuel dead, that guy was his only remaining lead. A mysterious lead, but his only one all the same.

As he climbed behind the wheel of his convertible and followed the SUV out of the parking lot with a screech of tires, Bolan wondered a moment how the guy had pegged him. Obviously the word was out about his assault on Santos's drug lab. What he couldn't understand was what relationship, if any, these men had to Manuel Rivas. Had they been sent to protect or to assassinate?

Bolan powered smoothly through the traffic, staying back far enough to avoid detection. It was a risk but one he was willing to take. It was possible his quarry knew Bolan was following him, and he'd lead him into a trap. Then again, he hadn't actually seen the Executioner take out Manuel because he'd been too busy trying to flee.

What bothered Bolan more than anything was that up to this point it seemed someone was always one step ahead of him. The guy who'd followed him to Cabeza's hadn't been fortunate to live long enough to tell him anything. Someone had obviously informed the ringleader of this operation of Bolan's hit on the Quito operation. And then these heavies just happen to show up in San Lorenzo at the same time he did?

Bolan couldn't accept that as dumb luck on the enemy's part. Either someone had been watching every move since his arrival in Ecuador, or the enemy had connections back in Wonderland. Either case painted a grim picture for Esposito and Gustavo. The fact they'd been hounding Bolan from the get-go spelled possible doom for this mission before it had barely got off the ground. In fact, the enemy might consider it better to take their chances with an alternate plan and just kill the hostages outright.

Bolan reached into his pocket and withdrew a cell phone. He pressed a speed-dial button and the phone was halfway through the first ring before the voice of Jack Grimaldi came on the line.

"What's up, boss?"

"Things aren't off to a good start," Bolan said.

"What happened?"

"Lead number one just went out of the picture."

Bolan heard Grimaldi sigh. "Anything I can do to help?"

"Yeah. See if you can get us a chopper, preferably a military type. I'm sure the Farm can get you the clearances you need."

"Check." There was a pause, then, "Any idea where we might be going?"

"Not yet," Bolan admitted, "but when I do, I get the feeling a plane won't do the trick."

"I'll get on it right away."

"Good. I'm following up on a lead and I'm not sure where it ends. I'll touch base again as soon as I can. Out here."

Bolan returned his full attention to the road. The traffic was dense enough that he could maintain a discreet distance. He hadn't been kidding Grimaldi about this trail—he really didn't know where it might lead—but he'd signed up for this War Everlasting long ago, so he was in it for the long haul. Bolan had hoped to shake trees to see who fell out.

Now it looked as if he was getting his wish.

CHAPTER SEVEN

It was close to noon when the small jet touched down at the private airfield in San Lorenzo. The plane was a loaner from President Gustavo and the pilot had orders to remain exclusively at the Quail Group's disposal. Curtis Kenney was appreciative of Gustavo's cooperation but he hadn't liked the old man's threat, and it had to have been showing in his expression because Pete Morristown picked up on it almost immediately.

"What's up?"

"My blood pressure," Kenney said as he washed down three aspirin with a sparkling water. "It looks like Gustavo plans to keep us on a short leash."

"How do you know?"

Kenney shrugged as they rose to help their teammates offload equipment and overnight bags. "Because he said as much."

"The problem with politicians is they don't understand the finesse in our kind of work," Morristown said, shaking his head. "Sometimes I wish we could just stick to business and skip all the bullshit. I'd take a straight fight anytime over a gig where we have to walk on eggshells the whole time."

Kenney chuckled. "You signed up for this stuff, chum. Better get used to it."

"If only the money weren't so good," Morristown replied with a frown. "Oh, well."

The four men busied themselves loading their bags and packs into the back of a Dodge Durango before climbing aboard. Morristown took the wheel with Kenney riding shotgun. The other two men of the Quail Group, Buford Jones and Louis Sturgis, sat in the rear. Jones was a big, hulking black man with tree-trunk legs and biceps the size of cantaloupes. A "walking tower of muscle" was the way Morristown had once described him. Jones was an ex-Marine with an impeccable record as a professional soldier and a history of duty tours doing things best not examined too closely. Sturgis was comparatively smaller than the rest of his team, sporting the lithe frame of a gymnast. His demure looks hid the fierce spirit within. Sturgis, a former demo expert with the Navy SEALs, was a firebrand combatant and quite capable of carrying the ball as far as needed.

Together, the four men of the Quail Group comprised a formidable team. They had a reputation for getting the job done no matter how tough or high-risk it might seem. They had never failed a mission to date, and Kenney didn't plan to start with this one.

As they left the airport tarmac, Kenney took out a

rough sketch composite of the mysterious American professional who had suddenly made an appearance. During the flight, Kenney had reached out to his contacts in the NSA and CIA. Neither of them could find any information on one Colonel Brandon Stone, either retired or currently serving in the U.S. armed forces. This led Kenney to his original assessment that Stone was nothing more than a paper ghost.

"This guy's definitely using an alias," Kenney announced to his crew. "My contacts at the CIA are usually able to get something for me, which tells me this guy's not operating through any normal channels."

"So if he's not Company and he's not NSA or DOD," Jones said, "that means black ops with an outfit that's not even on the books."

Kenney nodded. "That'd be my guess, as well. And since we can now assume he's not who he claims to be, I'm left wondering who sent him."

"And why," Morristown added.

"He definitely uses unconventional methods," Kenney replied with a nod. "And it doesn't seem like he gives a damn if he draws attention or not, considering the havoc he's wreaked around Quito. The guy's already blown some drug lab sky-high and killed a dozen men or so."

"I can't say I'll lose much sleep over that," Morristown said.

"Me, neither," Kenney admitted, "but I get the feeling he's just getting started. If he's here looking for Esposito or Gustavo, I'm concerned he might get in our way. The guy's a liability to our mission, in that case, and one we can't afford to let just run wild. I think we should do our best to avoid him if at all possible, but be ready if we do run into him."

"And what if we can't avoid him?" Morristown asked.

"Then we simply remove him from the equation," Kenney replied.

MACK BOLAN PARKED his car at the curb within two hundred yards of where his quarry had stopped. He'd followed the man along the main shoreline drive to the southern outskirts of San Lorenzo, eventually winding up at a massive seaside community that resembled an old Spanish villa. The enclave was really little more than a series of very expensive houses with a single street dividing the neighborhood. The abodes here could have been classified as anything but humble, and Bolan smelled old money mixed with blood money.

The Executioner reached to the field glasses he'd stowed in the glove box and raised them to his eyes. He watched as the small leader of the hit team he'd encountered turned into the drive of a house surrounded by tall, adobe walls and staffed by a pair of bruisers in three-piece suits. They pulled the guy from the SUV, relieved him of his firearm, then escorted him through the massive wrought-iron gate leading onto the property, leaving his car outside the gate.

Bolan lowered the binoculars and sat in contemplation a moment, then scanned several of the properties nearest him for house numbers. Once he had a pattern, he reached into the pocket of his blazer and withdrew a small notebook. A quick check confirmed it for him. Stony Man had managed to run down the last-known current address for Carmita Rivas, and the number pattern seemed to match. The warrior was a bit surprised his proverbial leprechaun would be sloppy enough to risk leading him straight to the pot of gold.

A moment later he realized there would be no treasure trove here. Six armed men emerged from the gate and spread out before rapidly converging on his Camaro. The weapons they brandished spoke to their intent.

Bolan turned the key in the ignition and the convertible's engine roared to life. He slapped the stick into Reverse, then tromped the gas as he popped the clutch. Tires squealed on pavement, churning smoke and dust as the Executioner powered his car into a speedy reverse. When he reached optimal speed, Bolan jerked the wheel and worked clutch and brake to power the sports car into a J-turn. The heavy front end swung 180 degrees; a quick second motion on the stick had Bolan accelerating away from the gunners.

In the rearview mirror Bolan saw a van emerge from the gate and pull onto the street. It stopped just long enough to pick up the foot pursuers, then accelerated toward Bolan. The soldier wanted to make it look as if he were attempting to escape, but not actually get away from this team. He was keeping the enemy on his—or her—toes and that seemed to be getting results. Bolan's very presence in San Lorenzo was making someone nervous enough to send out the big guns. That told him he was on the right track.

The Executioner put the convertible in fourth gear and powered away from the small, gentle community. He needed to get out in the open where he could exercise some combat stretch and not endanger innocents. He found his opportunity a moment later in a turnoff, whipped the vehicle around and pointed it back the way he came. He pulled onto the street just as the van was slowing to make its turn.

Bolan stuck his pistol out the window and fired at the driver, squeezing the trigger several times. The van's windshield spiderwebbed but the erratic steering told the Executioner he'd nailed the mark. The van fishtailed before slowing and bumping onto the curve. It crashed into a stand of trees on the opposite end of the side road where Bolan had executed his turnaround.

Bolan brought his vehicle to a halt, then reached into the bag next to him and procured an M-26 high-explosive grenade. He leaped off the front seat onto the back of the Camaro, and scrambled across the trunk until he dropped to the ground at the rear. He hit the pavement running, hoping to get close enough with the advantage of surprise before allowing his enemy to recover from the impact. Bolan reached the back doors of the panel van just as one swung open and produced its first occupant.

The gunner's expression transformed from confusion into surprise, but Bolan wiped that expression clean with a shot from the Beretta. A 9 mm Parabellum round punched through the man's lower jaw, ripping away a good portion of the fleshy part of his neck and cracking bone before lodging in his spine. The man came off his feet, his skull smacking the lip of the van roof, and sailed backward into the interior. Two of his comrades became entangled with the corpse, and Bolan dispatched them with equally deadly shots before they could recover.

The Executioner quickly moved to the front of the van and found the front-seat passenger still dazed by the crash. The driver was slumped on the steering wheel, dead. Bolan cleared away the broken window glass, unlocked and opened the van door from the inside, and yanked the passenger out. The man stumbled and staggered on wobbly legs as he muttered something totally unintelligible. The Executioner wondered for a moment if the guy was injured seriously enough to warrant taking him to a hospital, but he needed information first. As Bolan headed toward his car, he yanked the pin from the grenade and tossed it into the back of the van. He had reached the relative safety of the Camaro by the time it blew.

Bolan opened the passenger door and deposited his hostage in the front seat before climbing behind the wheel and powering away from the van, which was now engulfed in flames. He kept one eye on his prisoner, making several turns on side roads before bringing the vehicle to a halt behind a stand of trees bordering the shoulder of what appeared to be a crushed-rock access road. The warrior pulled a pistol and slapped the face of the man next to him a few times to rouse him into full consciousness.

Bolan could see this wasn't the man he'd followed to the house, so he was probably a hired gun. The guy he'd been tracking had either been in the back of the van or still at the house.

"W-who are you?" the man stammered, a glazed look still evident in his eyes. His English was broken but understandable.

"Shut up and listen," Bolan replied. The Executioner took a moment to assess the man more closely. Blood soaked through the prisoner's pants at both knees, probably where he'd smashed them against the dash of the van on impact. There was also a gaping laceration across the left ribs, the open skin bleeding mildly. No doubt he would need medical attention, but Bolan would deal with that shortly. Bolan put the muzzle of his Beretta to the man's head. "Answer my questions and I'll make sure to get you medical help. You understand?"

The man nodded.

"Who do you work for?"

"Arauca," the thug replied. "Chico Arauca."

The name didn't mean anything to Bolan. "He sent you after me?"

A nod.

"Who lives at that house you came from?"

There was a moment of silence, and Bolan shoved the muzzle harder against the guy's head to make him aware of what would happen should he not get the answers he sought. The Executioner didn't like these games but he didn't have a choice. The numbers were running down and the longer it took him to find Esposito and Gustavo the less chance he'd find them alive.

"It is owned by Señorita Rivas," the thug replied.

"Is this Arauca working for her?"

The man shook his head. "I can say no more. They will kill me."

"I'll kill you if you don't," Bolan said. "Provided you don't bleed to death first. Talk to me and at least you have a chance."

A long silence followed and the warrior let his prisoner chew on that thought. This one was obviously young and inexperienced; Bolan marked him at only nineteen or twenty. He was playing on that inexperience in hope the guy would be truthful.

"Now, is Arauca working for Carmita Rivas or not?"

"He come protect her," the man said.

"Two men were kidnapped day before last," Bolan said. "One of those men was President Gustavo's son. Is Arauca or Rivas responsible for this?"

The man shook his head. "I do not know about this."

Bolan swore under his breath. He could only believe the guy was telling him the truth. For a moment he entertained the idea of employing more forceful methods of interrogation to validate he was getting the information, but he dismissed it. Torturing this wounded animal probably wouldn't reveal any more intelligence than he already had. He'd have to put in a call to Stony Man directly to find out what he could on this Chico Arauca. But he had a name—and he'd confirmed the house was Carmita Rivas's residence—and for now that was enough.

Bolan turned the car around and pulled onto the street. He stopped long enough to go around the car and pull the man from it. He sat him on the ground and propped his back against a utility pole, then retrieved a medical kit from the bag. He quickly field-dressed the man's wounded side, slapped ice packs on his knees, then left the area. Once on the main road, he called the operator and requested an ambulance. Bolan surmised the injuries weren't serious enough that he'd actually bleed to death before help arrived, but it had made for a useful ploy. If nothing else, he had a name: Chico Arauca.

It was time to arrange a meeting—face-to-face.

ADRIANO RIVAS ENTERED El Encontrar under the escort of four of Arauca's biggest and best security men.

The club was deserted of any patrons, and only a few of the staff had arrived in preparation for the late-afternoon opening. Most of them didn't give him a second glance, obviously accustomed to the comings and goings of Erasmo Cabeza's "business" associates. It was just as well, since Rivas had come with good reasons to avoid attracting unwanted attention.

Rivas found the club owner in his office, alone. He smiled as he and his men entered Cabeza's office unchallenged. Rivas had never considered Erasmo Cabeza all that bright to begin with, and for a man in Cabeza's position to not have bodyguards with him at all times only served to reinforce Rivas's opinion. Apparently, Cabeza figured seclusion inside his club during off hours as security enough. That was going to prove unfortunate for the man.

"Good day, Erasmo," Rivas said.

The heavyset man looked up and blanched, the blood draining from the normally dark complexion that tinged rosy with any sort of exertion. Rivas wondered how there was even enough brain power to move that flab around. Cabeza had always been an obese slob, and Rivas could now see that in the few years since his absence time hadn't been any kinder to the man.

"Adriano?" Cabeza whispered hollowly.

"In the flesh," Rivas said as he took a chair.

Rivas's men spread through the room. One of them quickly circled Cabeza's desk and silently frisked him. He then gestured for Cabeza to move his chair back where they could watch his hands and he complied, though not without throwing the bodyguard a look of indignation. The man simply stepped back—arms folded with one hand inside his jacket—his expression cold and impassive.

Cabeza returned his attention to Rivas and his breath quickened. "So…so it's true. You are alive."

"Of course," Rivas replied. He waved Cabeza's statement away as a declaration of the obvious. "Do you honestly think I could be killed off so easily? Come now, Erasmo, where is your faith? I was certain we knew each other better than that."

"What do you want?"

Rivas looked around the room in mock study. Cabeza's tastes in decor did not mirror his own, although the club owner did betray a certain amount of class. The fact nature had cruelly robbed him of a Colombian birthright wasn't Cabeza's fault. Rivas had very little use for Ecuadorians, but he found men like Cabeza especially distasteful. The guy had made a fortune in the money-laundering business, then caved at the first sign of pressure from political and legal officials. Cabeza's former relationship with Mario Esposito was no secret in underworld circles.

"I've always liked you, Erasmo," Rivas lied. He stared at the man. "But news of your recent activities has reached me, and I'm disturbed by it."

"I don't know what the hell you're talking about," Cabeza said.

"I'm sure you don't." Rivas showed him a smile, and one into which he put no warmth. "Or at least that's what I thought you would say. You see, Erasmo, I understand how a man in your position could give in to outside pressure. Oh, I know of you and Esposito. Anyone with a marginal intellect could figure out quickly enough that someone would come to you after the good American senator was kidnapped so suddenly."

"Why don't you cut this shit and get to the point, Adriano?" Cabeza said, gesturing toward his desk. "I have a lot of work to do."

Rivas leaned forward and sneered. "Don't be insolent, my friend, or I'll have my men open you up from your pathetic pecker to your gullet, and display you in open public like a gutted whale."

Cabeza visibly swallowed hard.

Rivas continued quietly. "Now I know that several people have already called on you, some of them officials and others who are not so official. Any business they have with you doesn't concern me, but I am curious to know is what you told the American."

"What American?" Cabeza said. "I spoke to no American."

"So now you lie to me," Rivas said in a frosty tone.

Rivas nodded at his men and they immediately converged on Cabeza. Two of them pulled Cabeza's arms behind him while a third wrapped an inch-thick nylon rope around his throat and pulled up and back. The maneuver didn't really choke him as much as force his mouth closed so he had to struggle to breathe through his nostrils. Rivas took a small piece of satisfaction from watching Cabeza's smug expression turn to one of panic. The fat-assed club owner couldn't breathe that well through his nostrils, having become more dependent on mouth breathing through the years due to his ever-increasing girth.

Rivas stood calmly and walked around the desk to stand in front of Cabeza. He held out his palm and the fourth guard produced a long cylindrical object about as thick as a carpenter's pencil. The bodyguard twisted something at one end of the device and then dropped it into his hand. Rivas smiled as he studied the puzzled look in Cabeza's eyes and then at the object. It was a miniature blowtorch, the kind used for soldering components found in automobiles and portable electronics.

"You see, Erasmo," Rivas said as he withdrew a cigarette lighter from his pocket, "I have contacts who inform me you spoke to this American. At first I didn't make the connection because the American hit our lab just outside of town. You couldn't have possibly known about that, now could you? But then I was informed he was going to San Lorenzo. It wasn't until I arrived here to meet with an associate that I discovered the American had been followed here by one of my competitor's many spies. Unfortunately my own contacts were forced to eliminate this man before he could talk to the American."

Cabeza's eyes widened farther as Rivas lit the torch. Rivas blew out the lighter as he released it to add dramatic flair. He then dropped the lighter in his pocket and studied the blue-white flame issuing from the torch with interest. His eyes gleamed as he turned to focus on Cabeza once more.

"The man my people killed could not have had the time to tell this American about my dear brother and sister in San Lorenzo. Only *you* would have known about this. It's too bad you couldn't keep your fat lips closed. I had planned to approach you first about some laundering business, see if perhaps I could talk some sense into you. I could have made you a very rich man, Erasmo. Now, I'm going to make you a very dead man, and I'm going to do it slowly…just one piece at a time."

As Rivas brought the torch in close and waved the flame near Cabeza's groin, he added, "And I'm going to enjoy every minute of it."

CHAPTER EIGHT

"We ran down the name you gave us, Striker," Hal Brognola said, his expression visibly weary even over the laptop monitor. "You're not going to like it."

"Story of your life, eh?" Grimaldi cracked, nudging the Executioner with an elbow.

Bolan nodded grimly as he said, "Give it to me."

Barbara Price laid it out for him. "Geraldo 'Chico' Arauca has been in and out of trouble since he was eleven. Most of the information on his juvenile offenses was filed in the rectangular bin long ago."

"As you can probably guess," Brognola interjected, "Colombian officials didn't do a real good job of record-keeping prior to the 1990s."

"Any idea if there's a connection between Arauca and Adriano Rivas?" Bolan asked.

"No question," Price said. "Arauca is a known associate and chief enforcer for Rivas...or least he *was*. After Rivas's death, Arauca seemed to drop off the radar.

Apparently law enforcement in Colombia figured he'd
crawled under some rock since he no longer had Rivas's
protection. Not that he needed it. The guy was no angel.
Arauca and Rivas were apparently childhood friends
and came up together through the criminal ranks. Intelligence reports say wherever Rivas was, Arauca was
usually close by."

"You have a picture of him?" Bolan asked.

Price tapped the screen and a moment later her and
Brognola's faces were replaced by a grainy shot of
Arauca.

Price's voice continued coming through clearly as
she said, "This is the most recent mug shot the Colombian federal agencies had of Arauca. It's about eight
years old."

Bolan studied the photo for a long time, trying to
match it to any one of the many faces he'd already encountered. Finally he said, "This might be the one I ran
into at Manuel Rivas's condo. I only got a brief look before those goons tried to punch my ticket."

"Yes," Brognola said as the picture of Arauca disappeared and the monitor returned to the live display.
"That reminds me, I hear you're causing quite a com-
motion down there."

"Who'd that come from?"

Brognola frowned. "The Man…who else? I guess
Reynaldo Gustavo called and gave him an earful. He was
pretty upset from what I gathered. Wanted to know why
we were sending operatives down there without his permission, what the President was trying to pull, et cetera."

"I assume he denied any knowledge."

"Of course," Brognola said with a shrug. "He told Gustavo he didn't have a clue what he was talking about and that he hadn't authorized any 'official' missions into Ecuador. I took a little heat for that one. Drawing that kind of attention isn't your usual style, Striker."

"Sorry, Hal, but I was getting no place fast," Bolan said. "I needed to shake things up and see who jumped. Now I think we may be getting close to something. How did Gustavo take the President's denial?"

"It seemed to satisfy him," Brognola replied.

"Especially when the President reminded Gustavo that he'd allowed the operation of a private military company in the country without even consulting the American embassy," Price added.

"A PMC's operating down here?" Bolan asked, growing concerned.

Price nodded. "That's not exactly how we wanted to break it to you, but yes, that's the long and short of it. A four-man team known as the Quail Group has penetrated the country on official sanction from the government of Ecuador."

"For what purpose?"

"Same as yours, apparently," Brognola said. "We think they were hired by TOBA, but we haven't confirmed that. We know Fred Proctor took an unscheduled trip to Houston only hours after the Man received official word of the kidnapping. Shortly after that, the Quail Group lands in-country and we now have intelligence from the CIA desk that word among Gustavo's intelligence ranks says the Quail Group is handling the investigation from now until further notice. They also have the full cooperation of Gustavo's personal staff."

"Perhaps we would have been better off taking the direct approach after all," Price said. "If we'd just asked Gustavo to let you assist, we might not have had to insert you covertly."

"I don't think it would have made any difference," Bolan replied. "If Gustavo's cooperating with the Quail Group, it's for no reason other than he has to. I'm sure he didn't ask for TOBA's help."

"You're thinking they offered it and he was in no other position but to accept," Brognola concluded.

"Bingo," Bolan said.

"Okay, fine, but what carrot could they have possibly dangled over Gustavo's head?" Price asked.

"It wouldn't take much," Bolan said. "The hope of getting his son back alive would be enough. If they could convince him the U.S. didn't plan to do anything to assist in recovering the MIAs, it stands to reason Gustavo would take whatever help he could get."

"I see where you're going now," Price replied. "It wouldn't hurt TOBA, either."

Brognola snorted. "You're damn right it wouldn't. A whole bunch of Congressional finger-pointing went on when Fred Proctor was the first to propose cozying up to Ecuador. An exclusive supplier to the United States would not only make the Arabs sit up and take notice, but it would take the heat off TOBA to quit sitting on the reserves. They'd lose a lot of money if they had to start actually distributing U.S. reserve supply."

"More disconcerting is what happens if we had to start dipping into our reserves," Bolan said. "Wouldn't be long before the country was right back where she started. Except this time we'd have nothing to fall back on."

"Fair enough," Price said. "But I hate to be the one to point out that none of this seems to explain the involvement of someone like Rivas in the kidnappings. What could he possibly hope to gain?"

"That's the part I can't answer yet," Bolan said. "But I do know it has something to do with drugs, and it's important to keep the heat on them."

"So you believe the rumors about Rivas still being alive are true?" Brognola asked.

"Based on what you've just told me about Arauca?" Bolan nodded after a moment. "Yeah, I think Rivas is alive *and* about to make his play. I don't yet know for what, but I'm sure I'll figure that out once I have sissy to bargain with."

"Just watch out for this Quail Group," Brognola said. "We wouldn't want one of our own to fall under friendly fire."

"Agreed," the Executioner said, his face a grim mask. "With any luck I can hit Carmita Rivas's place, get the information I need, and get out before this crew comes anywhere near me."

"That might be more difficult than you think," Price said. "Bear just forwarded some intelligence to you on this Quail Group. It looks like they're already on their way to your area of operation, if they're not already there."

"I'll look it over," Bolan said. "Out here."

The Executioner killed the live feed and then turned to the encrypted information that had come through via a standard newsgroup link. Bolan quickly downloaded Kurtzman's intelligence to the local drive and then ran the program that would decipher the encryption. Within minutes, he had the dossier and all the intelligence Stony Man could glean on the Quail Group.

They were a registered and duly authorized private military company with impeccable references.

Grimaldi looked over Bolan's shoulder as he scanned the dossier of the Quail Group members, and whistled. "Damn, Sarge, these guys are the real biz."

The Executioner had to nod in agreement. The team was led by a Curtis Kenney, a decorated military veteran with a sterling service record. Kenney was undoubtedly in the caliber of the men of Phoenix Force and Able Team, although nowhere near as experienced. Still, it was apparent the Quail Group could hold its own. The other three members were equally matched, and there was no mistaking the success rate of their missions. Bolan knew professionals when he saw them and undoubtedly the Quail Group fit the bill.

"Only strange thing about these guys is their name," Grimaldi said.

"Not if you understand the bird," Bolan said.

"Huh? Okay, Sarge, I think you'll have to enlighten me on this one."

"Quails are part of the pheasant family. I used to do a lot of pheasant hunting with my dad." The very mention of Samuel Bolan caused nostalgia mixed with regret to surface in the Executioner's conscious. Some of those earliest memories flooded back to him in that brief spell, happy memories—memories of better times before Sam Bolan's untimely departure.

Before the Mafia.

"Quail will typically keep hidden until absolutely necessary, and in most cases they'll crawl away from a potential danger area rather than fly. They have the ability to blend into their surroundings and move with considerable stealth."

"Dandy," Grimaldi said. "That's all the addition we need to an already difficult mission."

"Like I told Hal, I'll be able to avoid them if my luck holds out."

"Which, up until this point, it hasn't."

The Executioner shook his head by way of agreement. "I can't argue with that."

"So what's the plan?"

"Well, I'd hoped to get in, grab Carmita Rivas and get out with minimal effort. From what I know, this place will be locked up tight, especially since my unscheduled run-in with some of the house crew. I don't have any intelligence on the interior layout. I'll have to go in hard and fast, and come out the same way."

"Anything I can do to help?" Grimaldi asked with a hopeful gleam in his eye.

"Yeah," Bolan replied. "I'll need you to run interference for me on my exit scenario. I'm sure Carmita Rivas will prove a handful. It'd be nice to know I've got someone watching my six."

Stony Man's ace pilot didn't often get the opportunity to work side by side with the Executioner in the combat zone. When flying sanctioned missions for Able Team or Phoenix Force, Grimaldi rarely saw action unless he needed to extract the boys from a hot zone. But missions with the Executioner were usually more exciting and unpredictable. Grimaldi loved it when Bolan chose to involve him in a greater support role because it kept things interesting. Then again, things were always interesting where Mack Bolan was concerned.

"Then I'm your guy," the Stony Man ace said, cracking his knuckles in anticipation.

"I DO NOT KNOW what strings you have pulled to get the cooperation of my government, *señor*," said Felipe Redondo, captain of the San Lorenzo police force, "but I can assure you I do not like it."

"We don't really give a shit if you like it or not," Pete Morristown snapped.

"Chill, Pete," Curtis Kenney said, gesturing sharply with a hand. "I'll handle this."

Morristown pinned Kenney with a furious look but fell silent. Kenney didn't like dressing down his colleagues, especially not his best friend, in front of outsiders, but they didn't have time for this. There were moments Morristown could be a bit temperamental and quick to join an argument; right then he couldn't afford to indulge Morristown's knock-down, drag-out approach.

The four men of the Quail Group were assembled just inside the perimeter of the residential complex now surrounded by police tape. Bodies were scattered everywhere, and from what Kenney had gathered it reeked of Brandon Stone's handiwork. They had learned of the incident via a telephone call from one of Gustavo's security people.

"All we want to determine is who's responsible for this," Kenney told Redondo. "Were there any witnesses?"

Redondo held up an index finger. "One witness…a young woman, and she is most unsettled right now by what she has seen."

"Can we talk with her?" Kenney asked, although he thought he already knew the answer.

"Not yet," Redondo replied. "She is our only witness and we cannot allow her to speak to anyone else until she has been thoroughly interrogated. She will remain in our custody and under my personal protection until we have finished with her. Then you may perhaps talk to her."

"It'll be too late by then," Morristown muttered.

"Fine," Kenney said, frowning at his friend's continued malice. "I guess I'll just have to call President Gustavo and let him know you don't wish to cooperate with us. That will be unfortunate."

Redondo visibly stiffened but he didn't lose his composure. "You may call whomever you wish, *señor*. But for now I think it better if you do not remain here."

Okay, so Redondo obviously realized it was an empty threat—it had been worth a try. He was treading on much thinner ground than the San Lorenzo policeman right now, since Gustavo had already made it clear the limits of what he would tolerate regardless of the fact his son's life was on the line. Kenney hadn't dared mention it to the Ecuadorian president when arriving in Quito, but he didn't believe either of the hostages was still alive. This Brandon Stone, though, he and his connection to the events of the past thirty-six hours interested Kenney. It was one of the reasons he'd elected to continue with the job following his meet with Gustavo.

"Hey, boss," Jones called.

Kenney turned as Jones handed him a photograph. "What's this?"

"A grainy picture of that Colonel Stone," Jones replied. "I just downloaded and printed it from information sent by the Ecuadorian intelligence service."

Morristown chuckled. "I guess they got the guy on camera, after all."

The comment gave Curtis Kenney an idea. He turned and produced the photograph for Redondo to see. He pointed and said, "We believe *this* man is responsible for what's happened here, as well as recent violence in Quito. We also think he might have had something to do with the kidnapping of President Gustavo's son. Now we're willing to cooperate here, but you need to help us."

Redondo took the picture and studied it for a long time. He nodded a few times and kept looking behind him at a nearby squad car. Kenney couldn't figure out what he was doing, but he guessed that their key witness was probably locked away safely inside that car. Kenney weighed the risks of a snatch-and-run play and decided against it. They had the cops outgunned but not outnumbered, and he couldn't get away from the echo of Gustavo's threat running through his head. He had a lot of money plus the reputation of his group riding on this deal.

Kenney had to make good on that.

Redondo scratched his chin as he looked at the picture. "Well, this does look like the man our witness saw. But she is claiming that he saved her life and she won't speak about whether he was responsible for this."

"Your country's intelligence officials say this guy's a murderer and a menace," Morristown said. "And you're telling me your witness claims just the opposite?"

Redondo held up the picture, keeping his attention on Kenney and effectively ignoring Morristown. "*Señor,* may I keep this photograph?"

Kenney nodded. "Of course, Captain. Call it a measure of good faith on our part. Would you be willing to give us a little information in return?"

Redondo folded the picture, tucked it away inside his uniform jacket, then said, "I will answer a few questions."

"Can you tell me if any of the individuals killed were people of importance?"

"Only one that we have identified so far," Redondo replied. "He is a man of some notoriety in San Lorenzo. His name is, or rather was, Manuel Rivas. He was the brother of Adriano Rivas, a major drug lord from Colombia. Adriano was a big criminal, and he eventually got what was coming to him."

"And what exactly was that?"

"He was killed during a military drug raid," Redondo replied in a way that almost made Kenney think he was elated by the very idea. "Adriano Rivas killed many. He liked to think of himself as a man of the people, but in fact he was a murderer and peddler of the white death. His departure from this existence was not met with many tears."

"Sounds like a nice guy," Morristown replied.

"What about this Manuel Rivas?" Kenney said quietly, hoping not to press his luck. "Is there anything else you can tell us about him? Something that might be useful?"

"There is nothing else I can tell you," Redondo replied, then turned on his heel and headed for the squad car.

Kenney turned and gestured for his men to follow him. Redondo hadn't been that helpful. Kenney could understand why. The policeman was protecting what he viewed as his territory, and he had no legal obligation to answer to what he viewed to be nothing more than a gang of American thugs with profit motive. The idea didn't sit real well with Kenney, but he also knew he couldn't do a thing about it.

As they were getting into their SUV, a petite woman approached the vehicle from the side not visible to the officers ranged around the parking lot. Kenney reached inside his jacket, ready for trouble, but the woman looked fairly harmless. Still, it wasn't as if Americans were necessarily safe in Ecuador. Many such demure women had bombs strapped to them beneath their skirts. Those things were as much a part of the present as they were the past.

"Pardon me, *señor*," the woman said.

"Yeah?"

"I saw you talking to the policeman." Her eyes flicked in the direction of the crime scene. Her tone dripped with venom as she continued, "Captain Redondo, he is not a nice man. Most of my people think he wants to be a dictator."

"Yeah," Morristown said from behind the wheel, ducking his head to study the woman through Kenney's open door. "He's a real pain in the ass."

The woman gave him only a brief look before returning her attention to Kenney. "The men who were killed today, they worked for Manuel. A big man came in and pretended to be a friend, and they went up to Manuel's office and talked."

"Do you know what they talked about?" Kenney asked.

"I could not hear them. But I saw the man who did this horrible thing. I know that Captain Redondo will do nothing. He did not like Manuel. He will not work too hard to find his killer, I think. But I saw the man who did this and I will not forget his face."

Kenney turned and exchanged wicked grins with the rest of his team. He nodded toward Sturgis, who turned the laptop screen in the woman's direction. It had the face of Colonel Brandon Stone still plastered across the screen.

Kenney jerked his thumb at the picture and said, "Is that him?"

She took a sharp breath and her hands went to her mouth as her eyes glistened very suddenly in the mid-afternoon sunlight. "That is him. That is the man who killed Manuel." She looked pleadingly at Kenney and said, "Manuel was my lover, my heart, *señor*. I do not have much money, but I will pay you everything I have to find this man and kill him. I will pay anything."

"Whoa, there, missy, we're not murderers," Kenney said. "But we do want to find him and stop him as badly as you do. Now, do you have any idea where he might have gone or where he might be now?"

"I see him follow one of Manuel's men after he killed all of them." She shuddered, obviously still traumatized by the immense violence she had experienced.

"Can you give us anything more specific than that?"

She nodded. "I have seen this man before. He will probably go and get more men. He is in charge of security for the whole family. He will probably go to Carmita's home."

"Carmita?"

"Manuel's sister."

"Do you know where she lives?"

"I will take you there."

"No way," Morristown said. "Curtis, you can't actually be thinking about going along with that. We don't need some woman we have to watch out for. This could be dangerous."

The woman's expression went stony. "I am not afraid

of death, *señor*. But I want to watch this man die. And the only way I will help you is if you let me come."

Kenney sighed deeply and finally said, "Okay, but once we're done we dump you off at the nearest civilized stop. Got it?"

"It is agreed," she replied.

Curtis Kenney couldn't help but wonder what kind of deal he'd just made for himself.

CHAPTER NINE

The Executioner launched a 40 mm grenade from the M-203 mounted to the underside of his M-16 A-2, completely decimating a flashy Mercedes-Benz parked in the winding drive of Carmita Rivas's estate. As the noise from the explosion abated, Bolan left cover and rushed the two guards at the front gate.

One of the guards spotted him and clawed inside his jacket for a weapon. He produced a machine pistol in time to take aim, but he didn't get a shot off. The Executioner triggered the M-16 on the run and pumped two hard-hitting NATO rounds through the guard's chest. His feet left the ground as his body lurched backward and slammed into the heavy front gate.

The second guard realized they were under fire and felt that attempting to call for reinforcements was better than trying to go against the enemy on his own. Bolan actually couldn't blame the guy.

When Bolan reached the guard shack he keyed up the

transceiver unit attached to his belt. "Striker to Eagle One— Do it!"

Bolan grabbed cover behind the guard shack just seconds before the front gate erupted in intense flame. The sudden application of explosive heat turned some parts of the wrought-iron a bright orange. The blast from the M-72 A-2 LAW shoulder-fired by Jack Grimaldi tore the heavy gates from their hinges and sent them flying in opposite directions.

The Executioner broke cover and passed unchallenged through the gap. He skirted the drive and maneuvered from one tree to the next on an approach vector designed to minimize risk of confrontation. A few guards positioned at various windows on the second floor of Carmita Rivas's sprawling hacienda-style house attempted to snipe Bolan with pistols and SMGs, but none came close enough to worry him. Hitting a moving target from that distance would have been difficult enough for a crack marksman, never mind near impossible for house guards who probably spent little to no time on the firing range.

Bolan reached a good vantage point from the drive and decided to deliver some heat of his own. The Executioner flipped the leaf sight on the M-203 into action, settled the one hundred yard mark on the second floor and squeezed the trigger. The stock bucked against his shoulder with no more force than 12-gauge shotgun as a hollow "plunk" reported from the muzzle. A puff of smoke issued from the breech as Bolan dropped the grenade shell and immediately loaded another. As he slammed it home, he was rewarded with sound of his first grenade erupting. The HE erupted with a fiery ball of superheated gas and belched from the upper window, carrying along with it the mangled body of a would-be sniper. The hard case hit the ground headfirst in front of the house, his fall cushioned by a manicured hedge.

Bolan delivered a similar message through another window, this one devoid of any occupants. The effect was the same—the fiery gases and heat from the explosion threatening to topple the entire residence to its foundation—and to Bolan's complete satisfaction. This was more the kind of mission offensive with which the Executioner was comfortable. Up to now, he'd been forced to play the games of others to a certain degree; to wait on information he would have normally acquired with significant ease. Not anymore.

The enemy would have to play by *his* rules from this point forward.

As THEIR SUV ROUNDED the corner of the deserted street, the afternoon peace was broken very suddenly by a red-orange ball of flame roiling into the air a couple of blocks ahead. A moment later the thunderclap of an explosion reached the ears of everyone in the vehicle. The sight was probably a horrific one for the woman whose name they had learned was Paloma, but for the men of the Quail Group it was a scene they knew all too well.

Morristown looked sharply at Kenney. "Stone?"

Kenney nodded as he turned his attention to the

woman seated between Jones and Sturgis in the back seat. "Has to be. Is that Carmita Rivas's house?"

The woman said nothing but simply nodded slowly.

Kenney slapped Morristown's shoulder. "Step on it!"

The men of the Quail Group went into combat mode as they had been trained a thousand times before. Sturgis reached into an equipment bag at his feet and withdrew a pair of HK-53s. He handed one to Jones, and the men simultaneously began checking the function of their respective weapons.

Kenney reached to a bag at his own feet and procured an M-16 A-3 carbine. It took a bit of work to maneuver the barrel inside the confines of the SUV without the risk of pointing it at someone inadvertently. He eventually got it into a position with which he could work on it, then pulled the charging handle to the rear. He looked into the chamber to see the golden glint from the 5.56 mm round and then released the charging handle to chamber the round before tapping the forward assist a couple of times.

With his weapon now in battery, Curtis Kenney prepared his mind and body to do battle with this mysterious Colonel Brandon Stone.

"EAGLE ONE TO Striker!" Grimaldi's voice boomed through the high-power microwave transmitter attached to Bolan's belt.

"Go," Bolan replied as he reached a side door.

"I've got a bogey coming down the street and she's running hot," Grimaldi replied.

Bolan considered the angles and then said, "Understood. Stay loose until you make a positive ID. We don't want to blow up the wrong people."

"Acknowledged. Out here."

Bolan kicked at the side door but it was solid and refused to cave under his strength. He stepped back, leveled the M-16 at the lock and squeezed the trigger. The heavy-caliber rounds ripped through the door lock as if it were paper. Bolan tried once more and was rewarded with the door flying inward. He stepped inside and ducked, prepared for any resistance. The response to his intrusion was immediate.

One of the house guards—who had been hiding behind a large stainless-steel refrigerator—opened up with a machine pistol, spraying the doorway where Bolan had stood with 9 mm Parabellum rounds. The heavy autofire choked the air with wood fragments and plaster dust, raining debris on Bolan and reducing visibility in the massive kitchen.

The soldier shimmied to a spot between a freestanding cabinet and one of the stainless-steel-topped islands. He brought the rifle stock to his shoulder and, from a kneeling position, triggered two short bursts. The first sent sparks flying from the modern cooler his enemy was using for cover and ripped deep furrows into the metal. The initial return fire from Bolan surprised the guard and caused him to backpedal into full view. The soldier's second volley caught the guard full-on, the short burst from Bolan's weapon punching holes through the man's chest and abdomen. The SMG flew from deadened fingers as the gunner slammed against a wall and slid to the floor.

Through an open doorway of the kitchen, Bolan saw several guards approaching from an adjacent room. He steadied the M-16/M-203 combo on the island counter-top and triggered the grenade launcher. A 40 mm grenade—this one filled with a TH3 incendiary mixture—exploded on impact and showered the area with white-hot phosphorus. Molten iron struck the bodies of the house guards and spontaneously ignited anything it touched. The rush of flame filled Bolan's nostrils with the rancid stench of burned hair, clothing and flesh.

Screams of agony filled the Executioner's ears as his enemy collapsed under the superheated destruction. He pushed the distraction of suffering from his mind and hurried through the living area now littered with dead or dying men. He crossed to a stairwell and quickly ascended it, his over-and-under assault rifle/grenade launcher held low, and ready for trouble. He reached the top of the stairs unchallenged and was about to begin a room-by-room search when the sound of Grimaldi's voice reached his ears.

"Eagle to Striker."

"Go."

"I've identified our bogey and it's definitely hostile. Utility vehicle with four males and one female. They got through the front gate before I could take them. The four males bailed and are converging on your position from multiple angles. My guess is they're our little birdie group."

Bolan swore under his breath. He'd hoped to avoid a confrontation with them, but he was out of options. If they got in the way or tried to deter him from the operation, he'd have to treat them the same as the enemy. He knew they were doing a job. So was he.

"Acknowledged," Bolan said. "You think the female's an innocent?"

"Could be," Grimaldi replied. "Or she led them here."

"Get her clear. I don't want to risk killing noncombatants."

"Acknowledged."

"Striker out."

Bolan started forward again when he suddenly realized it was time to get clear. A ravishing and dark-haired beauty stood less than twenty yards ahead of him, her feet shoulder-width apart, a massive Ruger Super Redhawk .44 Magnum revolver in her hands. Bolan dived for cover milliseconds before the woman squeezed the trigger.

The Executioner realized immediately who was gunning for him, even before the thunderclap of the pistol died away in his already ringing ears. Carmita Rivas obviously wasn't the sweet-little-rich-girl type. Someone had taught her a thing or two about killing over the years, because no ordinary woman would have chosen such a weapon for mere home defense.

The .44 Remington Magnum slug punched a neat hole in the wooden trim just above Bolan's head. A second round followed immediately thereafter. It zinged a few inches past his knee and slammed into the wall, leaving a large plume of dust and plaster in its wake. The soldier pulled a flash-bang grenade from his web belt, yanked the pin and tossed the bomb side-handed around the corner. He heard the sharp intake of breath—followed by a short mewing sound like the squeak of a kitten—before squeezing his eyes shut and clamping his hands over his ears as he opened his mouth.

As soon as the grenade exploded, Bolan looked around the corner and was rewarded with the sight of Carmita Rivas sitting on her backside, her legs spread out directly in front of her, her confused expression worn like a frozen mask. The woman was fortunate to have gone head-to-head with the Executioner and live to survive the tale. If she cooperated, she'd probably live long enough to tell these tales to her grandchildren.

Bolan climbed to his feet and moved toward her before she had a chance to react to his presence. He scooped the revolver from the floor and stuck it in his belt, then grabbed the woman's arm and hauled her to her feet. Her knees were a bit unsteady, but a quick inspection by Bolan revealed no serious injuries. She'd snap out of it eventually.

The Executioner pulled Rivas's arms behind her and snapped on a pair of plastic riot cuffs. He then moved her toward the stairwell. So far, the numbers had been with him. He didn't figure there would be much in the way of further resistance from the house guards as he made his escape; he'd obviously eliminated all of them. If the chips fell in his favor, he could get Carmita out of the house alive and avoid an encounter with the Quail Group.

They didn't.

As Bolan reached the bottom of the stairs, a glass window near the front door shattered under the impact of a small cylinder. The soldier immediately recognized the device even as it clattered across the hallway floor and struck the opposite wall. He acted quickly, opening a nearby closet door and shoving Rivas through it even as smoke began to pour from the cylinder. He knew the choking and stinging of the eyes would start soon.

The Executioner reached to a pouch on his belt and quickly retrieved a small wrapped bundle of plastic and rubber. He broke free a plastic tie and the bundle rapidly expanded into a fully functioning gas mask. Bolan donned the mask quickly, clamping his hands against the filters as he forcefully exhaled. The maneuver cleared all excess air from the mask; he then cinched the head straps to confirm the seal.

Bigger troubles came through the front door a moment later. It swung inward violently and the doorway was silhouetted by a huge, muscular man in civilian clothes. The guy also wore a mask, obscuring his face, but Bolan could tell from the hair and skin on his forearms he was black. The warrior raised his rifle but at the last second changed tactics and charged the black man with the buttstock of his weapon leading the way. The charge caught his opponent off guard and Bolan landed a successful buttstroke to the guy's solar plexus. Air audibly whooshed from the man's lungs. The Executioner followed with a snap-kick to the groin and a haymaker to the jaw. The black man fell prone on the marbled floor of the entryway, as if poleaxed.

Bolan returned to the closet and yanked out his prisoner. He pushed Rivas toward the front door. He was guessing the four new arrivals announced by Grimaldi had split up and decided to take the house from different directions. Assuming this was one of them—and based on the descriptions he'd received from Stony Man he recalled it was—his colleagues wouldn't breach the interior in time to encounter the Executioner. Bolan figured discretion was the better part of valor, and he didn't want to risk any further conflict with the Quail Group.

Mack Bolan had made enough enemies this day.

CURTIS KENNEY FOUND the side door of the mansion dangling off its broken hinges.

He entered with caution through the splintered door frame and into the kitchen. The M-16 carbine was in an up-and-ready position, its stock jammed against the meaty part of his shoulder. He held the weapon with the practiced ease and expertise that spoke volumes to his training regimen. Kenney swept all four directions with the rifle muzzle as he kept his body low and mobile. Even at close range, a moving target was more difficult to hit.

The area was somewhat smoky, and as Kenney cleared the kitchen and passed into a living area he saw the scattered bodies. He knew the sight—he'd seen it a thousand times before—and he'd become quite familiar with the effects of incendiary bombs. Someone had dumped a willie peter right into the middle of this crew, and Kenney was betting that someone was Colonel Stone.

The guy was effective, Kenney realized, but obviously he was also a goddamn psychopath. Stone seemed to have a thing about leaving destruction in his wake. What Kenney couldn't understand was why this maniac was running around Ecuador on a mission to blow everything and everybody to kingdom come. Revenge, perhaps? After all, it seemed obvious the people he'd brought down weren't exactly popular among the citizenry of the country. Stone seemed to be going to an awful lot of trouble here.

There was more to it than that; there had to be.

Kenney realized quickly he couldn't do a thing for any of these poor bastards and moved on. The smoke got thicker and the acrid stinging in his nostrils told Kenney this was no longer smoke from the incendiary chemicals; Jones had obviously laid down some CS gas. Kenney reached to the pouch at his side and immediately donned his military-issue NBC mask.

"Quebec Four to Quebec One, come in!" It was Sturgis's voice echoing in his ears, and Kenney could tell there was some uncharacteristic stress in the man's voice.

"Quebec One, here," Kenney replied immediately.

"Quebec Three is down. Repeat, Quebec Three is *down!*"

"Stay cool, Four," Kenney said. "How bad?"

"Can't tell, but our target is flying the coop."

"All right, do what you can to stop him," Kenney said. "I want him alive if possible. What's your position?"

"South side of the building," Sturgis replied. "Target is headed south, toward the street."

"Stay put. Don't move on him until I'm in position."

"Number Two to One," Morristown chimed in. "I'm on it, too. We need to do it now or we may not get a second chance."

"Understood, but you go nonlethal. You copy, Two?"

Silence greeted Kenney as he turned and headed back the way he'd come. Damn it, if those two went after Stone without waiting for him, he'd personally wring their necks. They couldn't be certain yet that Stone was a murdering nutcase. Kenney wanted a chance to try to bring him down and to question him before just blowing the guy away, and he knew Morristown had a tendency to go off half-cocked sometimes.

He could only hope he wouldn't be too late.

As Bolan passed the SUV, he glanced quickly inside and verified it was empty. Good old Jack. The Stony Man ace had come through once more.

The Executioner continued to run with Carmita in tow. He was only twenty yards from the front gate when a swarm of hot lead suddenly zinged over his head and headed into a downward arc. Bolan skidded to a halt, preparing to change directions, but lost his footing on a slippery patch of ground moss. He fell backward, taking his prisoner with him as he landed hard on his back. The wind exploded from his lungs and his wrist hit something hard. The impact jarred the nerves in his hand, and he felt the M-16/M-203 combo slip from his fingers.

Bolan quickly assessed Carmita to insure she wasn't

hurt, then rolled onto his stomach. Another man matching the description of one of the Quail Group was sprinting madly toward him clutching an HK-53. Bolan reached to the holster on his hip and withdrew the Desert Eagle. He snap-aimed and squeezed the trigger twice. The weapon bucked in his grip as a pair of 300-grain slugs rocketed toward the target. Bolan gritted his teeth with regret even as he scrambled to his feet. The first round took the guy in the shoulder. He started to spin but never completed it as the second caught him in the side of the face. The bone cracked under the impact of the high-velocity .44 Magnum round, and the man's head exploded.

Bolan heard a scream, but he didn't try to find the source. He could tell it was coming from one of the man's teammates because a moment later the air came virtually alive with high-velocity slugs. He continued toward the front gate as fast as his legs would carry him, deciding it was easier to haul the cursing Carmita onto his shoulder and beat feet than to continue to drag her behind him.

As the Executioner cleared the front gate, Grimaldi screeched up in the Camaro, the convertible top back. Bolan dumped Carmita into the back seat with a heavy sigh of relief and then jumped in after her. The Stony Man pilot nearly tossed him out the back as he tromped the accelerator and powered away from the scene of chaos and pandemonium.

"I see you got what you came for," Grimaldi called over the rush of wind.

"Yeah," Bolan said. He couldn't hide the regret in his tone. "But I also had to take down one of our mercenary friends the hard way."

"I'm sorry, Sarge," Grimaldi said.

"Me, too, Jack," the Executioner replied.

And somehow, in that moment, Mack Bolan could take no solace in the fact that he had survived the encounter.

CHAPTER TEN

"What did you say?" Adriano Rivas's voice hissed like a snake. "You're telling me that this scum not only killed Manuel, but then you also let him take my beloved Carmita from under your noses?"

Rivas took the silence from Arauca on the other end of the line as deference and apology rather than insolence. He'd known the man too long to believe it could be anything else.

"Have we put a name to this bastard yet?" Rivas added, "This man who fights like ten devils?"

"Our contacts inside Quito have positively identified him as a former colonel in the American military. His name is Stone."

"And that's what I want him as cold as, Chico," Rivas replied. "Do you hear me? I want you to get every man you can find, every single one still loyal to us, and I want you to hunt down this Stone and bury him. Do it tonight and don't fail me again. Do you understand?"

"I understand, boss."

"And the next time you call me it will be to report that the job's done?"

"Yes, Adriano."

"Good. And you get Carmita back in one piece. If anything bad happens to her, Chico, I will hold you personally responsible."

With that, Rivas hung up the phone.

He could hardly believe what he'd been told. Of course, Rivas didn't really blame Arauca for the situation at hand. He knew a good part of this was his fault. He'd played his cards too soon and after his conversation with Cabeza—a conversation he had to admit had been considerably enlightening—Rivas had a much better idea of what they were up against.

Once more the American had outclassed his very best people. This man was good, and Rivas knew they could no longer afford to underestimate him. That mistake had proved fatal to his brother. He would miss Manuel, although his brother hadn't agreed with Rivas's way of conducting business. Rivas wondered how much of Manuel's timidity had contributed to his death. Still, blood was blood and he was now compelled to avenge his brother's death.

According to the way Chico told it, Manuel had died protecting his business. This Stone had killed him in cold blood, murdered him in front of scores of people. The cops had apparently put out word on the streets of San Lorenzo looking for anyone who might know how to find the American. That was just fine with Rivas, since he usually got his best information from the cops. Most of the policemen in Ecuador were a joke, and a good number that did have some street sense were also usually smart enough to take a bit of graft on the side. People seemed to have forgotten that Rivas had once ruled that city. In fact, he probably would again since moving within Colombia was so difficult without being recognized. He had much more freedom and mobility in Ecuador, and he would have even more when he reached the United States.

For now, however, he needed to concentrate on his plans. Cabeza had been his one weak link. With that fat slob out of the way, Rivas knew he could move forward without having to look over his shoulder every second. Losing the Quito operation had still been quite a blow to him, but it was hardly crippling. In just days he'd accompany his first major shipment out of San Lorenzo, and he'd do it right under the noses of all those who brokered the deal. The Americans were probably getting edgy in trying to find Esposito and Gustavo.

Let them be edgy. They would make more mistakes that way. Besides, he'd have Esposito returned within the next twelve hours, and the deal would follow shortly thereafter. Once Esposito was safe, they could start moving the exports out of port. Everything would fall in perfectly to his plan, because he had a perfect plan. By the time all of them realized what had happened, it would be too late and Rivas would have both himself and his product inside the country.

It would be a glorious day.

CURTIS KENNEY STOOD outside the doors leading into the hospital morgue and waited impatiently for the coroner to finish talking to the police.

Much to Kenney's dismay, Captain Redondo had shown up with an army of uniforms *and* plainclothes. This time their meeting would be in a much more official capacity. He hated to admit it, but it looked as though Redondo held all the cards on this one. The guy definitely had cause to take them all to jail if he really wanted to, and Kenney already knew President Gustavo wouldn't break his neck to bail them out. It looked like they were on their own, which was fine. Kenney understood Gustavo couldn't undertake an "official" position on sanctioning the Quail Group to operate in the country legally. It would be a violation of both national and international laws to permit a PMC to conduct military-style operations in proximity to any civilian populace.

As they waited outside the morgue, Morristown paced angrily. Kenney could feel for his state of mind. He and Sturgis had been pretty good friends and now this had to happen. What bothered Kenney even more than that was the fact Sturgis had died at the hands of Brandon Stone, who Kenney had wanted to give a fair shake from the beginning.

"Damn it!" Kenney slammed his fist against the veneer-panel wall. He whirled and looked at Jones and Morristown, soured by the bile rising from his stomach. "I hope this demonstrates why we follow fucking orders, gentlemen. You get me?"

"Hey, look, Curt—" Jones began.

"Shut up, both of you. It's listen time now." He focused on Morristown. "I ordered you guys to wait until I got there to provide support. Did I not speak English?"

Morristown's face reddened. "Now, just wait one goddamn minute, Curt, you are *not* blaming this on me. I was following orders. I can't help it if Lou went a bit crazy there."

"Oh, yes, you can help it," Kenney said. "We can all help it, Petey."

"Hey, I didn't tell him to go hard-charging at this Stone guy," Morristown replied. "I *knew* what kind of a psychopath he was. I'm the one who tried convincing the rest of you this guy was a fucking nut job. Now if you think you're going to turn this on me…"

Kenney shook his head slowly, choking back any emotion in his voice. The words still sounded hollow and unconvincing even in his own ears. "I'm not turning it on you and I'm not blaming you. I'm just saying in the future—"

Kenney never got to finish his statement as the doors to the morgue opened and several uniformed officers emerged ahead of Redondo. The policeman's face said it all as he looked at Kenney. Redondo did nothing to hide his disgust for the soldier. Well, that was too damn bad. It wasn't Redondo who had lost a good man today, and Kenney wasn't in the mood to take any shit off Redondo.

"If I thought it worth the effort, *señor*," Redondo said, "and you had not lost one of your friends today, I would arrest you right now and lock you away for a very long time."

Kenney didn't have much to say to that, because he knew the man could and would do exactly that if Kenney protested. Sometimes just keeping quiet and taking no action was actually the best action, and something in Kenney's gut told him this was one of those times.

"I will give you and your men exactly two hours to get out of San Lorenzo," Redondo said. "In fact, you have two hours to get out of my country. I don't care where your authority comes from. You will leave Ecuador and you will not return. If you do, my men have orders to shoot you on sight."

Kenney sighed deeply but before he could reply, Morristown stepped up. "What about Sturgis's body?"

"It will be released to your country once our investigation is complete and we have this Brandon Stone in custody," Redondo said as he waved dismissively and then turned to speak to one of his men.

"We're not leaving," Kenney said quietly.

Redondo turned and showed Kenney a deadly smile. "What did you say?"

"I said, we're not leaving. At least, not without the body of our man. If you don't like that, Captain, throw us in prison. But we don't leave Ecuador without Louis Sturgis's body, and that's not negotiable."

"You are correct, Señor Kenney," Redondo said. "It is not negotiable because you are not in any such position to negotiate. Right now I have you for kidnapping, murder and endangerment of the Ecuadorian public, not to mention illegal possession of firearms. Those are just the local charges, to say nothing of the fact you have violated at least two known statutes pertaining to international laws and treaties. Your conduct of military operations notwithstanding, I could turn you over to your government immediately and ask you be charged with matters of international terrorism. But again, I do not feel this serves the purpose of my people. We have more important matters to look after. And since up to this point nobody innocent has been killed, or nobody I care about, I am willing to let you go. Consider yourselves fortunate."

"That still doesn't answer the question about our—"

"Yes, your body," Redondo said with a curt nod. "Very well, gentlemen. Since you seem so persistent on the subject, I will see what I can do to hasten the process and grant you a reprieve until you can take possession. Until then, my men will escort you to a hotel where you will stay until the body is released."

"That won't be necessary, Captain," Kenney said. "We can look after ourselves."

"On the contrary," Redondo said. "It will be my pleasure."

CARMITA RIVAS couldn't believe her terrible misfortune.

In all her time watching over her brother's affairs, Carmita couldn't believe that she would have suffered humiliation at the hands of a barbarian such as this. The man who now sat in front of her—whose chiseled features it took some effort to bring into proper focus—was a ruggedly handsome brute. Still, Carmita held no interest in him beyond the most animal. The man was still an enemy of the Rivas empire, and when Adriano got hold of him, he would be sorry.

Carmita tried to warn him, but it didn't seem the man who called himself Colonel Stone was all that intimidated by ranting. In fact, he seemed rather calm in spite of the recent mayhem he'd caused. Carmita had been too confused to see the extent of damage he'd inflicted on her place, but things were replaceable. What she didn't know is how many of her house guards had fallen under this maniac's guns. It didn't matter. Her brother would see to it he paid for that, too. Of course, there was a small chance Adriano didn't yet know this Stone had kidnapped her, especially if Chico Arauca hadn't survived the battle at her hacienda. But even if he didn't know, Manuel would hear of it quite soon, and he would come after her immediately. He didn't have the same machismo of Adriano, but there was no question of Manuel's loyalty to his family.

He would come even if he didn't know where to look.

Carmita mused for just a moment how she'd ever come to be in a business like Adriano's. Things had been just fine on her return from the all-woman's college in Spain, a college that was more of a convent and boarding school than a legitimate institution for educating young women. At twenty-two and holding a business degree from a coveted university, Carmita had opened her boutique shops with money that came straight from Adriano's drug coffers. As a result, Carmita knew a lot of people, *important* people who would do just about anything, including risk their lives, to see she was returned unharmed.

Naturally, because of Adriano's loyalty to his sister and her business ventures, Carmita had felt it her absolute duty to return his favors. When he'd asked her to look over the business while he disappeared, Carmita hadn't hesitated for a moment. Despite the fact she knew very little about keeping things afloat in this business, Carmita had taken most of her cues from Chico. During these past few years she had not spoken with Adriano at all; of course, she hadn't told Manuel he was still alive. Adriano had insisted he not know, convincing Carmita that their little brother would be much safer that way. Carmita hadn't argued the point.

Now things were going to be different. Soon, very soon, Adriano was going to have to reveal himself to Manuel. He wouldn't be able to keep his "resurrection" a secret from their brother once the word got out he was still alive. Especially not when Manuel found out that Carmita had known all of this time.

Of much greater interest than any of that, however, was this Colonel Stone. The guy who hung with him— and who for some strange reason kept calling him "Sarge"—was, from all she could surmise, some kind of assistant. He was definitely a pilot as he'd asked Stone a couple of times about next possible destinations and what type of wings they would need. There was also something in his cocksure gait that told Carmita he was an American pilot—they all seemed to have the same arrogance and self-assurance. At the moment, he wasn't present and that left her alone with this big, mean brute.

Stone was a man of authority, no question there, and she knew he was someone who was quite accustomed to commanding others. He wore the authority on him like an aura. His eyes were intense, the ice-blue gaze appearing to look right through her. Carmita sensed the big man could read her like an open book. It was disconcerting the way this man looked at her. She didn't like it one damn bit. And it wasn't in any predatory or sexual fashion. No, there was nothing but a sterile and precise analysis in his gaze, something almost…instinctual about his look, as if he were reading her every thought.

She wondered if he knew what she was thinking right at the moment.

His smile lacked warmth. "It seems you've been busy minding the store while your brother hides like some scared animal."

"My brother is not the animal here, American," Carmita said, putting forth the words like a cobra spitting venom. "When he finds you he is going to kill you."

"He won't have to find me, lady," Bolan said. "I plan to find him first. And you're going to help me."

"I will never help you."

Stone smoothly withdrew a pistol from the shoulder holster he wore over his skintight black outfit. If there had been any warmth in his face at all, it was gone now. Carmita wasn't afraid to die, but she also knew there were a lot of ways to die. Some were slow and some mercifully quick, some excruciating and others painless.

Stone looked as though he knew how to deal them all as a man who had also experienced them. This was no amateur she was dealing with.

"You can torture me or kill me," she said, knowing her voice lacked conviction. She pretended haughtiness as she continued. "But I will not tell you anything about Adriano. I will not tell you anything."

"You already have," Bolan said with another frosty smile. He set the pistol on the table next to the two chairs they sat in. He shoved his chair back some, stretched his legs and interlaced his hands behind his head. "You just didn't know it."

"What are you talking about?"

"I got answers from you even before I laid eyes on you, Carmita," Bolan replied. "I got them when Arauca sent a bunch of his goons to try to erase me. I also got them when your brother Manuel tried to kill me. By the way, don't expect him to come to your rescue. He's dead."

Carmita inhaled sharply. "I don't believe it."

"Believe it," Stone said.

The big man rose and walked to a compact refrigerator. He filled a plastic cup with ice water from the full pitcher sitting on top of the refrigerator, walked over and offered it to her. She turned her head to the side and tightly pressed her lips together.

Bolan shrugged and tossed half the contents back before setting the cup on the table. "I say you're going to help me find your brother because of the very reason he's going to come looking for you. If he's not too afraid, of course."

Carmita tried to lash out and kick her captor in the shin, but the big man easily deflected it with a karate chop to the shin. The blow stung, but it wasn't debilitating. She bit back an outcry of pain. She wouldn't give this American pig the satisfaction of seeing weakness. She would defy him until the very end. In fact, she considered her other options. Adriano had always told her that when captured by the enemy the most important thing was to attempt escape.

She formulated a plan. "Are you going to take me?"

Bolan looked surprised. "What do you mean? Rape you? You think I'm going to rape you?"

Carmita said nothing.

"You must really think I am some kind of animal," Bolan replied. "No, Carmita, I have no such intention. You see, I don't need to lay a hand on you. If you don't tell me a thing, it won't matter. I have what I need you for, and that's bait. Up until now, everyone's been trying to make me believe that your brother's some walking spirit who actually died three years ago."

"Silly myths and superstitions," Carmita said.

"I'm glad we agree," Bolan replied. "I didn't believe it, either. You see, I couldn't figure out at first what your brother was up to. I didn't even know if he had anything to do with the kidnapping of Mario Esposito and Hernando Gustavo. But when that private military company showed up at your house the same time I did, I was sure of it."

"I am not going to tell you anything," Carmita insisted.

"You don't have to. Like I said, I know what's going

on now. Adriano kidnapped Esposito and Gustavo to stall for time. It seems this trade agreement would stand to put him to considerable inconvenience. Why? I don't know that yet, but I'm guessing it has something to do with drugs. I'm also guessing it has something to do with the contracts for oil delivery. I'd be willing to guess that you and Manuel were watching over his holdings while he made his plans. The trade agreement for oil threw some sort of monkey wrench into his plans. So he's delaying."

"You do not know what you're talking about."

"Don't I?" Bolan said, crouching to one side of her chair and leaning close. "I think I'm right on the money. In fact, I'd bet even *you* didn't know exactly what your brother had planned. Now it's obvious. He's planning to run drugs into the U.S., and he's going to use this agreement to do it. Well, his little plan just fell apart because there's one thing he hadn't counted on."

"And what is that?"

"Me."

Carmita wanted to laugh, but something in Stone's tone caused her to hold back. She had seen what he was capable of, and she knew her brother might not be able to take the American alone. He would need a small army, in fact. Carmita had watched this man single-handedly eradicate her entire security force.

"But you might be able to help yourself," Bolan continued. "You might be able to keep your brother alive."

Carmita didn't want to listen, but something compelled her to hear him out. Something that sounded like the bare truth echoed in his words. She remembered again her brother's counsel. *If someone ever takes you hostage, the most important thing is finding a way to escape.* Maybe, just maybe, this was her chance to do that. If she decided to cooperate with Stone, he might let her go and she could warn her brother before Stone led him into a trap.

"What do you want to know?"

"Where's his base of operations?" Bolan asked, taking the chair once more. "I know he has one. Tell me where it is."

"I don't know," she said. It was the truth. "Nobody knows that except..."

"Except who?"

"I cannot say," she said. "I cannot betray Adriano."

The big American simply studied her features intently. Carmita tried not to meet his gaze, tried to push him and everything around her from her mind. She knew he could read her thoughts easily enough. It wouldn't take a very smart person to guess what she had almost revealed. She squeezed her eyes tighter, trying not to give him an edge in case he could read into her very thoughts. Those eyes might be able to even penetrate her very soul.

"Arauca," Bolan whispered. "Chico Arauca knows where it is, doesn't he?"

Carmita refused to look at him.

"He wasn't at the house." A look of sudden realization spread across Bolan's face. He grabbed her by the shoulders and shook her. "Why not? Where is he, Carmita? Where did he go?"

Carmita opened her eyes and stared at her captor with rock-hard defiance. Suddenly she became giddy with laughter as she thought about it. It had been so foolish to think she had to talk to this one. Chico would find her soon enough. Stone couldn't wait in this hotel room forever. Eventually he'd have to move, and when he did, Chico would be waiting—along with Adriano.

"He is gathering the supporters loyal to my brother. And when he has completed that, there will be no escape for you, American. You are as good as dead."

CHAPTER ELEVEN

Stony Man Farm, Virginia

Barbara Price would have given anything for a hot bath, a decent night's sleep and a good cup of coffee. Unfortunately she would see none of them until she could provide some hard intelligence that would help Striker accomplish his mission.

This vigil was routine for Price, but one she would be the first to admit was self-imposed. There weren't many other women like her, and she knew it, but then that wasn't anything unusual since there weren't many women who did the kind of work she did. There were moments Price wondered if it was all worth it. Sure, she'd chosen this life, but sometimes she wondered what it would be like to just live a normal life. Then she would remember her short-lived marriage to an unfaithful husband, and all those memories that came flooding back to her were reminders of why she had chosen her present path.

Price was concise and insightful in everything she did. The position of mission controller was one of the hardest and most trusted positions within the ultrasecret Stony Man organization. She tried to handle everything with efficiency and speed, and diplomacy wasn't really part of her game. She left that to charmers like Rosario "Politician" Blancanales, one of Able Team's warriors and a master tactician. Politics just weren't her bailiwick, and Price avoided playing at any costs. In most cases, she would let Hal Brognola handle those matters; he was certainly a lot better at it.

The phone rang and the screen identifier showed it was Aaron Kurtzman calling her.

Price sat forward and stabbed the intercom button. "Hello, Bear. What can I do for you?"

"It's what I can do for you, Barb," Kurtzman's booming and cheerful voice replied. "I think you ought to come over to my neck of the woods and quick. I've finally broken through the computer systems at the intelligence headquarters of the Colombian government."

"I'll be right over," Price said.

She rose from her chair in the conference room of the Annex and headed for the Computer Room. Its size defied the very term, since Bear's area of operation was massive. Several computer monitors of varying sizes and types lined one wall, each with a very specific purpose. In concert the colorful lights winking and blinking throughout those displays were enough to leave one with either the spirit of Christmas or an eye-splitting headache.

It never seemed to have an effect on Aaron Kurtzman in the least. He sat erect in a wheelchair near his workstation. Powerful forearms rested in front of him as his fingers danced across a keyboard with grace and speed that would have left any court transcriber green with envy.

He acknowledged her with only a cursory nod and then pointed to the computer screen.

"It took me a while, but I finally got into the federal justice network of Colombia." He grinned with showmanship and added, "Their security was a bit tougher than I first anticipated."

"Yes, you're a true hero in the cyberspace universe," Price teased. "So tell me what you've found that we can actually use to help Striker?"

Kurtzman showed her a sideways glance. "A bit testy tonight, are we?"

"I'm sorry," she said quickly. He was right, of course. Kurtzman knew her pretty well, which meant he also knew what exactly was bothering her. Damn him. Bear was one of the few who could get under her skin. "If you're thinking I've felt useless to Striker up until now, you're right. So please tell me you have something worthwhile."

"Oh, I do," Kurtzman said. "But first, tell me again how wonderful you think I am."

She slapped his shoulder playfully. "Get on with it."

"Okay, so I cracked their system and found out the flyboys in Colombia might see an operation going on right under their noses and they're not even aware of it."

"How so?"

"The Colombian police, and sometimes the army, do regular aerial reconnaissance of the high-traffic areas for drugs and arms. They're mostly looking for drug-runners, but occasionally they turn up small militia cells, FARC remnants mostly, operating in the mountains."

Price furrowed her brow, now becoming more interested in what Kurtzman was telling her. Although the mission controller was very technically savvy, she didn't possess anywhere near Kurtzman's uncanny abilities. The guy was a walking wealth of information, and there was very little he didn't know about when it came to the technical aspects of his job. He was *that* good.

"These are photographs taken by an observation plane three months ago," Kurtzman said. He pointed toward a small area on the map. "You see this? See the line of infrared heat circling all the way around here?"

"Sure," Price said. "Looks mostly like a hot spot to me."

"Aha. And all other things being equal, I'd say you were right on the money." He flashed a quick grin, the playful gleam evident in his eyes. "But let us not forget in our business almost nothing is equal, neither are things as they would appear."

"Okay, so enlighten me," Price said, folding her arms in mock skepticism. "Show me some real magic."

Kurtzman ceremoniously tapped a button on the keyboard and gestured toward a massive screen behind them. "If you would be so kind as to direct your attention there, m'lady, you will see I have enlarged and enhanced that same picture."

True to his words, the photograph appeared on the

screen and the reddish hue of the infrared line was now much more crisp and clear than on the tiny screen where she'd first viewed it. As soon as she saw the enhanced picture, it became immediately evident to her what had Kurtzman so excited. The outline was entirely too regular to be a natural phenomenon. No, this was definitely heat being generated by a construction of some type and magnitude.

"Okay, so I'll buy what you're saying. There is definitely something man-made there, most probably a base of operations. But I don't get how you would tie that to Adriano Rivas."

"Simple deductive reasoning." Kurtzman tapped another key and a very similar map displayed next to the other one. "The picture on the right was taken by the police, army, whoever…three years ago."

Price's eyes widened. "Nothing."

"Right. Now take a look at two years ago." He tapped a key and the line was definitely visible. It wasn't nearly as comprehensive or large as the one in the present-day picture, but there had undoubtedly been a change and it wasn't one of nature. Since the first picture had been taken, things had changed considerably.

"The before picture you see was taken just a few months prior to Adriano Rivas's disappearance."

Price nodded. "And then suddenly these area photographs begin to change. That's too much to chalk up to a coincidence."

"Right," Kurtzman replied. "Especially when you consider the location of this find."

"Which is?"

"Based on the coordinates and map traces I've already conducted, it's in the mountain jungle region bordering Colombia and Ecuador. The computer's still doing exact estimates, but I'd say from the preliminary we're talking about a hundred klicks southeast of San Lorenzo."

Price looked at him. "On the Colombian side?"

"Yep."

"Okay, so it's a good bet that's where Rivas has been operating since his alleged death. I know Hal's going to be especially happy when he hears what you've come up with. We need to get the information into Striker's hands as quickly as possible. I'll call Hal while you arrange that."

"Sounds good."

As she headed out of his office, Price stopped and turned to smile at him. "Good work, Aaron. Damn good work."

THE SETTING SUN CAST brilliant oranges and reds on the low-hanging clouds. Darkness would come very quickly, and as soon as it did Mack Bolan would move Carmita Rivas to a more secure location—or at least a more remote one. Jack Grimaldi was at the airport setting up a base of operations. It was the last place either of them figured Rivas and his men would look for Carmita. Plus, if they determined they had to leave the area quickly, they wouldn't have to spend a lot of time getting her to air transport if necessary.

Once Bolan had moved Carmita Rivas safely to that location, he could concentrate on finding Chico Arauca before Arauca found him. The Executioner was now convinced that once he found Arauca he would find Rivas. It wouldn't mean he could pinpoint their base of operations, where he now strongly suspected they were holding Esposito and Gustavo, but it would allow him to continue on the offensive.

Bolan's first suspicion was that Rivas's headquarters was somewhere in the nearby jungle mountains. First of all, it was the only place that made sense. Rivas was much too notorious to risk showing his face in the cities, and he would have needed someplace to hole up for the past three or so years. Second, they would need the same out-of-the-way place to stow the hostages; somewhere remote and uncivilized that would make it difficult not only for someone to find them, but for them to mount any type of decent rescue mission.

Carmita had probably been telling him the truth about Arauca. The guy would come looking for him. When word got out to Rivas about Carmita being taken, he'd pull out all the stops and order Arauca to find her and get her back unharmed. That meant the best tactic would be to put Arauca on the offensive rather than wait for him to find Bolan. Oh, he'd allow himself to be "found" by Arauca, but it would be on the Executioner's terms.

Their other prisoner, a woman named Paloma Guerra, had proved stubborn and useless as an information source. Bolan had immediately recognized her as the one behind the desk at Manuel Rivas's condominiums. How she'd come to figure out where to lead the Quail Group was anybody's guess, but he was chalking it up to coincidence since he lacked any evidence to the contrary. Mostly, she had spit obscenities at him and accused him of murdering her boss, who had also apparently doubled as her lover. What Bolan figured had Paloma most angry was she'd lost her meal ticket to the big time, which meant she'd have to start all over in exploiting someone else with the cash necessary to keep her in the way she'd obviously become accustomed.

The Executioner decided to use her to his advantage, letting it slip that he would be at one of the local hangouts that evening. He then had Grimaldi dump her off in the downtown area—hoping she'd get the word around—and that eventually the information he'd leaked would wind up in the ears of Chico Arauca. It seemed like a good plan and Bolan was counting on it to work.

As soon as the sun had dipped below the horizon, Bolan woke Carmita and took her to his car. After dropping them off at the hotel, Grimaldi had returned the rental and traded it for something a bit less conspicuous, a midnight-blue Ford Focus. He dropped the car back at the hotel before hopping a bus to the airport, tugging much of the Executioner's equipment along with him.

Bolan quickly dropped a bag filled with armament onto the floor of the back seat and then opened the door for Carmita. He looked around and noticed only an old woman watching him. She was seated on the porch in front of the office, and the warrior recognized her as the night clerk. She was ancient with a mouth filled with black teeth, the stain no doubt mostly due to the thin, long pipe that seemed stuck between her dark lips.

Carmita's hands had been secured with a pair of riot cuffs in front of her, and Bolan had draped a beach towel over them to conceal the restraints. They looked like a normal couple going out for an evening on some secluded part of the beach. The old woman didn't give them a second glance, and Bolan maneuvered his car out of the lot and into the ever-thickening night traffic.

They reached the airport without incident. Grimaldi had managed to get a small hangar rented for the plane, which would double nicely as a strategic base for now. The Stony Man ace had already set up the communications equipment that allowed them to talk via secured satellite link directly with Stony Man. Something in the pilot's expression, maybe the ear-to-ear grin he wore, told Bolan he had good news. Well, the Executioner was all for that. He'd heard just about all the bad news he wanted for this trip.

"What is it?"

Grimaldi cleared his throat, looked at Carmita and said, "Your buddy called. Says he has some very important information for you that shouldn't wait." He pointed to the computer and added, "It's waiting for you now."

"Okay," Bolan said with a nod. "Why don't you get our guest here aboard the plane? Probably the best place to hide her, since she'll be out of the way and can't cause any trouble."

Grimaldi nodded and took custody of Carmita while Bolan went to the desk and sat in front of the terminal. He typed in his security information and the information appeared on the screen with a video message from Kurtzman. Bolan had nothing but the highest respect for Aaron Kurtzman. The Bear had lost his ability to walk following a vicious attack by Russian operatives on Stony Man Farm. What they had been unable to take away was Kurtzman's indomitable spirit, and Stony Man had benefited from that spirit ever since.

"Hey, buddy," Kurtzman's voice boomed. "The MLIC told me to get this out to you right away."

Bolan couldn't repress a laugh. MLIC was short for main lady in charge, a humorous reference to Barbara.

Kurtzman continued, "We've located what we believe is Adriano Rivas's base of operations. I've included a map and coordinates of the location. Be advised we're standing by to provide you whatever support you request. We're not solid this is where the hostages are being held, but it's the best lead we can give you. Good luck, Striker."

The recording ended and Bolan sat back with a contented sigh to think about what he'd just heard. If Stony Man was convinced that was the location where Rivas was operating, then he wouldn't be the one to dispute it. They had way more resources at their disposal than Bolan could ever hope to muster in the field. He'd have to go with it and hope it panned out.

Jack Grimaldi returned a few minutes later. "Your wild card is secured, and I do mean 'wild.'"

"Yeah, she's a real pistol," Bolan replied.

Grimaldi chuckled. "A true Latin firebrand. So what's up, Sarge? Is it good news like you were promised?"

"Could very well be," Bolan said. "It looks like I'm not going to have to work nearly as hard as I thought to find Rivas's operation. The Farm thinks they've pinpointed it."

"What's the lowdown?"

"Jungle terrain, thick and mountainous."

"Yuck. Doesn't sound very air-friendly."

"Probably not," the Executioner said. "It's about sixty miles southwest of our position, which means I'll have to tackle it by vehicle."

"And I would assume," Grimaldi interjected, the disappointment evident on his face, "you're going to do it alone."

"I have to, Jack. I don't know what I'm going up against. And if I find either Esposito or Gustavo still alive, I'll need you to extract us in hurry. I can't risk losing you or anybody else in this right now if I can afford to go it alone."

"I understand," Grimaldi said. "So, you're leaving right away?"

Bolan shook his head. "I'll need to arrange some wheels for me, and perhaps find me a guide who won't ask any questions. Do whatever you have to, but be ready when I get back."

"Where are you going?"

"I have another appointment to keep first," the Executioner replied. "With Chico Arauca."

CHAPTER TWELVE

The nightclub was deserted except for a few staff members, yet it stunk of sweat intermingled with the dust of the day. An unseen disc jockey cranked out Latin rhythms at a deafening level even though the dance floor was vacant.

Mack Bolan sat patiently in a rear booth watching the entrance and waiting for Chico Arauca. He knew the numbers were running down, and he also knew it wouldn't be much longer before he'd have to give up on this plan and head for Rivas's base. However, it was important to the overall operation that he eliminate as much resistance as possible. The bottom line was he'd have to fight Arauca's people either here or somewhere else, and here was better because he could fight them by his own rules.

With most of Rivas's people spread throughout San Lorenzo in a vain effort to take him out, Bolan surmised security at the jungle complex would be minimal.

It was another good reason for him to take out Arauca and his crew here rather than face him on totally unfamiliar territory.

It looked as if he would get his chance.

Arauca entered the club with a group of his thugs in tow. There was no mistaking Rivas's chief enforcer: the short and lithe build; the dark hair; the eyes of a killer. Bolan had known many men like Arauca, and he'd come to believe they were pretty much all the same. This kind preyed on the innocent, feeding off their helplessness like a jackal or buzzard fed off desert carrion. No, there was no mistaking what drove men like Chico Arauca. Well, his time had come.

Bolan watched as Arauca's men spread throughout the club; he knew they were looking for him. But like a good chess grandmaster, the Executioner had no intention of making his move before all the pieces were in their proper places. He had been playing this game too long to allow the enemy an upper hand. The booth he was seated in occupied an upper area of the club. Bolan observed two of Arauca's team begin to search the lower area, and two more accompanied Arauca up the steps to the soldier's level. The club was dark, which made it much more difficult for them to spot him immediately. Then again, that's what the soldier was counting on.

Bolan did one more brief inventory of the hard cases combing the club, then let his eyes return to the entrance. The two men who had occupied places on either side of the front door were gone, replaced by men who had "thugs" written all over them. It was obvious they were both packing hardware beneath their suit coats just by the way they stood.

The Executioner sat calmly in the booth and waited for Arauca and his men to approach. He kept one fist wrapped around the bottle of lukewarm beer he'd nursed for the past hour, and held his other hand beneath the table. Another minute elapsed before Arauca and his men got close enough to notice him. Bolan could tell there was a bit of surprise in Arauca's expression, but he remained impassive and nonthreatening.

"I was beginning to think you weren't going to show," Bolan said with a smile.

Arauca didn't appear amused. "You're the most fortunate son of a whore I've ever met, Stone."

"You know my name," Bolan replied. "Looks like your intelligence is better than I gave you credit for."

"As is yours," Arauca said, inclining his head in deference.

"So what do we do now?"

"It would seem you've made a fatal mistake this time. I believed you were acting with the sanction of your government, but my employer feels you're doing this on your own. If you had come to him first, we might have been able to work this out."

"I know you work for Adriano Rivas," the Executioner said. "I also know he's still alive. I'd be willing to bet I even know what he has planned. So what makes you think I want to work anything out with your kind of scum, Arauca?"

"It doesn't matter anymore," Arauca replied. "I have orders to kill you and that is exactly what I'm going to do. But first, you're going to tell me where Carmita Rivas is."

"What makes you think I'm going to tell you anything?"

"We shall find out very quickly what you know," Arauca replied. He sat across from Bolan and produced an Imbel pistol. It was difficult to tell what caliber, but Bolan knew it didn't matter; it was real and it was loaded. Arauca had made his point; he wasn't here to chat. "I won't ask you again."

"Are you sure you don't want to negotiate?"

"There will be no negotiations. It's too late for that."

Bolan's expression turned into a cold, unyielding mask of death. He replied quietly, "You said it."

The Executioner flipped the arming switch on the wireless transmitter he'd been holding concealed beneath the table and pressed a button. The club was suddenly rocked by an explosion at the front entrance. Arauca and his men turned at the blast that ripped through the two men posted there. The concussion dismembered them and the heat seared the skin from their flesh.

In the moment of distraction, Bolan overturned the table and stood as he smoothly drew the Beretta from shoulder leather. He squeezed the trigger just milliseconds after the surprise registered on Arauca's face. That expression disappeared abruptly, replaced by the impact of the 9 mm Parabellum round that punched into the

bridge of his nose and split open the better part of his
face and upper skull.

Both of Arauca's shadow men reacted with incredi-
ble speed, but it was useless against the Executioner's
lifetime experience. He caught the man on the left with
a double-tap to the chest, one of the rounds punching
first through the hand he'd stuck inside his jacket in a
reach for hardware. The gunman on the right managed
to clear his pistol, but he never acquired his target. Bolan's first round cored through his throat and the second smashed his breastbone. The gunman reeled from
the close-range blast and crashed into a nearby table.

The Executioner wasted no time in meeting four others now headed for his position. They reached the steps
just as Bolan moved to the railing with an M-67 fragmentation grenade. He overturned another table for
cover as the grenade exploded in midair. Two of Arauca's soldiers were ascending the small flight of steps and
closest to the grenade when it went. Razor-sharp steel
fragments sliced through their flesh, penetrating bone
and muscle. The other pair was knocked from their feet
by the concussion.

Bolan vaulted the railing, hit the floor eight feet
below and shoulder-rolled to absorb impact. He came
out of the roll on one knee and tracked the pair as they
tried to get up. The blast that had disoriented them stole
any chance they might have had in making a stand.
Bolan took the first one with a shot to the gut. The guy
doubled over and hit his knees as the Executioner got
the second with a 9 mm stinger through the thigh.

The nonlethal shot was by design. Bolan needed at least one of Arauca's heavies alive, otherwise he'd be unable to verify Stony Man's intel on Rivas's jungle base. The warrior rose and stepped over to the wounded man. He grabbed him by the back of the shirt collar and dragged him from the club, exiting through a back way he'd scoped out earlier.

The plan had worked perfectly.

Bolan had given five grand U.S. in cash to the owner to "rent" the club for two hours, and another five to cover any possible damages. The proprietor had made a killing, since the explosive charges Bolan planted had been only decent enough to take out hostile personnel and not to do any significant structural damage.

The Executioner reached his vehicle unmolested, tossed his prisoner in the front seat, then jumped behind the wheel and tore away from the scene. A pair of police vehicles zipped past him two blocks from the club, obviously now alerted to the trouble that had gone down. The entire operation had taken less than four minutes with no innocent lives endangered and Chico Arauca off the predator list forever.

It took him only ten minutes to reach the airport. He parked alongside the rented hangar-turned-operations center and hauled his prisoner out of the car. The man wasn't bearing weight on his injured limb, so Bolan had to assist him into the hangar. He shoved the guy into a padded cot on a near wall, then slammed the door securely shut behind him. The man roared in pain, but the Executioner couldn't have cared less.

Jack Grimaldi rushed into the office from the main hangar area and studied the new arrival with indifference. "Looks like he picked the wrong side to be on."

"Yeah," Bolan said. "You got the first-aid kit handy?"

"On board the plane," the pilot said. "I'll get it."

As he rushed for the hangar, Bolan called after him, "Bring lots of large field dressings. Bullet went through his thigh."

Grimaldi waved his acknowledgment.

Bolan whirled on the prisoner and pinned him with an icy gaze. "You speak English, I assume?"

"Yes," the man replied weakly.

"Good. Your boss is dead and you're out of options, so listen carefully because I'm about to offer you the deal of a lifetime."

PETE MORRISTOWN felt like he was about to go insane, and he didn't mind giving Curtis Kenney a ration of shit for it.

They wouldn't have been in this situation if Kenney had just decided to pass on this job. Sure, he'd agreed to the mission, but hostage rescues were about the worse kind of missions because they always stood so little chance of success. It either turned out to be some sort of misunderstanding, or the kidnapped person usually ended up dead in some alley or river before a rescue could be effected. Morristown knew that—anybody who had done this kind of thing before knew it—so why didn't Kenney?

Frankly, the thing had been doomed to fail from the

start. Kenney had given him practically verbatim his conversation with President Gustavo during the plane ride to this pesthole. Now they were seated in some seedy hotel room near the airfield awaiting their pseudo-extradition. To make it worse, Sturgis was dead and they were going to have to explain to his family what had happened to the poor bastard.

And all because Kenney wouldn't listen.

Well, he couldn't blame the death of a comrade on his best friend. Sturgis had understood the risks right along with the rest of them. Still, it wasn't supposed to have gone down this way. They had been stripped of their weapons and pride, and practically emasculated by Redondo and his crew of ass-kissing goons. And what chaffed Morristown's ass the most was the fact they'd been defeated by one man. Buford Jones was still complaining of pain following his encounter with this Stone dude, and he knew if Jonesey was belly-aching, the big guy was undoubtedly hurting.

Morristown threw a phone book across the room. "This is horseshit, Curt!"

"Settle down," Kenney replied.

"Don't tell me to settle the fuck down. We shouldn't be sitting here on our asses while the bastard that killed Sturgis is out running around free as a bird." Morristown looked in Jones's direction. "What do you think, Jonesey? You feel like we should be sitting here?"

Jones didn't say a word. He just stared at Morristown for a minute before lowering his eyes and shaking his head.

"I'm not running a democracy here, Pete," Kenney said, the threat obvious in his voice. His manner suggested he was getting irritated. "Nobody feels worse about Lou than I do, but I'm still in charge of this group. Everybody voted."

"Everybody's not here anymore, Kenney."

There was a jiggling at the door handle—the sound of a key being inserted—then the door swung inward to admit four uniformed officers followed by Redondo. "What is the trouble in here?"

Morristown's face turned a dark and dangerous hue of red. "Get the fuck out of here!"

The officer seemed to get nervous, but Redondo appeared relatively unaffected. He was obviously accustomed to dealing with worse threats, and Morristown realized he wasn't easily intimidated. Morristown imagined for just a moment what it would have been like to cut the throat of that smug bastard from ear to ear. Yeah, an old-fashioned Colombian necktie—it would have been almost poetic justice from Morristown's point of view. He danced back to reality and decided to hold his peace. But only for now, since he didn't see how their situation could get much more abysmal.

As if nothing had happened, Redondo said, "You may be pleased to know that I am releasing your friend's body. It is being brought to your plane as we speak. My men will escort you there now, then you will do as we have agreed. If you ever show your faces here again—"

"Yeah, we know, we know," Kenney said. "You'll shoot us on sight."

"I see we understand each other," Redondo said. "This is good. But now I am sorry to say I cannot see you off personally, but I have another matter to which I must attend. You see, we believe we have located our mutual friend. Very near here. In fact, we have very reliable information that he and his associate have rented a hangar at the airport. So we're going to go there now and arrest him."

Morristown snorted. "You think he's going to let you take him alive? I've been up against him personally. He'll kill a whole bunch of you before he let's you take him alive."

Redondo's smile was cool. "We shall see."

And then it happened—Buford Jones came alive in the way Pete Morristown knew he could. The big, black man came out of his seat and managed to knock together the heads of two of the four officers before anyone knew what was happening. The pair of officers dropped like stones to the floor, and before anyone could react to what was happening, Jones had his hands around Redondo's throat.

Pandemonium erupted in the room.

Morristown and Kenney reacted with blinding speed. Morristown stepped forward and launched a low kick to one of the officer's knees. The man grunted with pain as he went down. Morristown followed with a palm strike behind the ear and the cop flopped prone to threadbare carpet.

Kenney was equally formidable, catching the other cop with an uppercut to the chin that took him off his feet and slammed him into the wall. The paper-thin dry-wall collapsed under the force of Kenney's enthusiasm. The officer was stunned but still apparently had enough presence of thought to reach for his side arm. Kenney and Morristown tackled the guy in a random but coordinated fashion, one that had come from years of hand-to-hand combat training. They dragged the officer to the ground and a punch to the back of the head by Kenney ended the struggle.

Redondo was gasping for breath by the time Morristown and Kenney had regained their feet. Kenney now had the unconscious officer's pistol in his hand. He stuck the tip of the barrel against Redondo's left nostril and then looked at Jones.

"Enough, Jonesey," Kenney said, panting with the exertion. "We don't want to kill any cops. Especially not since the good captain has been so hospitable with us."

Morristown had busied himself with disarming the other three officers, and now turned to watch the show. It looked for just a moment as if Jones didn't plan on letting go of Redondo's throat until he'd choked the man to death, but at the last second he released his hold. Redondo gulped the first few breaths, guttural sounds escaping with each breath. Another moment and Jones probably would have crushed his windpipe.

"Now listen very carefully, Redondo, because we're not planning on asking twice. You're going to tell us *exactly* where we can find Stone. We owe him, and it's time to repay. And then as soon as we've taken care of him, we promise to get on the plane and go back to our own country."

"Yeah," Morristown added gleefully. "And then we won't ever bother you again."

THE PRIVATE LINE aboard Adriano Rivas's jet buzzed for attention and startled the drug lord from a sound sleep.

"Yeah," he huffed.

"Mr. Rivas, this is Hector," the voice replied in Spanish. "I work for Chico, and I was told to call you and give you a message."

So Chico had gotten someone else to play message boy. The news was either bad—so bad that Chico had decided he didn't want to be the one to deliver it—or he had failed in his mission and was now on the run. Rivas wouldn't have actually made good on his threat to bury his friend, but he had to keep discipline in the ranks. He'd ruled by fear most of his life, and that was what he knew and with what he was most familiar.

"You woke me up, Hector. You had better hope this is good news."

For a moment Rivas smiled because the voice on the other line began to stammer. "I'm afraid it…it isn't good news, Mr. Rivas."

Rivas sighed. "I'm listening."

"Chico is dead."

Rivas felt his heart plunge into his stomach. He could hear his pulse begin to race in his ears, feel blood rushing to his cheeks as an almost instant migraine took control. Blinding-white streaks of light seemed to lance to the front of his eyes from somewhere deep in the back of his head, and it took every bit of self-control to keep from lashing out at the messenger. Chico Arauca may have been a lot of things, but he'd been Adriano Rivas's friend since childhood.

"Who is responsible for this, Hector?"

"I do not know his name, sir," Hector replied. "But I do know he's an American. The same man Chico hired me to help find."

Rivas clenched his teeth. He knew exactly who was responsible: Stone. "First this American kills my brother, then he steals my sister, and now he has taken the life of my best man. What of Carmita? Is she safe?"

"Yes, Mr. Rivas. She is safe here with me."

"Let me speak with her."

There was a long silence…then, "She is sleeping. This bastard American put her through quite an ordeal. He drugged her and she has not yet awakened."

"Where are you?"

Hector told him where he was waiting; a small club in San Lorenzo. Rivas remembered the place—basically a hangout for scum and not a very popular one at that. Rivas ordered Hector to stay put and broke the connection. He sat back in the reclining seat of his plane to think through what he'd been told. Rivas smelled a trap, but he was willing to take the chance. He had adequate protection with him, and even if they fell, Rivas would make sure he took care of this Stone.

"DID I DO WELL, *señor?*" Hector asked as he hung up the phone.

"Perfect," the Executioner replied. He tossed the man the keys to the rental. "You just bought your life back. Take that car out there and return it to the rental place on the paperwork. Then get to a hospital. Do as I say or I'll hunt you down."

The man wasn't fast enough to grab the keys when they were tossed to him, but he certainly recovered quickly enough to scoop them off the macadam floor in the hangar. He got to his feet and through some means Bolan would never be able to understand, managed to get out the door under his own power. The guy was tenacious, if nothing else, and the warrior wished more good men had such mettle.

"What now, Sarge?" Grimaldi asked Bolan once they heard the rental pull away.

"Assuming Rivas took the bait, I just bought myself the additional time I need to get to this base of operations and see if I can find Esposito and Gustavo."

"Okay, but something's bugging me." Grimaldi scratched his head.

"What's that?"

"If Rivas is coming here, why not just take him down now?"

"Because if this intel from the Farm doesn't pan out, he's my last information source. And I'll need his sister to bargain with."

"Ah," Grimaldi said. "Now I get it. Smart play, Sarge."

"I'm touched," Bolan said with a grin. "Did you find me a rough-terrain vehicle?"

"Yep." Grimaldi smiled and jerked his thumb behind him. "Parked outside next to the plane. It's a Land Rover LR3, and man, is she sweet. Plus I packed plenty of extras from the plane. But no could do on the guide. Sorry. I guess all the locals around here are a bit superstitious, and nobody really wanted to guide the American into the woods."

Bolan shrugged. "I'll manage on my own. Thanks, Jack."

Grimaldi clapped Bolan in friendship on the shoulder and the two men walked out into the main part of the hangar. True to Grimaldi's words, an LR3 sat packed and waiting for the Executioner. His mission would take him deep into rugged country, and he'd need a dependable vehicle. It didn't get much more dependable than that.

"Well, I'd better get moving," Bolan said. "It's going to be tough enough even negotiating that kind of terrain in the dark."

"There's a map on the front seat," Grimaldi said. "I used the computer linkup at the Farm to get you within spitting distance on some fairly clear trails. It gets thick toward the end."

"Understood."

Bolan opened the door to and started to climb aboard, but the sound of a roaring engine suddenly commanded the attention of both men. A moment later a pair of police vehicles swung into view, lights blazing. Two men bailed from one of the vehicles and a third man from the other, but none of them was dressed in uniforms. Instead they wore black fatigues and were loaded for bear with assault rifles, bandoliers of ammunition strapped to their bodies.

It looked as if the quails had been flushed.

CHAPTER THIRTEEN

Mack Bolan had fought many battles.

Some had been small and others much grander. Sometimes he'd fought alone, without support or respite—pushing himself for days or even weeks at a time—and sometimes he'd fought side by side with the finest warriors on earth. But if Mack Bolan had learned one thing throughout his War Everlasting, it was only those who fought with the deepest and strongest convictions that what they were doing was for the cause of right would emerge victorious.

The enemy wasn't to be treated as some inhumane monster; an enemy had to be treated with respect. Bolan had learned never to underestimate his enemy and the Quail Group had been no exception.

Bolan had never judged the convictions of others because they weren't his to judge. There was nobody accountable to him for their personal beliefs. He'd never appointed himself as a judge or jury, merely the *judg-*

ment. It was a difficult concept for most to understand because they considered his methods as little more than moral zeal or vigilantism. But it didn't matter to the Executioner because he knew deep in his heart the real reasons for this crusade. To him the justification for fighting such a war hadn't come from some lofty idealism that the end justified the means—the end had already been written.

The laws of society were, for the most part, in place to protect the innocent. But too many times social order wasn't enough to defend the rights of people to live free and in peace. That was the justification for Mack Bolan's war—he did what he did out of duty. And if there was one thing he could respect it was when another soldier did what they saw to be his duty. So the Executioner understood exactly why he was watching the barrels of three heavy assault rifles being leveled in his direction.

Yeah, he understood it…but that didn't mean he'd succumb to it.

The firestorm laid on Bolan and Grimaldi was as thick as a swarm of hornets rousted from their nest during a sticky summer afternoon. Bullets peppered the brand-new LR3, punching holes in the grille and spider-webbing the windshield to the point that it buckled within seconds.

Bolan knew he'd waited a little too long to head for the deep mountainous terrain where he hoped Rivas had secreted the captives he sought, but he was glad he hadn't left Grimaldi to suffer some horrific fate on his own.

As the pair reached the relative safety of the LR3, Grimaldi said, "Seems like the band just played this tune."

"Seems like," Bolan replied.

The warrior risked standing long enough to smash the back window of the vehicle with his Beretta 93-R and reach through to pull the weapons bag from the back. He passed the 93-R to Grimaldi and pulled the M-16/M-203 combo he'd used earlier from the bag. Fortune smiled on him as he found a stack of 40 mm HE grenades accompanying the weapon.

Bolan dropped a high-velocity grenade into the breech, slammed it home, then rose and fired from the hip. The grenade bounced once off the hood of one of the police cars, exploding when the nose struck the windshield. The scorching effect of the HE instantaneously peeled paint from the vehicle and charred the insides. The front doors were blown off their hinges and the vehicle came off the ground about four inches.

The Executioner took the advantage of surprise to get Grimaldi's attention. "Get to the plane and do everything you can to protect it."

"Where are you going?"

"To lead them away from here," Bolan replied.

"Live large, pal."

"You, too."

Bolan lunged from his position and managed to get behind the wheel of the Land Rover without getting his head blown off. He turned the key, hoping the hail of AR rounds hadn't turned the engine to mush. Bolan was rewarded with a powerful roar, and he put it in gear and peeled out of the hangar with a squeal of tires.

The Executioner put some distance between him and the hangar in a hurry, then slowed in the hope he could lure away the men of the Quail Group. They took the bait. Bolan waited until they started to close the distance, then poured on the speed once more. He still couldn't understand their angle in all this. If TOBA had hired them to come to Ecuador to find Esposito, as Brognola theorized, then why the hell were they bothering with him? It didn't make a lot of sense, and the Executioner knew it wouldn't until he could get a better handle on the situation.

For now, he had enough to occupy his mind as the car started to gain on him. Bolan left the airport through the exit gate. He didn't bother stopping for the guard who came out of the security shack and tried waving him down, but he did make sure to swing wide enough to avoid any risk of hitting the poor, unsuspecting man. The guy was just trying to do his job and didn't deserve to get run over.

Bolan turned the wheel steadily and merged smoothly onto a main thoroughfare leading from the airport. This was the second time in the same day he'd been forced to lure the enemy from a critical target. As far as he was concerned, he was wasting time fighting the wrong people. Rivas was the real enemy that needed his unique attention. This Quail Group had been thrown into the mix by others who obviously didn't know what was at stake.

Bolan pressed the accelerator harder and kept checking the lights in the rearview mirror to insure his pursuers didn't lose him. For a moment he considered the oddity in the fact he wasn't actually trying to escape them. The Executioner didn't really want to fight these men, but they weren't giving him much of a choice.

Once they were a few miles from the airport, Bolan increased his speed until it redlined at 90 mph. The engine began to smoke, and Bolan knew he'd have to make his move soon. He saw an exit coming up and decided he had his opportunity. The acrid smell of freshly burned oil assailed his nostrils as he suddenly veered off the highway and pumped the brakes. He missed the concrete median separating the highway from the exit by less than a yard.

Bolan reached the traffic signals at the end of the ramp and slowed only enough to make sure no pedestrians or unwary motorists could be hurt. He then continued into the intersection, pumped his brakes, then jerked the steering wheel. The Land Rover nearly went up on two wheels, but the Executioner managed to hold it together.

The soldier pressed onward and traffic began to dissipate somewhat. Another minute ticked by and now the smoke coming from the engine was obscuring his view. Bolan rolled down the windows and turned on the heater, switching the air from recirculation to fresh-air intake. Some of the smoke entered the car and was immediately flushed out through the open windows.

As Bolan continued down the road, all traffic seemed to disappear and the shadowy outlines of what looked like a cluster of factories loomed on the horizon. Bolan gauged his distance and wondered if he'd be left with any place to go at the end of the road. He considered the circumstances now presented—the road would probably dead end. That meant there wouldn't be much time for improvisation if it did. He'd have to make a decision and make it fast.

Bolan blew past a large object and jammed on his brakes while simultaneously killing his headlights. The Land Rover rocked to a halt with a loud squeal. He slammed the gearshift into reverse and backed up his vehicle until the moonlight reflected what he had passed. It was the thick, stone balustrade of a small bridge. Bolan peered through the back window and saw the bridge spanned a dry creek bed. He swung the back end of the Land Rover off the shoulder, then put it in neutral and let the vehicle roll backward. When the roof of the Land Rover was below the top of the balustrade, he went EVA.

Bolan crossed the creek bed, charged up the opposing incline and dropped prone. He yanked the charging handle on the M-16 to load a round, palmed the forward assist and pressed the rifle stock tightly against his cheek. Bolan kept himself as low to the ground as possible and watched the police vehicle approach, its lights flashing. Bolan aligned the sights between the headlights and the blue lights, took a breath, let half of it out, and squeezed the trigger.

The M-16's light recoil was barely noticeable to Bolan. He squeezed off a second shot, adjusting level by pure estimation. This round contacted the grille and

Bolan could see the sparks from the ricochet. The Executioner smiled with satisfaction; another adjustment did the trick. The third round blew out a front tire. No driver, no matter how good, would be able to maintain control with a blowout at that speed. Bolan saw the headlights swerve back and forth, in and out of his line of vision, then veer onto the powdery surface of the shoulder. The vehicle spun out of control and slammed into a large stand of trees on the far side of the road. It stopped less than a hundred yards from the road.

Bolan jumped to his feet, watched the vehicle a moment to confirm movement inside, then returned to the Land Rover. He turned the key in the ignition and at first the engine sputtered, but it came to life. He'd probably be able to nurse it back to the airport. As he drove up the incline, swung onto the road and headed back the way he'd come, he passed the vehicle slowly to insure there were no serious injuries. All three occupants appeared to be exiting the car, albeit a bit slowly, and Bolan nodded with satisfaction.

For the moment he'd taken the Quail Group out of commission and out of the picture. There was no way they'd be able to track him to Rivas's base of operations before he could get there and do what had to be done. It was time to wrap things up in Ecuador. He had a feeling that even if he did find Esposito and Gustavo alive and returned them safely to Quito, the mission would hardly be over.

Bolan still planned to deal with Adriano Rivas, but he needed to wait it out until he could discover exactly what the drug lord had planned. For now, he figured it was better to hold on to Carmita. Rivas would do what he could to rescue her, but Bolan didn't believe the guy would actually shut down his operations for it. He was loyal, but he wasn't *that* loyal. Bolan knew he was pushing all the right buttons where Adriano Rivas was concerned. Rivas would probably act with a fair amount of predictability, and he would have to act sooner than perhaps he planned. That meant he'd make mistakes and show his hand too early.

And when he did, Mack Bolan would call it.

A DAMP, COOL WIND buffeted the muscular form of Mack Bolan as he stood in the doorway of the Lear-jet 36A.

Despite his attempts to avoid it, Bolan had been forced to begin his reconnaissance on Rivas's complex with a low-altitude, nighttime parachute jump into treacherous jungle terrain. It was a tremendous risk even when considering the payoff. For all the Executioner knew, Stony Man was completely off the mark and this would turn out to be either a wash or some other operation of no bearing on his current mission goals. Yet Bolan was still willing to trust the expertise of his friends. He could count on one hand the number of times they'd failed him, and have several fingers left over.

"You have a green light, Sarge," Grimaldi said through the headset. "Thirty seconds to the drop point. There's no real wind to speak of, so you should come down on a fairly literal vector."

"Understood," Bolan replied. He looked back at Carmita Rivas, who was secured to one of the passenger seats and staring daggers into him. "Take care of our little package here, and I'll see you for pickup at the coordinates we discussed."

"Acknowledged."

"And, Jack?"

"Yeah."

"Don't forget our agreement. We meet in four hours and—"

"I know, I know…if you're not there I don't wait. But you could get hung up or something. How will I know if you're really out of the game just because you don't show in four hours?"

"You don't," Bolan said in a matter-of-fact tone. "But if I'm not there on time you can be sure I'm out of it. Trust me."

"Stay hard, guy," Grimaldi said.

Bolan bailed. The initial exit was like it always was for a parachutist. A noisome rush of wind, the sound of jet engines roaring in the ears, then a silence as deafening as what had prevailed on the senses just seconds earlier. Less than ten of those seconds following his leap, Bolan knew he was in trouble. There was no sound of the nylon crackling in the breeze as it expanded; no sudden jerking of the harness; no upward thrust as the chute hit opening peak.

Nothing!

Bolan went into high gear, reaching to his chest for the Colt combat knife. The Executioner yanked the knife free and cut away the main chute. The seconds ticked off as fast in his consciousness as the freefall air rushing past his ears. Bolan secured the knife and yanked the cord on the reserve chute at the front, rearing his head to avoid rope burns from the risers. The chute expanded and the familiar yank came as a painful but welcome relief to Bolan. He looked below and realized an outline of the thick jungle canopy of trees loomed close.

Bolan braced for what came next. He first felt the brush of jungle treetops against his boots and a moment later was rocketing past the trees. He tucked his chin to his chest, closed his eyes and kept his arms pressed tightly against his side, hands clutching the reserve chute pouch. As he suspected would occur, he never touched ground.

He jerked to a halt about thirty yards above the jungle floor.

The soldier took a quick inventory—everything seemed to be in its place. After unloading his equipment bag and letting it fall to the earth, he unclipped the flashlight from his military web belt and shone the beam upward. The chute was definitely hung up; visible tears were evident in the nylon. Bolan returned the flashlight to its place and then began climbing up the thin chute cords to the where the chute was entangled in the trees.

Bolan wrapped his legs around a thick vinelike branch and began to cut the cords from the chute. When he'd cut a significant length, he tied them together with rigger knots. That accomplished, Bolan took one end of his extended rope and tied it to the branch. He then wrapped the cord around his hand and released his leg-hold. Slowly but steadily, Bolan played out a bit more of the parachute cord until he'd reduced his drop distance to within four yards.

Bolan released the cord and dropped to the ground. He crouched and sat watching the darkness and listening to the silence of the jungle. Nothing.

The soldier gathered his pack and opened it. He retrieved the Beretta 93-R and .44 Magnum Desert Eagle, restoring them to their respective places. The bag also contained everything he'd need for a full-scale assault, including spare ammunition for both pistols and the FN-FNC Para. He'd packed jungle fatigues and boots for the captives since they'd have to hoof it to the drop zone. He had water and rations enough to last them three days, a compact military field surgeon's kit, and an analog homing beacon. He also had a fanny pack containing five pounds of C-4 plastique, and all the accessories for blowing same. Additionally he'd replenished the grenades on his web belt with four Diehl DM-51s.

Yeah, he was ready for just about anything.

After securing the pack, Bolan double-checked his compass against a small map before heading toward the coordinates Kurtzman had provided. It was a quarter mile journey, maybe less. In either case, it was little more than a fresh-air stroll for Mack Bolan.

The Executioner planned to bring a wide cast of characters to the show, and Death had the lead role.

CHAPTER FOURTEEN

San Lorenzo

Adriano Rivas knew as soon as he arrived at the club that he'd been deceived. A sign posted on the front door advised it was closed for repairs, and some cash to a nearby vagrant—one who made it a point to let Rivas know he knew what he was talking about—told the story of gunfire and a battle. When pressed for when this occurred, the drunken old man couldn't be certain but from what he said Rivas assumed it was *before* he'd received the call from Hector.

"A diversion to be sure," Rivas told his new chief of security, Antonio Prospera. "I want you to send some men and find this Hector. If he is alive, I want to know who hired him to deceive us. And if he refuses to talk to you, then I'm confident you'll find some creative way of getting the information we desire."

Prospera nodded, but as usual he didn't say much.

Rivas actually didn't know that much about Prospera personally, except that he had served faithfully as Arauca's lieutenant for a long time. He was also respected by the other men, and carried with him a natural air of authority. Prospera was also reputed to be a crack pistol marksman and a formidable opponent in hand-to-hand encounters.

Rivas returned to his Mercedes with Prospera and ordered the driver to take him to his next meeting. He wouldn't have admitted to anyone else, but he was very concerned for Carmita's safety and her life. He was hoping this meet with Hector would have at least uncovered some clues as to her whereabouts. Rivas couldn't believe Hector would have pulled this stunt on his own. First of all, nobody working under Chico Arauca would have been stupid enough to cross Rivas. Second, Hector stood to make money, a lot of money, if he had produced Carmita unharmed. So Hector calls under the pressure of someone else, Rivas was guessing Brandon Stone, and hands him a story about how he has Carmita and wants Rivas to meet him.

"This story Hector told me was carefully thought through," Rivas said. "I think this mysterious Colonel Stone was behind it."

"You believe this man is trying to stall us?"

"Yes, but it hardly matters," Rivas replied. He couldn't resist a smile. "This American was sent here by someone for a reason. If he's not working for his government, then he would have to be doing it on his own. That's unlikely, since to the rest of the world I've been deceased for three years. I don't believe he knew about my involvement. I think he discovered it once he was here. We know that Erasmo mentioned it."

"It seems like a very reasonable assumption," Prospera said. "If we can believe what Erasmo told us."

"We can believe it." Rivas's smile was hard and cold.

"What do you want me to do about this Stone?"

"Kill him, of course," Rivas said in a very nonchalant tone. "But first I must complete my plans. We are here now. We shall speak no more of this until after I have talked to our benefactor."

They arrived at a palatial estate on the outskirts of the city. It was beachfront property, large and well-kept without any disturbance to the natural elements. The estate was two stories, about twenty rooms, and its grounds covered at least five acres. The owner of the place was an American, and he had long been an unofficial business associate to Rivas. Rivas felt he owed this man his life in some ways, although he would have never openly admitted it.

Adriano Rivas was not and never had been comfortable dealing with Americans. In fact, Rutherford Emerson was probably one of the only Americans for whom Rivas had any respect. He'd first met Emerson in Mexico City ten years earlier. Emerson had affiliations with a number of the big cocks there, affiliations built mostly on Emerson's passion for bullfighting. When Rivas first met the man, he was still very much up-and-coming in the drug business. Most of those men at that time viewed him as little more than another Colombian thug, but Rivas's nose for business soon had them convinced he was capable of more.

Emerson and his other lackeys put up the money to invest in Rivas's plans for distribution throughout Ecuador, simultaneously gaining the money-laundering contacts his new business associates needed to keep covered their less-than-legitimate business interests. Rivas's schemes made Emerson and the others very rich in short order, and consequently put Rivas on the map as a drug lord.

Other than Carmita and Arauca—and of course the private army Rivas had been building in the jungle of southern Colombia—Emerson was the only other person who knew Rivas was alive and well. In fact, Emerson had sunk quite a bit of his own money into this latest deal, so Rivas had to treat him with the respect due any business associate. Not that he didn't already have it. Despite Emerson's age and senility, the old cock was a man who simply commanded respect, and one of the few who continued to believe in the kind of good old-fashioned services Rivas had proved so talented in providing. There were many men Rivas might have crossed; Emerson wasn't one of them.

The men greeted each other with a warm handshake on the massive, decoratively lit veranda overlooking Emerson's beachfront property. The veranda had a full bar and a massive table covered with delicacies and appetizers prepared in a variety of ways. Emerson had a known passion for seafood, especially, and the table sported everything from shrimp cocktail to sautéed mussels. There were also sweet cakes, streusels and coffee available, and a full-service staff on call.

The muscle was present, too. Several men stood close to Emerson, who sat in a wheelchair when walking was too painful, and a number more roamed the grounds. Some of them Rivas knew he couldn't see, but that was okay because it just meant they were doing their job. Prospera was allowed to keep his gun—it was protocol as he was responsible for Rivas's personal security—but the others were required to surrender their weapons to the house staff. There were limits to hospitality in a business like this. Prospera had told his men to allow it without argument.

Rivas was impressed with that; Chico Arauca had trained Prospera well.

"It's good to see you well, my friend," Rivas said.

Emerson nodded. "I'm not all that well." He had a sudden coughing fit, then added from behind a handkerchief, "Let's face it. I'm going to be one among the departed here very soon. It's only a matter of time."

Rivas inclined his head out of respect.

"I'm sorry to hear about Chico," Emerson continued. "That was a tough break. Please let me know where you're going to do the services so I can send something. I'm afraid I won't be well enough to attend."

"The services will be held in private by his men and me only," Rivas said. "I'm sure you understand."

"Yes," Emerson said. "I should have realized that."

"These events do seem to be putting some undue problems into your plan," Rivas said.

"This was *our* plan, son," Emerson said. "You won't forget that again, right?"

Rivas bit back the more terse reply he'd conjured and smiled. Slowly he said, "I misspoke. Yes, *our* plan does seem to be having some problems."

"Are you talking about this American?"

"Yes." Rivas didn't hide his surprise. "You know about him?"

Emerson shrugged. "Of course, Adriano. I make it my business to know about everything. I had hoped the Quail Group would have dealt with him. I went to considerable expense and effort to insure they ran into one another. This Stone moves very quickly, and he's effective. If I thought it would help, I'd have him brought here and offer him the opportunity to come work for us."

"From what I know of this man, he'd never do it," Rivas said.

"I know." Another fit of coughing, and then, "But he's a nuisance as I see it."

"A nuisance? No disrespect, my friend, but this 'nuisance' has killed quite a number of my men, including Chico. He's also kidnapped my sister."

"He won't hurt your sister," Emerson said. "He's not that kind of man. You see, I also know something about Brandon Stone. One of the things I know is that he doesn't really exist. It's a cover, probably developed by someone working for my government. I know of other such operations conducted by a man who matches his description. We're dealing with more than just a run-of-the-mill CIA man. This guy is a professional operative with plenty of experience. We will overcome him as a hurdle, maybe not easily, but we will overcome him all the same."

"Your confidence is admirable," Rivas said. "I just hope you're right."

This brought forth a raspy laugh from Emerson. "You think I didn't expect this? I'll tell you what, Adriano, you worry about making sure the shipment goes correctly, and I'll take care of the American."

"Any other time I wouldn't argue with you," Rivas replied. "In this case, you must understand I have a personal score to settle with this American."

"I do understand," Emerson said. "But this is business we're talking about here, Adriano. You want to be back at the top when this is through, and I can make sure you get there. But I've made promises, you see, and this could go very wrong."

"Are you saying you don't believe I'll come through on this deal?"

Emerson frowned and something hard flashed in his eyes. "I never said that. I never even thought it. Don't be so quick to join a fight, son. You'll live longer. What I'm trying to do is tell you that the business comes first and should *always* come first. That's the first true mark of a pro, which you've proved you are. Settle your personal scores after this deal is done, Adriano. I'm telling you don't rush to find this Stone now. Such a move will only bring you trouble. That's why I say, you let me worry about Stone."

Rivas gave careful thought to what Emerson was

saying. The old man was right; there was no point in throwing all his energy and focus into Stone. In the grand scheme of things, Stone *had* been little more than a nuisance. While his biggest worry was Carmita, Rivas knew she would be safe. The American wasn't an animal. He wouldn't brutalize her, or steal her virtue. The guy was probably using her as leverage to wield against Rivas, and so far he'd allowed the man to do it.

Finally, Rivas said, "I will defer to your judgment for now. You've never lied to me. But please understand I must deal with this man and soon. He has murdered my brother and my friend. They must be avenged."

"I will insure he's taken alive," Emerson said. "In fact, I will give you my word on it. How is packaging of the shipment progressing?"

"Excellent," Rivas replied. "It will be ready for tomorrow morning's journey to America. I'm sure you will be very pleased with the quality of this product."

Emerson took a long pull from his mixed drink. There was an uncomfortably long silence, and Rivas couldn't have sworn to it but it almost looked as if Emerson didn't believe him. Of course, he'd omitted the story of Erasmo Cabeza and how he'd spoken with the American about operations occurring with San Lorenzo, but obviously Emerson hadn't caught on to that.

"You're not telling me everything, Adriano," Emerson said. "I'm disappointed in that."

"What do you mean, 'everything'? What is it you think I haven't told you?"

"You didn't mention how your entire Quito operation

went up in smoke yesterday morning. Or how Pascual Santos is now on the run and nobody can locate him."

Rivas smiled although there was nothing ingenuous about it. "First, Pascual was one of my major manufacturers, yes, but not my *only* one. The operations in Quito are still going strong. Besides, the loss is entirely mine and none of yours, so I wouldn't concern myself with it. Second, and I wasn't going to mention this, but one of my business contacts decided to go shooting off his mouth to the American. He told just enough lies mixed with truth to sound convincing."

"Did he give the American my name?"

"I don't believe so," Rivas said, shaking his head. "But he certainly gave him mine, and he told him where to find my family. Needless to say, Erasmo Cabeza is no longer in my employ. In fact, he's no longer in anyone's employ. I do not tolerate disloyalty in my operations, Mr. Emerson. I'm sure you can understand the need for maintaining my reputation as one who rewards loyalty and punishes those who betray me. Such consequences must be immediate and final."

"I'm satisfied you did whatever you had to do," Emerson replied.

"So now, the shipment will leave tomorrow morning from the San Lorenzo airfield. It will stop to refuel in Mexico City and then continue on to Houston. You have all the official documentation prepared?"

"Yes."

"Excellent. My men will be acting as the work crew. There will be U.S. Customs officials on-site, but you will not have to let that concern you. The operation will all look very legitimate. In fact, we've even told our friends in Washington, D.C., about it."

"It's a good plan," Rivas said. "I'm assured we will have no difficulties making the trip. I will be there personally to insure there are no problems."

"Good," Emerson said. "I have complete faith you will do whatever is necessary to see this succeeds. In the meantime, I'll keep those puppies in TOBA on a short leash. And I will find a way to make contact with the Quail Group and offer my support. They've already lost one of their men. I know this Curtis Kenney would be willing to take help if I offered it to him. Stone has embarrassed them, and Kenney will want his money. Speaking of which, when are we planning to release the information on Gustavo and Esposito?"

"You may proceed with this at any time of your choosing," Rivas said. "They've served their purpose as an insurance policy for me. And now that we know the shipment will go out tomorrow and arrive in Houston okay, I see no reason why you can't leak it to this Quail Group of yours."

"You will, of course, make it look convincing?"

Rivas nodded. "The complex has lived out its usefulness, as have some of the men I've had to pay to feed and house there for these past few years. It will be like leading the wolves to the lambs."

"That is good news, then," Emerson said. "This will be the largest and most valuable shipment of its kind my country has ever seen. The money to be made from the

Proctor Initiative and the political good will it produces
is only of secondary value."

"Agreed," Rivas said. "And you're right. In just one
more day we shall make history."

MARIO ESPOSITO COULDN'T believe his good fortune.
Of course, many men who were in his position might
not have seen it that way, but then they didn't now have
a literal key to freedom in their hands.

Esposito did.

He'd found a loose piece of metal left carelessly near
his left hand. Esposito had discovered the hard way that
the metal was razor-sharp on one side, and with some
effort he'd managed to position it in such a way as to
saw through the leather strap binding his wrist. It had
taken him a number of painful cuts and what he estimated had to have been about ten hours to cut through
the binding to make it loose enough he could slip his
hand free.

Esposito looked up at the high window above his
head and realized it was pitch-dark. His prison was so
deep into the ground he'd experienced some problems
determining if it was night or day. It didn't matter. With
his hand free he stood a good chance of getting out of
this hellhole. Esposito tore off a strip from the pajama-
style clothes provided by his captors and used it to bandage his sore, weak hand. He was glad it was his left
hand and not his right; that meant he could still fire a gun.

One thing at a time, Mario, he told himself. First
thing you got to do is to find a gun.

The other thing he had to do was to find Hernando Gustavo. Of course, he could just go for help and bring back the cavalry, but Esposito had come up differently. He'd served as U.S. Army Ranger and the Rangers didn't leave anyone behind. Despite the fact Esposito had neither a personal responsibility nor a loyalty to Gustavo, he still couldn't bring himself to run away with his tail between his legs and leave someone else to suffer an unknown fate at the hands of a man like Rivas. Then again, Gustavo might already be dead.

It was a weak justification—even ethically wrong to think in those terms—and Esposito damn well knew it. He had to make an attempt to find Gustavo, or he wouldn't be able to look in the mirror every morning. Besides, he had the training and background, and even perhaps some of the skills. Those things had never left him, just as they never really left any former field operative in the CIA. Some "analyst" desks were easier and cushier assignments than others; the Ecuadorian desk hadn't been one of them.

Esposito unfastened the remaining leather restraints that bound him and then stood, gingerly at first, to see if he could bear his weight. It was painful, but the wound in his leg had apparently not damaged any of the major muscle groups, which was something to at least be thankful for. It still hurt like hell, despite the pain drugs they had tried to force-feed him the past two days. He hadn't consumed them fully, instead making a good show of popping them and washing them down with water, then crushing them between his fingers when the guards departed.

They had been putting something in his food, too, although Esposito couldn't be sure what it was. Maybe it was a drug to make him more receptive to the power of suggestion, maybe just antibiotics or something to help him sleep. Whatever the hell it was, Esposito didn't feel topping it with opiates would be conducive to clearing his mind so he could formulate a worthwhile escape plan.

Esposito took a couple of unsteady steps and grit his teeth against the pain, letting his training and discipline take over with each new step. Surprisingly, the exercise made him feel stronger as he walked, and although it was agonizing to ascend the steep, massive flight of stone steps to the prison door, Esposito managed. He pressed his ear to the heavy wooden door. The entire scenario made Esposito feel as if he was in some sort of really bad B movie, some twisted remake of *Frankenstein* or *Count Dracula*.

Esposito tried the handle and found the door opened easily to his touch. He wondered if it would squeak on the hinges and give him away before he'd had a fair shake, but fate or something else was with him. The door swung open smoothly and quietly. Esposito peered both ways down a darkened hallway. At one end, a sliver of light showed from a cracked-open door, and Esposito could hear several men's voices. They were laughing and talking and—from what he smelled—smoking marijuana.

Esposito smiled because he knew what that meant: Rivas was nowhere near here. He didn't tolerate drug use by his people while on duty, and even then he rarely

allowed anyone to work security for him who had a
habit of any kind. Okay, so they were smoking some
grass, which meant they were relaxed. Esposito also
guessed that with Rivas off the premises, security forces
were at a minimum. He actually stood a chance of getting out of here as soon as he found Gustavo. Esposito
crept down the hallway, moving away from the room
housing an indeterminable number of guards.

The lighting was poor, and Esposito took the time to
let his eyes adjust as he kept to the sides of the hall. He
reached a door in the hallway and tried the handle. It
turned smoothly and came unlatched with a soft click.
He checked both directions, then slipped through the
small opening and closed the door behind him. It was
even darker in here without the light of the lamps interspersed throughout the hallway. The senator put his
back to the wall to rest and give his eyes an opportunity
to further adjust to the dimness.

Then he heard it, a sound he hadn't detected on first
entering the room as his heart had been thudding in his
ears. It was hard to be certain at first, but Esposito settled on what he was hearing: it was snoring. As his eyes
began to adjust, he could feel the rapid heartbeat return.
In his somewhat involuntary stupor, he realized he'd
walked right into the bunking area for Rivas's men.
Some of his fear abated when he was able to see that
only a single bunk was occupied.

Get it together, he thought.

Esposito was ashamed of himself, acting like he'd
never handled a dangerous situation in his life. He'd

been shot, stabbed and even had the snot kicked out of him a few dozen times; this would be kitten's play by comparison. Esposito cat-footed to the sleeper's side. He couldn't see the man's face, but the guy seemed to be sleeping heavily. The ex-CIA man almost felt sorry he had to do it, but he couldn't risk taking the guard's equipment only to have the man awake and raise an alarm.

Esposito considered this as he pinned the guard to the bed with a good knee in his belly. Simultaneously, he grabbed the top portion of the sheet and quickly wrapped it around the guard's neck, twisting it tightly as he pulled up and to the side. Within a minute, the man passed out as the blood was blocked from reaching his brain. The senator continued to tighten his makeshift garrote, waiting a significant time to insure he'd completed the job. A quick check of the carotid pulse confirmed he had.

Esposito tried to calm his breathing as he found a flashlight among the equipment. He clicked the switch and began rummaging through the guard's belongings, finding his equipment belt, which included a holstered 9 mm SIG-Sauer P-226 with four spare clips. He also found a Para AUG leaning against the wall. Esposito considered that kind of weaponry odd for this area, but then there was no telling where Rivas might have acquired his hardware. He certainly wouldn't have been able to deal with local suppliers if he'd wanted to keep his "death" a secret.

Esposito donned the belt, cinching it against his narrower waist, and then took the Para AUG and checked the action. It was all starting to come back to him. These bastards had kidnapped the wrong dude. Yeah, he was about to open up a fifty-five-gallon can of whup-ass on them, and the funny thing was he actually stood a chance of succeeding.

Mario Esposito had been reborn.

CHAPTER FIFTEEN

Mack Bolan reached the jungle complex in under an hour.

He crouched near a tree and studied the perimeter through NVDs. Mosquitoes stabbed into his neck, but Bolan ignored them. He'd experienced worse, and without knowing the security measures he couldn't risk any sound. For all he knew there were ten sentries staring at him right now through infrared scopes, just waiting for an opportunity to cut him down.

The Executioner put thoughts of death from his mind and focused on the task at hand. He watched the perimeter and counted the timing between the roving sentries. Best as he could tell, they patrolled the perimeter in pairs, and there were a total of six walking the exterior. There seemed to be no regular pattern of time or movement between each pair, which would make entry to the complex more difficult.

Bolan stripped the NVDs from his face, packed them carefully away, then considered his options. He didn't know the total number of enemy gunners, and he had no layout to the complex. Even if he'd had such a layout he still didn't know exactly where the prisoners were located. To make matters worse, he didn't know what condition either of these men was in. Would they even be mobile under their own power?

Bolan was glad for one thing, and that was the Quail Group acting when they did. There was no way the Executioner would have managed to get the Land Rover to this point easily. Not when he considered the kind of terrain he'd just had to navigate. Well, he wasn't going to get the job done thinking about the past. It was time to make some decisions for better or worse. Experience had taught Bolan that the decision was never wrong or right, but it was the plan to deal with the consequences of a decision that often failed.

The most obvious course of action would be to get inside the complex and locate the prisoners, then see if he could extract them quietly. There were too many variables to go in hard and even more to come out that way. It would make it much easier to get to Esposito and Gustavo just before first light, when the enemy would be tired and the least alert. It meant their discovery of their prisoners' departures would happen much sooner, but not soon enough for them to do anything about it.

Assuming the light of dawn had broken and that Esposito and Gustavo were well enough to travel, Bolan would be able to move rapidly to the rendezvous point. If all went well, the Executioner would have his charges safe and sound in Quito by noon this day.

Bolan did a quick check of his equipment to make sure nothing would make noise, then ventured toward the perimeter. He kept low, stopping every few steps to listen for any threat or opposition. The camp was quiet, the silence broken only on occasion by the sound of predators and other beasts in the surrounding jungle. Bolan reached the first outbuilding, a cabana-style hut about a foot off the ground. The Executioner figured it for a guard shack.

Bolan stopped and crawled beneath the building. He reached into his fanny pack and removed a stick of C-4 and a blasting cap. He used a hollow pen body to core through the plastique and make a hole for the explosive, then stuck the wireless blasting cap into it. There was a large, cylindrical metal object crowding him, and from the smell Bolan figured the guard house also had a makeshift toilet in it. The methane gas would make a great accelerant, so Bolan carefully molded the plastic to the floor of the shack where it met the lip of the metal cylinder.

Bolan quietly rolled from under the outbuilding and continued toward the main structure. From the outline he estimated the building was probably about three thousand square feet. It was rather impressive, considering the remote location. Bolan reached one end of it and peered around a corner. Two guards stood at the entrance door. He cursed his luck. Now he was faced with a choice: try to take the guards out quietly and risk alerting the entire camp, or find another way in.

It wasn't much of a choice.

MARIO ESPOSITO was becoming frustrated.

Despite his earnest searching, he still hadn't found Hernando Gustavo. He was beginning to think that he might have to give up hope. Rivas had said he had other plans for Gustavo. Maybe he'd meant he was going to kill him. Esposito wouldn't have put it past him.

Esposito was so wrapped up in his own concerns that he almost missed it. For a second, he thought he was imagining things, but after blinking a few times and shaking his head, he knew it wasn't the drugs. A golden sliver of light, there in the floor at the end of the hall-way. He took a few uncertain steps, moving a little closer until he was absolutely certain about what he was seeing.

The senator checked the hallway once more, then stepped from the shadows and passed his hand over the floor. It was definitely light, and it had a regular pattern and shape. He finally determined he was looking at a trapdoor. There it was, as big as all get-out, right in the middle of the floor. Who would have thought?

He found the release bolt set into the trapdoor, eased it back slowly and lifted the door.

THE ONLY WAY he could have taken both guards simulta-neously without risking detection was with a silenced pis-tol. That wouldn't be possible since the subsonic cartridges he fired from the Beretta still made enough noise to be heard over the dead quiet. He couldn't risk hand-to-hand, such as with a knife or garrote, for all the obvious reasons.

That left the tranquilizer darts he always carried in his belt.

While they were very small and fired from a small tube attached to a CO_2 cartridge, they packed a hell of a punch. They contained a heavy sedative called Thorazine, but this was a concentrated form used by veterinarians to sedate large animals such as bears or elephants. Bolan loaded the first dart, primed the cartridge and steadied his forearms against the side of the main building.

The report was whisper-quiet, catching the first guard in the neck. The man opened his mouth as his hand went to his neck but no sound came out. The Thorazine rushed to his brain, and the dazed look crossed his expression a moment later. He dropped like stone, much to the surprise of his partner. The second guard started to bend, and Bolan tracked along his back. He fired the second dart and it struck the guard at just a point above his left kidney. The guy stood erect, swatting at the area as if he'd been stung by a wasp. The effect was much the same as that on his friend. Within thirty seconds he toppled to the pavement.

Bolan broke cover and sprinted to their position. He scanned the immediate area, then picked up the first guard and dragged him through the front door. He found a closet just inside the vestibule, stowed the guard there and went back for the second. When the job was complete, the Executioner closed and locked the front door. He stopped a moment to study the interior. The size was impressive, but the decor rather foreboding. It was lit like a dungeon, artificial torches lining the walls at regular intervals.

At one side there were doors that led into individual rooms. At the other corner a short flight of steps led up to a second floor built into the back of the structure in an architectural style similar to a raised ranch. Bolan decided to try the lower rooms first. He was about to proceed along that wall and start a room-to-room search when the sound of movement attracted his attention. The Executioner cocked his head and listened. At first he couldn't orient himself to determine where the noise originated, but another few seconds and he realized it was coming from the hallway on the second floor.

Bolan changed tactics and proceeded toward the steps. He kept his back pressed to the wall, the FN-FNC Para held in front of him. He took the stairs slowly, methodically, pausing with every small creak they made under his weight. Every time he heard a creak, he would stop to listen and continue to hear the noises in the hallway at the top of those steps.

He reached the top of the steps and crouched, keeping to the shadows of the wall. Straight ahead he saw it, an armed man peering through the trapdoor in a hallway floor. It only took Bolan a moment to recognize that face: Mario Esposito! The Executioner quickly recovered from the surprise and started forward but then thought better of it. Esposito would be scared and nervous, and if Bolan approached—dressed as he was and armed to the teeth—the senator could possibly shoot him.

Okay, calling out to him wasn't really an option.

Bolan decided to wait and see what Esposito had planned. The Executioner remained in the shadows and studied the man as he gingerly put one foot into the trapdoor, then the other. In the light coming from the opening, Bolan noticed the bandage wrapped around the man's leg. He was injured, no doubt, and the Executioner wondered just how far he'd be able to travel.

Bolan waited until Esposito disappeared beneath the floor, then started forward. Before he could get halfway down the hall, several doors opened in the surrounding walls and four men suddenly emerged from them. They immediately started to converge on the trapdoor, the first one dropping into it and being followed by a second. It was an obvious trap, and one Bolan should have seen coming.

Bolan drew the Beretta 93-R, sighted on the first enemy target and squeezed the trigger. The 115-grain 9 mm Parabellum round punched through the side of the first man's skull, splitting it down the middle and dousing the other two with blood and brain matter. The soldier tracked on the second one and delivered a similar two-round message. Both bullets ripped through his chest and punctured his left lung, the impact driving him into the wall. He bounced off it like a rubber ball and fell to the decking facefirst.

The third guard shouted a warning at his man halfway through the trapdoor as he fumbled to bring his SMG into play. Bolan triggered the pistol again. The 9 mm slug cored through his abdomen and ripped open his liver; it exited his lower back leaving an apple-size

hole. The man fell onto his partner who had started back up the ladder leading beneath the hallway floor. The weight of his fall drove the man into the hole and his head disappeared from view.

Bolan charged up the hallway and dragged the corpse aside. He peered into the hole and found the guard below still trying to recover from the short fall. The Executioner thumbed the selector switch to 3-round-burst mode and pointed the muzzle into the hole. The man looked up and saw his predicament. He scrambled for his own weapon although he stood no chance of implementing an effective defense. Bolan squeezed the trigger. The Beretta 93-R recoiled in his grip as all three rounds crashed through the top of the man's skull. His head disintegrated under the brutal assault.

Bolan holstered the pistol and scrambled down the ladder. He dropped into the low-hanging room and tracked it with the FN-FNC Para. Mario Esposito stood in the corner, an assault rifle pointed in Bolan's direction. There was a hesitation and Bolan raised the muzzle of his weapon to demonstrate his nonaggressive position.

"Who are you?"

"No time to explain," Bolan said. "But you can trust I'm on your side, Senator."

That seemed to satisfy Esposito and he lowered his weapon.

Bolan saw Esposito crouched next to a bunk. He couldn't distinguish the features of the man lying on top of it, but he could guess it was Hernando Gustavo. Bolan

let the rifle dangle on its sling as he moved over quickly and helped Esposito untie Gustavo's restraints. He cut the filthy rag used as a gag from the man's mouth. At first, the fear was obvious in Gustavo's eyes but Bolan showed him a brief smile.

"You're all right, son," the Executioner said quietly.

"W-who are you?" the young Ecuadorian stammered.

"A friend," Bolan replied, then looked at Esposito. "Rivas was holding you here?"

Esposito nodded. "Yeah, and if I find that bastard I'm going to put a bullet between his eyes."

"Maybe, but there's not time for that now." Bolan gestured toward Esposito's bandaged thigh. "You well enough to travel?"

"You going to take us out of here?"

Bolan grinned. "Bet on it."

"Then I'm well enough," Esposito said.

The two men didn't waste any more time in helping Gustavo to his feet. He assured them he wasn't hurt. Bolan went to the dead guard at the bottom of the ladder and retrieved the man's weapon. It was a Chinese-made Kalashnikov, a variant Bolan hadn't seen in some time. The Executioner checked the action on the weapon and then returned to the bunk and handed it to Gustavo.

"You ever fire one of these?"

Gustavo took the rifle gingerly and shook his head, studying the weapon with interest.

"Short lesson. Hold it low and tight, aim at the target, squeeze the trigger. Don't pull." He pointed to the selector switch. "The red line means safe. I've set it to sin-

gle shot. The next mode is automatic. Keep it off of that unless you have plenty of targets to take. Understood?"

The uncertainty was evident in Gustavo's expression, but he murmured his acknowledgment. Bolan nodded with satisfaction. When a man's life was on the line, he could learn quite a bit in a very short time. He'd have to make sure they kept Gustavo between him and Esposito. He'd let the former CIA man stay to the rear while he took up the lead; it would be a lost cause from the start if he allowed a wounded man to take point.

"Let's go," Bolan said.

The Executioner bounded up the steps to make sure the hallway was clear, then assisted the other two men out of the hole. They proceeded down the hallway slowly, Bolan checking his rear to make sure the two could keep up. He had to admire Esposito. The guy hadn't let the years of soft living work too much on him. He had guts, and sometimes guts were enough.

The trio reached the end of the hallway and descended the steps just as trouble came through the front door. Six guards fanned out and brought weapons to bear on their position. Bolan went into motion, pushing Gustavo toward the cover of a cherrywood table to the left. The young man didn't need to be told this was the real deal; the weapons held by Rivas's trained soldiers were evidence enough.

Bolan removed one of the DM-51s from his web belt. The Executioner ripped away the pin and let the grenade fly, tossing it into the center of the room. He dragged Esposito to the nearby cover of a freestanding oak shelving unit seconds before the grenade exploded. Six thousand steel balls whistled through the room at an effective kill radius of fifteen meters. Two of the guards fell under the deadly missiles as the wooden floorboards vibrated beneath Bolan's feet, and the concussion disoriented the remaining four.

Bolan knelt and opened up with the FN-FNC Para from behind one end of the shelving unit as Esposito took a similar posture on the other end. They sprayed the room with autofire, keeping their bursts short and controlled. The soldier took the first gunner with a rising, corkscrew burst that stitched the man from crotch to sternum. The man danced backward under the force of the shots and his weapon clattered to the floor, followed a moment later by its deceased owner.

Esposito got the second hardman with shots to the legs and abdomen. The assault rifle chattered its song of destruction as the man's entrails protruded from his shredded stomach. He dropped to his knees and screamed with agony. Esposito finished the job with a 3-round burst that blew the guy's head wide open.

Bolan risked a glance toward Gustavo. The kid was doing his best to find a target, and with a few more seconds he succeeded. He took as careful aim as he could and pulled the trigger repeatedly. He didn't execute the shots by squeezing slowly and carefully, but he got results. One of the guards who had been searching for cover fell under Gustavo's novice marksmanship all the same, three of the seven rounds striking the man in the chest.

The Executioner returned his attention to the final

target who had found cover behind one of the doorjambs leading into a room. He was trading shots with Esposito, flooding the area with autofire that was obviously designed to keep heads down more than to hit anything. Bolan seized the advantage, waiting until the guard revealed himself again to deliver another burst. Bolan squeezed the trigger of his assault rifle when he had the man's head in sight. The first few rounds sent wood chips flying about the guard's face, distracting him enough for Bolan to reacquire his sight picture. A second burst ended the argument neatly, ripping the man's lower jaw from his face and tearing the flesh and bone of his neck. His head bounced oddly on the shredded flesh before his body toppled to the ground.

"Look out!"

Esposito's cry caused Bolan to whirl in time to see a guard rushing down the steps and leveling his weapon in the warrior's direction. The Executioner swung his weapon into target acquisition but something beat him to the punch. Two shots struck the guard in the side, the first getting his arm and the second his head. The man's body canted sideways before tumbling down the remainder of the steps. Bolan turned to see Gustavo standing at full height. The Kalashnikov was snug against his shoulder and the muzzle smoking.

Bolan nodded, and Gustavo smiled his acknowledgment.

The threesome regrouped and headed for the front door. As they reached it, Esposito said, "Is there a back way out?"

"Don't know," Bolan said as he peered into the darkness. The sound of men shouting was now audible. "But I still have a few surprises either way."

The Executioner retrieved the wireless detonator from a concealed slit pocket on his blacksuit and thumbed the switch. He jerked his head to indicate the other two should follow him out, then thumbed the switch as he burst into the darkness. The guard shack exploded, lighting the night as the methane gas ignited and produced a secondary explosion. More shouting could be heard in the aftermath as flames rose twenty yards into the night air. A few of the guards screamed, some of them caught by the intense heat of the blast.

Bolan beelined across the open complex, Gustavo on his heels and Esposito doing his best to keep up with them. The Executioner could hear the man grunt with each agonizing stride. There was no way in hell Esposito could make the journey through the jungle without assistance. Bolan would have to switch to Plan B if they had any hope of escaping. A wounded man would just slow them down long enough for the guards to recover.

As they reached the perimeter, the area still darkened and obviously not patrolled, Bolan gestured for Gustavo to keep going as he went back to retrieve Esposito. He found the CIA man on one knee, panting and holding his injured leg. Bolan could see blood was starting to soak through the bandage. Bolan slung his weapon, then pulled the guy to his feet. He hauled Esposito onto his shoulder, adjusted the weight for balance, then turned and continued back the way he'd come. Within a minute, he had merged with the jungle darkness. The rescue operation had been a success.

What happened next would be determined partly by fate and partly by the skill and tenacity of a man called the Executioner.

Anything, he told himself, before she announced she was pregnant or he found a wife she was it didn't sure... that apart, then would he even accept that party... hazard of he didn't have sure enough, he finally knew him...

CHAPTER SIXTEEN

Sometimes, good fortune smiled on a man and he couldn't explain why.

This was the case with Curtis Kenney, although he wasn't sure if he could have called the information good fortune. Maybe it would work out that way. With the money they stood to make from this deal—Lou Sturgis's portion going to his kids notwithstanding—Kenney entertained the idea of retiring. He could live comfortably the rest of his life on five hundred thousand dollars. While the Quail Group had accepted only one other truly lucrative job prior to this mission, it had been enough for him to pay all his debts and put something away for a rainy day. Adding this to it would set his portfolio at about two million; that was more than adequate for a man who lived as simply as he did.

Kenney knew he was kidding himself, however. He wouldn't be able to stand being out of the field. He knew there might come a day where he accepted his last assignment—the kind from which he wouldn't return—but he sure as hell didn't plan it to be this one. That's why he accepted an invitation to hook up with a guy who claimed Rutherford Emerson of TOBA had sent him.

Kenney and Jones met the guy at a remote location outside of San Lorenzo, a meeting observed from a distance through a high-power sniper scope by Pete Morristown. The man had told him how Emerson had connections inside Ecuador, and how he knew it violated protocol to maintain communications silence, but the information was too valuable to pass up. Kenney listened carefully as the man told him about the American named Brandon Stone. He nodded with enthusiasm, keeping quiet even as he listened to the entire cockamamie story of how Stone had been sent by the government to find Esposito and shut him up. He tried to look attentive as the man explained that Emerson had interests that required protection, interests outside those of the TOBA group, and how Emerson would double the offer if the Quail Group brought Esposito and Gustavo back to Quito alive.

Kenney had no trouble believing most of what he'd been told until he heard about how Stone may have already found this hidden complex of drug smugglers. Emerson wanted the Quail Group to make absolutely sure that if they ran into Stone the guy wouldn't come out of the encounter alive. That's when Curtis Kenney knew the entire deal stank like a rotting corpse. And yet, he agreed to do it because it would accomplish his original mission.

"As to Stone," Kenney told the man, "we'll make sure he's taken care of."

Now they bounced and jounced through the jungle terrain in a specially equipped Jeep, a native guide at the wheel, following a map provided by Emerson. The "trail" the guy had chosen to take them into the jungle mountains was anything but, yet Kenney decided to keep an open mind. The little man who barely spoke English supposedly knew the area better than they did, and they were going to need the guy to get them out once they found the hostages.

Kenney couldn't stop thinking about the enigmatic Colonel Brandon Stone. He sure as hell didn't believe what the guy from Emerson had told him. Something didn't wash about that story. They had twice handed Stone the opportunity to kill all of them, and twice Stone had opted not to do it. Kenney couldn't even bring himself to hate Stone for the death of Sturgis. The guy had been defending his life, and Kenney had to respect that. He'd have done the exact same thing had he been in Stone's shoes.

Stone wasn't the assassin type. First, he'd made entirely too much noise. Second, the U.S. government didn't send men of Stone's caliber to commit political assassination. Esposito had been sent to broker a deal that would benefit America; it didn't make sense to then have him killed. It would have been stupid to send Stone—a guy who was obviously a soldier and not a government assassin—to eliminate a man who was doing something for his country. And Esposito's background in the CIA just wasn't enough incentive for the government to go to such trouble.

No, there was a lot more going on here than this man of Emerson's had let on. In fact, Kenney thought it strange Emerson would act at all outside the parameters of TOBA. Kenney had never met Emerson personally, or any of the others in TOBA save for Weygand, but he knew he didn't like this one damn bit. He wasn't going to just kill Stone without finding out the man's true intentions. Like Stone, he was a soldier not a thug.

"How much farther do you think?" Kenney asked, directing his voice to the back so he could be heard over the straining engine.

"Shouldn't be too far," Morristown replied. He'd been studying the map with Jones since their departure.

"Hey, Curt, I've been wondering something," Jones said.

"What's that?"

"Well, I wonder just where the hell Emerson got this information. I mean, if it was that damn easy for him to find out, why didn't they just do it to start with?"

"Yeah, I was wondering the same thing."

"Well, it seems pretty obvious to me," Morristown interjected. "They're setting us up."

"Okay, but setting us up for what? We're helping them by taking this mission. Nobody else would have bothered with a job like this. Too political and too hopeless."

"Maybe they figure we'll buy the farm out here and they won't have to pay us," Jones replied. "Maybe they know Esposito and this Gustavo boy are already dead."

"Doesn't make any sense," Kenney said. "The two million they offered us is chump change to a group like TOBA. Even Emerson's doubling the deal is nothing. Every man in that group is a millionaire more times over than I'd care to count. This isn't about money."

"I don't even think it's about oil," Morristown said in agreement.

"Me, neither," Kenney replied.

As they continued slowly and methodically through the jungle, dawn turned to morning. The sun was rising higher in the sky and soon it would start to get hot and sticky. It also meant they were going to have to hit this place in the light of day. Kenney would have preferred to conduct the operation before dawn, but he didn't get to call the shots on this one. They were running out of time.

"Hold it!" He held up his hand to the driver.

The engine wound down as the vehicle lurched to a halt and nearly threw Kenney through the front windshield. He cursed softly, then pushed it from his mind. He reached over and turned the key to kill the engine, then studied the area ahead of them.

"What the hell—?" Morristown began.

"Quiet," Kenney whispered. "I saw something. Some kind of movement, about one o'clock."

He spun his finger in the air and then grabbed his M-16 carbine from the floor in front of him. Morristown and Jones obediently followed suit and the three men went EVA. Kenney ordered Jones to go to the left and Morristown to the right while indicating he'd take the center. The three stood abreast of one another, put about twenty-five yards distance between them, and then on cue from Kenney started moving slowly and methodically through the dense undergrowth.

Kenney was positive he'd seen something, and it wasn't one of the many creatures populating the jungle. Animals weren't made of metal. A stream of sunlight had reflected off something metallic. That meant human beings. Kenney had spent many hours in terrain like this, and he knew when he was being watched.

Yeah, there were definitely eyes on them. Human eyes.

MACK BOLAN HEARD the vehicle well before he saw it.

He quickly indicated for Gustavo to take cover behind a nearby tree root protruding from the ground, then he slowly eased his burden to a soft spot of moss beneath a thick batch of tree fronds. He checked Esposito's pulse and nodded with satisfaction at the slow but steady throbbing beneath his fingers. The man had lost consciousness about an hour before dawn. They'd kept up a fairly steady pace for the past two hours, and they weren't far from the landing zone, maybe four hundred yards. Forty minutes remained before his rendezvous with Grimaldi.

Bolan felt light on his feet after unburdening his load. Esposito wasn't a big guy, but the deadweight was heavy nonetheless when navigating through the Colombian jungle. It was okay. He'd carried much heavier than Esposito much farther than this. Bolan whipped a pair of nonreflective binoculars from his belt and scanned the jungle ahead. After careful searching, he spotted the vehicle.

Much of it was concealed by the jungle vegetation, but he could see the driver clearly. The man was small and dark-skinned, clearly native. Okay, so maybe he wasn't faced with enemy, maybe it was a border patrol unit or hunters. Maybe not. In either case, Bolan didn't have time to find an alternate route. He needed to find a quick way past them. Risking an encounter now would mean they were stranded for certain. He'd ordered Grimaldi to scratch the pickup if he wasn't on time. While he knew the Stony Man ace might not obey orders, he couldn't take that risk. Whoever blocked the path ahead stood as much of a risk to the extraction as they did to the hostages. Bolan checked his watch. At the outside he had five minutes at best to neutralize any threat.

The Executioner prayed it was enough.

BUFORD JONES WAS no stranger to the jungle.

As a career Marine, Jones had been stationed or fought on nearly every continent and in almost every kind of terrain. His tour of service had started with Lebanon, and he'd participated in Grenada and Desert Storm. He'd attempted to reenlist for Operation Iraqi Freedom, but his age combined with his inactive reserve status made him ineligible for any front-line action. It was when he'd attempted to reenter service that Kenney came to be acquainted with him, a tip offered by the recruiter who rejected his application.

When Curtis Kenney presented the Quail Group's intent and showed him some of the after-action reports,

Jones didn't hesitate to join up. He'd just suffered a bitter divorce—one where his wife somehow managed to see to it that not only did she get sole custody of their one teenage daughter but also severely limit his visitation—so it seemed like the right thing to do.

Jones was frustrated with the current situation. Like Morristown, he hadn't been enthusiastic about taking this job to start with. While the money seemed right, the mission had been one disaster after another. Jones felt as though they weren't coming close to accomplishing their objective, and to have gone through what they had—including the loss of a good man—only to have the information just fall into their laps didn't sit right with him.

Jones pushed the problems from his mind and concentrated on the job at hand. One wrong move in a place like this could get a soldier killed; Jones understood that if he didn't understand anything else. He crept through the jungle overgrowth, moving with a grace and silence belied by his mammoth size. He wasn't sure if Kenney had really seen what he thought he'd seen, but he trusted the guy. Curtis Kenney was a good soldier; hell, they were all good soldiers. They had survived this long listening to Kenney, and Jones wasn't about to switch gears now.

Jones froze in place for a moment. He could hear something, not sure what exactly, but for just a second it had sounded almost like a…moan? Jones looked to right but he couldn't see Kenney or Morristown. Okay, so maybe that wasn't anything to be worried about, but it still wasn't good. They were supposed to stay close enough to one another that they could use hand signals.

Where the hell had they gotten off to now?

PETE MORRISTOWN DIDN'T see it coming; he couldn't have possibly seen it coming. He would have hoped his skills allowed him to hear it coming, but apparently he'd been outfoxed by someone of more skill and cunning.

A muscular forearm encircled his neck and yanked backward. Stars popped instantly in front of his eyes as air and blood flow was instantly cut off from his brain. Morristown reacted with the first and best tactic he knew, twisting his body into a position such that he could stomp on the attacker's instep. It was ineffective as his assailant had positioned his body in such a way that Morristown couldn't gain leverage enough to reach the booted foot.

Morristown reached for the sheathed Ka-Bar fighting knife dangling from his belt. He managed to get the knife partially free before there was a jarring blow to his wrist. The stinging pain wasn't enough to cause him to drop the knife, but seconds after the blow his arm went numb from fingertips to elbow and he found his muscles no longer wanted to work. He clawed at the arm around his neck, but the muscles were hard and rigid, and Morristown knew that grip would be immovable.

Morristown had one option left and he exercised it; he rammed his skull backward and was rewarded with a successful crack that would have knocked lesser men unconscious. The hold slackened, and it was enough for

Morristown to gain the leverage he needed to throw the attacker off balance. He stepped back a couple of steps and almost lost his footing on an uprooted tree root as he gasped for life-giving air.

Morristown now had a clear view of his attacker's face, even through the blackened cosmetics and trickle of blood now running from a head laceration. Colonel Brandon Stone! Stone came immediately to his feet in a defensive posture. Morristown quickly regained his composure and took up a Shotokan-style karate stance. It was his first chance to see Stone close up, and Morristown had to admit the man made for an intimidating inspection. He was tall and muscular with the coldest blue eyes Morristown had ever seen. His face was a grim visage to behold, and the intensity of his aura would have made devils flee him with dread. Morristown had never quite experienced fear of this kind before, but he did as soon as he looked at Stone.

"We're not your enemy," Morristown said, not sure why he'd even said it.

"I don't care," Bolan replied evenly. "You're stopping me from completing my mission. I can't allow that."

Well, Morristown sure as well wasn't going to allow it, either. He charged Stone as if he were going low, shouting a battle cry he hoped his comrades would hear. He'd been well-trained and had a lot of experience, but he wasn't sure he could take Stone alive on his own. That had been Kenney's instruction: if they encountered Stone they were *not* to automatically try to kill him as Emerson's man had ordered.

At the last moment Morristown went low and tried for a single-leg takedown. It was an old move but had proved useful in the past. Not this time, unfortunately, as Stone swung the leg out of reach at the last second and drove a fist into Morristown's right shoulder. He scraped his palms on rock covered by slippery lichen but managed to regain his balance. He whirled and studied his opponent's face with determination. Morristown was not going to let this guy defeat him. No way in hell he would let that happen.

He charged once more.

MACK BOLAN HELD his position as the Quail Group's Peter Morristown charged him for a second time. He didn't have time to fight with this man, but he hadn't expected to have the tables turned on him. What worried him was the idea Morristown probably wasn't alone; his teammates were certainly nearby and would soon arrive to assist. Bolan had to take the guy down quickly and get to the LZ with Esposito and Gustavo.

As Morristown reached out for his throat, Bolan grabbed his wrist and forearm. He twisted inward and wrenched the wrist in such a way as to be extremely painful but not debilitating. Morristown yelped with pain and swung his free hand toward Bolan's side. The Executioner spun farther inward, taking the blow to his back rather than his ribs. He gritted his teeth but kept in motion as he stuck out his right foot. Morristown lost his balance and fell backward, the tripping motion slamming him to the ground.

Bolan stepped backward and immediately felt his back smack something hard but not natural. Before he could react, two black arms encompassed his chest and shoulders. The soldier felt his feet leave the ground and the hot breath of the assailant on his neck. He swung his legs backward and drove the heels of his boots into his opponent's shins. There was a grunt and the bear hug slackened.

The Executioner twisted out of the hold and dropped to the ground. He followed with a combination punch to the abdomen and an elbow strike to the groin. The breath escaped his enemy with an explosive burst, and Bolan got his first view of the newcomer. He was a hulk of a man dressed in jungle camouflage identical to that of Morristown: Buford Jones. Bolan landed a rock-hard punch to the back of Jones's left ear and toppled him. A moan escaped and Jones stopped moving, obviously rendered unconscious from the blow.

The Executioner turned to the sound of scrambling in the brush on his left and drew his Desert Eagle. He aimed in the direction of the sound just milliseconds before Curtis Kenney burst through it, an M-16 carbine clutched in his hands. Bolan thumbed away the safety and sighted down the barrel center mass. Kenney stopped short and leveled his own weapon in Bolan's direction.

Both men hesitated a fraction of a second, their eyes locking on to each other, their fingers poised over the triggers of their respective firearms.

Kenney was the first to speak. "Why are you doing this?"

"Why are you?" Bolan returned.

"Because we've been told by some rather reliable people that you're here to betray your own country."

"And just who's feeding you that line?"

"Uh-uh," Kenney said. "I answered one of your questions, now you answer one of mine."

"Fine," Bolan replied. He inclined his head in the direction of the groaning Morristown and said, "As I've already explained to your pal there, you're keeping me from my mission."

"Which is?"

"Hostage rescue," Bolan replied. "That's the only detail you need."

"So you weren't sent here to assassinate Senator Mario Esposito?"

"Hardly," Bolan said. "Is that what you've been thinking all this time?"

"That's what we were told just last night," Kenney replied.

"A lie."

"I don't think Rutherford Emerson has any reason to lie."

Bolan didn't recognize the name. "Well, this Emerson, whoever he is, is a big windbag. You've been set up."

"So why did you kill one of our men?"

"Because he was trying to kill me," Bolan said. "You and your team didn't even bother to ask what was going on before you jumped into the middle of it. You just assumed, and you acted without any plan or forethought."

"We were paid to do a job," Kenney said. "We're just

trying to do that job. Esposito and Gustavo represent cash to us."

"No, they don't," Bolan said simply and quietly. "They represent trouble. The kind of trouble you don't want. Now, I'm short on time, so I'm going to walk away and so are you."

"No, afraid you're not," Kenney replied.

There was an all too familiar click and a voice said quietly, "Yes, he is."

All eyes turned toward the sound of the voice. Esposito and Gustavo stood just inside the clearing now, weapons drawn and aimed in Kenney's direction. Jones was just coming awake and Morristown had become a statue, obviously unsure of what to do next. Everyone there knew that one wrong move could bring the entire standoff to a very sudden and bloody end.

"As you can see," Bolan said with a grin, "Esposito and Gustavo are alive. They're going to stay that way. Now drop the hardware."

Kenney looked toward his men and realized they were helpless to assist. Bolan could see the shame in the private soldier's expression, and he could understand it. He'd been defeated one too many times by Bolan, and this wasn't going to do a thing for his ego. Frankly, Bolan didn't give a damn; there wasn't time for self-congratulation. He could get his pat on the back somewhere else because it wasn't Bolan's job.

As he took Kenney's rifle and pistol and dropped the magazines from them before tossing them away, Bolan said, "Look on the bright side. You could have ended up getting yourselves killed at Rivas's base. I saved you the trouble, and your lives."

"Who?"

"Adriano Rivas," Bolan said. "He's the one behind all of this. You didn't know that?"

"Who the fuck is Adriano Rivas?" Morristown asked.

The sound of vehicle engines in the distance left Bolan convinced there was no more time to chat. It would probably be Rivas's forces on a manhunt for the escapees. And Bolan had very little time to get his people to the rendezvous point.

"Sorry, boys," the Executioner said, "but we'll need to borrow your guide."

"Like hell—" Morristown began.

"No arguments," Bolan said. "I'll make sure he comes back for you. In the meantime, I'd stay out of sight until Rivas's men get past you. They'll be long gone by the time the guide returns for you. You'll have no trouble avoiding them then."

Bolan left the pair to help Jones recover as they quickly got to the guide. Gustavo very quickly explained to the guide that he was to take them to a particular point as directed on Bolan's map and then return for the other three men. The guide shrugged and motioned them to get aboard. What the hell did he care? He'd been paid for his services and it didn't really matter who he drove where. If these Americans wanted to ride around and play army men, what was it to him?

As they pulled away, Bolan thought of the men in the Quail Group. He didn't really have much cause to feel as though he'd landed any sort of real victory. They had been duped, just as he had, and he couldn't help but feel a bit sorry for them. Still, they had their rules and he had his. Fighting former American soldiers like himself was generally a violation of those rules, unless they had decided to play on the wrong side of things. Bolan didn't get that from Kenney. No, this guy was someone Bolan thought he could get to like. He'd have to make sure he saw to it they got a fair shake. For the Executioner had a feeling he hadn't seen the last of the Quail Group.

Yeah, this wasn't over yet.

CHAPTER SEVENTEEN

Quito, Ecuador

News of Mario Esposito and Hernando Gustavo's rescue spread through the city.

As soon as he'd delivered them safely to an initial meeting location, Mack Bolan made himself scarce in short order. He needed to get to Stony Man Farm and get some things worked out. The Proctor Initiative could go forward, but there was still the issue of Adriano Rivas. Bolan had arranged for the arrest and detainment of one Carmita Rivas, but he was certain that wouldn't draw Rivas out of the woodwork.

As Grimaldi helmed the Learjet 36A homeward, Bolan contacted Stony Man across the satellite link.

"That was a great job you did, Striker," Brognola said, congratulating him.

"Not as smooth as I would have preferred," Bolan replied. "But thanks."

"What's next for you?"

"Rivas," Bolan replied.

"What?" Price asked. "Rivas wasn't part of the objective. You got Esposito and Gustavo's son back okay. You're taking on a private mission?"

"No, I'm completing this one," Bolan said. "And I'm going to need all the support I can get."

"You want to try explaining it?" Brognola asked.

"Maybe later," Bolan said. "Right now, I need you to do a couple of things. First, I need everything you can find on a Rutherford Emerson, and I need you to get this to Curtis Kenney, the guy who heads up the Quail Group."

Brognola furrowed his brow and yanked an unlit cigar from his mouth. "Rutherford Emerson? You mean *the* Rutherford Emerson, oil tycoon?"

"Oil tycoon," Bolan repeated absently. "I don't suppose he happens to be a member of TOBA, does he?"

"One of the senior members," Brognola said. "And a close and personal friend of Frederick Proctor."

"I don't know how he figures into this, Hal, but if Proctor's on the level, then Emerson's no friend. I think he's as rotten as they come. I think he's somehow connected to Rivas. I just don't know how, or even how to prove it. Yet."

"That might be easier said than done, Striker," Price interjected. "Emerson has some very powerful friends, including a few inside the White House. He's well-known and respected throughout the business community. He has financial ties from here to Oman, and is both an entrepreneur and philanthropist of some credentials. I doubt he could or would be involved with the likes of Adriano Rivas."

"Well, he managed to convince Kenney that I was sent to assassinate Rivas," Bolan said. "So he's made the mistake of making himself *my* enemy. I think he's rotten, and I'd like to see the Quail Group get the opportunity to dish out some of what they've had to take."

"You want to maybe start from the beginning, Striker?"

Bolan told them about all of the trouble he'd encountered from the moment he'd set foot inside Ecuador. He also detailed his encounters with the Quail Group over the past eighteen hours, and how they had told him of Emerson's offer to double their payment if they managed to kill Bolan and get Esposito and Gustavo out alive.

"I think we should get with the Man on this," Brognola said when Bolan had finished. "If there's some kind of trouble, maybe he can use Proctor as leverage and get TOBA to back off."

"I get it," Bolan said with a nod. "You're thinking if you could get TOBA to shut it down, anything Emerson did on his own would bring more attention because he'd still be acting outside the influence of the group even though they didn't know it."

Brognola nodded. "Exactly. It would make it a damn sight easier to figure out what he's up to."

"That sounds like a plan. The other thing I need from you is to know if anything unusual is planned for the next two days. Particularly anything that might be connected with the deal Esposito was supposed to broker."

Price went to check with a nod from Brognola, and in less than a minute she returned with a sheet of paper.

"There's a small commercial venture going on, something with a lot of political clout behind it," Price said. "It's all supposed to be quite legit. You'll recall one of the agreements in the Proctor Initiative was our willingness to help Ecuador improve its refinement techniques. There's supposed to be a very large sample of mixed refined and unrefined product flown into Houston. TOBA has apparently appointed a team of scientists to start looking at the samples immediately."

"When is this product supposed to arrive?"

"It came in about two hours ago. Customs officials and every known representative were on site. I guess they wanted to keep it out of the press, hence the reason it didn't go through all of the usual channels."

Damn it! The entire thing had been a stall tactic. All this time Bolan had been sent on a wild-goose chase while Rivas pursued his real plans.

"I don't suppose there's any way to stop that shipment from getting in-country," Bolan said.

"Doubtful," Brognola replied. "But with the ton of federal officials who were supposed to be present, that shipment would have been screened pretty carefully before being allowed to clear customs."

"Maybe," Bolan said. "But somehow I think Rivas, and Emerson if he's in on it, probably got all of that covered. Those barrels might have oil, but I'd be willing to bet they're stockpiled with drugs, too."

"What makes you think so?" Brognola asked.

"The sample's too small for anybody to be overly concerned about it," Bolan replied. "Think about it, Hal. People are tired of the energy crisis, and they're willing to do just about anything to make this work."

"They won't see it because they don't want to," Brognola said. "You're right, of course."

"We need to find a way to track that shipment," Bolan said. "Never mind a trip to the Farm. I'm going to head straight to Houston to see if I can stop this thing before it gets out of control."

"What do you need from us?"

"Manifest records, shipping documents, every scrap of information you can get me on this shipment and its final destination."

"Roger that. We'll get started right away."

"Let's have the Man start putting heat on Proctor, as well. The sooner we can get TOBA to ease up, the sooner Emerson will show us his cards. And when we know where and how it's going down, I want to make sure Curtis Kenney's involved. He's a good man, Hal. Let's give him a chance to prove it. That'll keep him out of my path, too."

Brognola nodded. "I'll do everything I can on that, Striker. After all, we can't grant him official sanction any more than we can grant it to you."

"If Kenney finds out Emerson set him up, he'll do something about it. I can't be in two places at once. Maybe we can get Kenney's cooperation."

Houston, Texas

AS SOON AS HE ARRIVED in Houston, Bolan cleaned up, changed clothes, then took a rental to the Gentry Tower.

The Executioner wasn't sure what part TOBA had in Emerson's activities, but he'd managed to get a meeting with TOBA's chairman, Hoover Weygand, and attorney Benjamin Samson. Bolan was now sporting Justice Department credentials that identified him as Matthew Cooper, Special Agent. Brognola had managed to cop the identity papers on short notice, and had left it to Bolan to actually handle the angles on his story.

As soon as they'd verified his credentials and appointment with Weygand, the guards escorted Bolan to the elevator that would take him straight to the top floor. The Executioner didn't like walking into an environment with only one exit, but then he didn't have too much reason to be concerned. Guys like Weygand were strictly businessmen and not accustomed to dirtying their hands. Even if he did have contacts with those in the drug world, he wouldn't have tried anything in front of so many witnesses. He'd wait until the moment was right, and that's what Bolan was counting on.

"Agent Cooper?" Weygand said, extending a hand as soon as Bolan stepped off the elevator. "Welcome to Gentry Tower. Please come in and be comfortable. May I offer you something?"

"Coffee," Bolan replied. "Black."

"Of course," Weygand replied, waving to the man

hovering near him, who departed obediently for the drink. He then showed Bolan to a comfortable sitting room and offered him a luxurious leather chair across from a matching love seat. "Please, make yourself comfortable."

They sat, and it took Bolan only a moment to see the room was a study of Old World navy. A set of thick, hardback volumes stood rigid next to each other like a line of foot soldiers, obviously a law library of some type. The furniture in the room was of finely crafted dark woods, including teak, mahogany and cherry. Lamps and other decorative items were made of brass or copper, and there was a fully stocked bar lining one wall. It was all very…masculine. Obviously, it was also supposed to double as intimidating for visitors.

It had no such effect on Mack Bolan.

"I understand you're here on a matter of some urgency," Weygand said. "I hope you don't mind if I ask you to come right to the point."

"I'd be happy to," Bolan said with a smile. "Although I thought someone else would be joining us. Your attorney?"

"Benjamin Samson, yes," Weygand replied with a genial smile. "He was called away on some urgent matter for the association at the last minute. My sincere apologies he couldn't join us."

"No need to apologize," Bolan replied. "In short, the United States government sent me here because we suspect TOBA, or members of TOBA, may have violated U.S. State Department statutes regarding affiliation with known members of the drug smuggling underworld."

The surprise that registered on Weygand's face appeared genuine to Bolan. He would have even gone so far as to say the man appeared insulted. Still, Weygand kept his composure and did nothing to either confirm or deny Bolan's statement. He just sat back in the supple leather of the love seat, crossed his legs and studied his guest.

"That's a very serious allegation, Agent Cooper," Weygand finally said. "Do you have any evidence to support such a ridiculous hypothesis?"

"How about the shipment of oil you received this afternoon," Bolan said. "If I could prove there were drugs in that shipment, would that be enough evidence for you?"

"Well, it would except for the fact that would be a very big 'if,'" Weygand replied. "Not to mention, sir, that U.S. customs inspectors and representatives from half a dozen law-enforcement agencies were on site to insure nothing hazardous or illegal entered the United States. We followed all of the import laws to the letter. This was at the behest of the U.S. government, and now they suspect us of illegal activity?"

"Then each and every member of TOBA knew exactly what was going on during this entire transaction," Bolan said.

"Of course." Weygand kept the smile like it was frozen to his face.

"Then you must also be aware that one of the men among the group escorting the product to its final destination was Adriano Rivas. Do you know the name?"

"Nothing about it comes immediately to mind."

"Then let me enlighten you," Bolan replied. "Not long ago, Adriano Rivas was one of the most feared and powerful drug lords in Colombia. He was not only responsible for most of the cocaine distribution throughout Ecuador, he was also suspected of ordering his own personal death squad to murder hundreds of people, including competitors and their families or anybody else who stood to get in his way."

"That's all very interesting, Agent Cooper, but I don't see—"

"That's right, Mr. Weygand," Bolan cut in. "You don't see. You don't see at all what's going on. Now the government believes something has gone very wrong here, and as far as I'm concerned everyone within TOBA is a suspect until I can prove otherwise."

Weygand sat back and sighed. "What can I do to help?"

"You can take me to where they were storing that shipment," Bolan said. "Let me look at it for myself. If there's nothing there, then I'll split and you won't ever see my face again."

"I couldn't do that," Weygand said. "Not without a warrant or our attorney present, and certainly not without the approval of the other TOBA members."

"Which would you rather have, Mr. Weygand, a legal precedence to hide behind or a clear conscience?"

"What are you talking about?"

"Well, let's suppose just for a moment I'm right," Bolan said, turning the knife a little. It was time to put the screws to this guy and get him to cooperate. He didn't want to have to go searching for this shipment on his own. "If I have to go through this lengthy process, I'll have to assume it was your attempt to delay me and you'll be arrested along with the rest of your group."

"You would never be able to prove that," Weygand said, trying to sound convincing even though his tone had started to waver.

"Maybe not, but then I won't have to prove it," Bolan replied. "All I have to do is make the arrests. The rest then gets out to the press. The story might also mention how you and TOBA have been sitting on the reserves while America continues to pay ridiculously inflated prices."

"We don't regulate reserve releases, Agent Cooper," Weygand said, rising from his love seat. "And I think you've outstayed your welcome. I'm afraid I have no more time. You'll have to come back with a warrant."

"You're making a mistake," Bolan said.

"I'm afraid it's you who has made a mistake, Colonel Stone," a voice said behind him.

Bolan turned and found himself staring at a large man with gray eyes and blond hair. He was dressed in a dapper suit and stood with his arms crossed in blatant defiance. Two large men stood behind him, holding pistols. They looked like they meant business, and without a word they sent a very clear message that if Bolan so much as moved in the wrong direction they wouldn't hesitate to punch his ticket.

"Samson!" Weygand jumped up and stood in a rigid position. "What's the meaning of this?"

"Be quiet, Hoover," Samson replied. "You're always

trying to take control. This time I think it's best you realize you're not in charge of things right now."

"You bastard," Weygand said in a tight whisper.

"Benjamin Samson," Bolan said quietly. "You know, you did just what I thought you'd do."

"And what's that, Stone?"

"You showed your hand a little too soon. You should have waited a little longer and you might have gotten away with it. Now that I know you're involved, I'm going to shut down your little operation. Permanently."

"Who the hell is Stone?" Weygand demanded, walking around the table and strolling toward Samson.

"Careful," Samson said, raising a meaty hand as both flankers swung their pistols in Weygand's direction. "I'd hate to see anything happen to you. I've always liked you, Hoover. I thought you had the makings of one of the smart ones. It's too bad you proved me wrong. Rutherford said you couldn't be trusted. I'm glad I listened to him."

"Rutherford?" Weygand asked, astounded by the revelation. "He's in on this, too?"

"Of course," Samson replied. "Don't tell me you actually believe all the money I've made him over these years was acquired through completely legitimate means. There's much more that must happen in today's business world to stay competitive. Men like you and Emerson don't get ahead on sound financial planning. We must take what's offered and take it when it's offered. Most of our associates are too shortsighted. It was up to me to protect our investments. I did it for TOBA. I did it for *us*."

"All you've done is let drug-peddling scum profit from the depravity on American streets," Bolan replied. "I can't allow that to continue."

Samson looked at him scornfully. "Well, I don't think there's much you can do about it."

Bolan's smile was frosty. "Want to bet?"

The Executioner had only a second to vault the chair he'd occupied and reach Weygand. It seemed as if he was moving in slow motion, although he knew that the subtle motion he'd made by tapping his watch just before turning to face Samson and his crew would solicit a direct and immediate response. He knew it with certainty because he'd planned it that way, and he couldn't ever recall a time when Jack Grimaldi had let him down.

Just as Bolan reached Weygand and managed to get his hands on the businessman's shoulders, the neighboring room seemed to implode in a massive ball of hot flame. Wood, metal and plaster flew in every direction, and it felt to Bolan as he crashed to the floor behind a heavy table with Weygand as though the very breath was being sucked from his lungs by that intense heat.

Bolan overturned the table and pressed himself tightly against it, shielding Weygand's body with his own. After nearly thirty seconds, the debris had settled for the most part and he knew it was safe to rise. He pulled Weygand to his feet and quickly scanned the room. The explosion had taken out all three of the opposition. Both gunmen had been thrown into the opposite wall headfirst, and their bodies lay at its base in crumpled heaps. Samson's body had been shielded for the most part by the explosion, but he'd been tossed completely over the shredded leather sofa and his head sat on his shoulders at an odd angle while lifeless eyes peered upward.

Bolan reached to the transceiver on his belt and adjusted an earpiece attached to it. "Striker to Eagle One."

"Eagle One, here," Grimaldi replied immediately.

"Nice job, Eagle One," Bolan replied. "Give me two minutes to get topside for pickup."

"Eagle One copies," Grimaldi replied.

"Let's go, Weygand," Bolan said, grabbing the oil tycoon and steering him toward the penthouse roof where Grimaldi would be waiting to take them away.

"Where are we going?" the still dazed man asked.

"To find that shipment," Mack Bolan replied. "And you're going to show me exactly where it is."

CHAPTER EIGHTEEN

San Lorenzo, Ecuador

Curtis Kenney surveyed the massive beachfront house and surrounding property.

No question remained in his mind that the place was well-guarded. According to the information provided by Stone's contacts—information that only a covert government agency could have probably acquired—the property was owned by Rutherford B. Emerson. As far as Kenney was concerned, that was all he needed to proceed with his operation. He had a score to settle with Emerson, and he planned to do just that.

Stone had sent the guide back to pick up the Quail Group and return them safely to San Lorenzo. By the time they arrived, announcements were being made on the television regarding the safe return of Esposito and Gustavo to Quito. Less than hour later Stone contacted Kenney by telephone and advised him Emerson had a large estate in San Lorenzo. He gave him the location and the details, and he advised Kenney to do whatever he thought necessary.

As far as Kenney was concerned, Stone was the only one left he could trust. Whether one or more men of TOBA had betrayed him was no longer important. He'd been fed a lot of bogus information on this deal from the beginning, information Stone convinced him had come from Emerson. Stone theorized Emerson had set up the deal to pit them against each other, and that action had cost Lou Sturgis his life.

Kenney was determined to return that treachery in kind, and collect a blood debt that wasn't owed by Stone but by Rutherford Emerson.

Kenney and his crew were equipped for the bloody action ahead of them. He had traded jungle camouflage for a fresh set of black fatigues, and his M-16 carbine was cleaned and loaded with high-velocity 5.56 mm NATO rounds. Morristown and Jones were attired in identical battle dress, and both carried MP-5s. All three men were also carrying MP-5 K machine pistols in 9 mm. Additionally, they were equipped with Ka-Bar fighting knives and stun grenades.

Kenney lowered the binoculars and signaled for the other pair watching from the opposite side of a stand of palm trees to fan out. It was time to go seek payback for the death of their friend. Morristown and Jones moved without a sound, approaching quickly and with the stealth bred into well-trained professionals. Kenney kept the approach covered from a distance with a Rangefinder 20 sniper scope attached to his carbine.

Morristown and Jones used their Ka-Bars to take out the pair of guards patrolling the base of the massive beach house. Kenney maintained a steady sweep of the area with the M-16, watchful of any opposition that might appear to assist their comrades. When his teammates successfully dragged the bodies out of sight, Kenney left the cover of the large boulder and sprinted toward the east end of the house. He'd crossed half the fifty-yard distance when a guard emerged from sliding-glass doors and stepped to the edge of the veranda.

The guy started to light a cigarette and spotted Kenney. The mercenary had already dropped to one knee and was sighting on the guard through the scope. Kenney watched the electronic vertical and horizontal lines align and turn green, then stroked the trigger. Three rounds of ball ammunition hit the man, two striking the breast bone and the third drilling through the skull. The man's head split open wide and his body dropped from view.

Kenney jumped to his feet and continued toward the house. He reached the base unchallenged and pressed his back to a thick corner upright. He risked a glance around the corner and saw Morristown skirting the back toward a rear door. Two armed men charged through the doorway when he was within a few yards of it. Morristown leveled his MP-5 and triggered a pair of controlled bursts. The men fell under his expert marksmanship before either could respond to the threat.

Kenney joined his teammate, and they took up a position on either side of the door. "Where's Jones?"

"Looking for another way in."

Kenney nodded. He yanked a concussion grenade from his harness, primed it, then tossed the bomb through the open door. It blew a few seconds later, the blast threatening to rattle his teeth from his head. He nodded and followed on Morristown's heels. His friend stayed low while Kenney tracked for any upright targets. Nobody challenged them. They proceeded up the hallway, which opened onto a main room. As they swept the room with their muzzles, they could hear the sound of footfalls to their right. They turned to see four men descending a flight of steps.

Kenney flicked the selector on his weapon to full-auto and opened up on the crew. He swept the weapon side-to-side, scattering the opposition. They stumbled over themselves, one of them hitting a step chin-first, to avoid being ventilated by the autofire spitting from Kenney's and Morristown's chattering weapons. One of them wasn't so lucky. A double burst of high-velocity slugs ripped through tender flesh and cracked bones. Blood splattered the wall and his comrades, and the guy bounced down the remaining steps and rolled to a stop at the base of the stairwell.

The remaining three brought their weapons to bear and triggered a return volley. Morristown answered one of the gunmen with a controlled burst from his MP-5. The 9 mm Parabellum rounds ripped through the man's stomach and perforated his spleen. He stepped awkwardly back on a step and went down hard on his buttocks, a look of shock mixed with surprise crossing his face. The expression quickly melted to one of death, and he lay back slowly and closed his eyes.

Kenney took another with a steady burst that caught the gunner in the chest. The impact spun him sideways, and he tumbled over the banister and landed on the hardwood floor below with a wet smack. The remaining gunner crouched and unloaded a sustained burst. Kenney dived for cover behind a wingback chair, but Morristown couldn't avoid the deadly missiles in time. The blast caught him full in the chest and slammed him against a tall, stone statue.

Kenney felt panic rise from his stomach and sting his chest, settling there like a knot, but some of it subsided as Morristown let out a wail of pain and slid to the ground. Kenney didn't see any blood—Morristown's Kevlar vest had held under the vicious assault. Before Kenney could react, the last gunman's head disappeared under a short burst from an unseen weapon. A moment later, Jones made entrance from another room.

"What the hell you sitting in the corner taking a break for?" Jones asked with a mischievous smile. "Let's find this Emerson bastard."

Kenney nodded, then the pair moved to help Morristown to his feet. They gave their friend a minute to catch his breath, then they lined up a few feet apart and proceeded up the stairs, Kenney in the lead and Jones on rear guard. They reached the second-floor landing and spread out, Jones heading down one hallway and Kenney taking the other while Morristown covered them from the head of the stairs. He would hold position and make sure they weren't flanked by any new arrivals that might still be patrolling the grounds.

Kenney started searching the second-floor hallway, methodically kicking in doors and clearing the room before moving on to the next one. When he reached the end of the hallway, Kenney kicked a door at the end inward and then stepped aside. A plethora of angry rounds whizzed past him.

He procured another flash-bang grenade from his harness, primed it and counted off a few seconds before releasing it. He closed his eyes, covered his ears and opened his mouth a moment before it blew. He was rewarded with a few screams and groans, a clear indication the grenade had done its work. He went through the doorway that opened onto a massive veranda facing the ocean. One man who had apparently survived the concussion peered from around a large upright pillar and triggered a short burst from an Uzi SMG.

Kenney triggered his weapon and sent a hail of 5.56 mm slugs in the gunman's direction. A couple struck the pole and sent wood chips flying into his face. One lodged in his eye, and he dropped his weapon and staggered into view, screaming and holding his hands over the right side of his face. Kenney blew the man away with a gut-level burst. The impact drove the guard backward over the railing. He disappeared from sight.

Kenney turned to find two other guards lying on the ground. One of them was unconscious and the other was holding his eyes as watery blood leaked from one ear. The leader of the Quail Group stopped cold and saw a decrepit-looking old man seated in a wheelchair. The man was calmly smoking a cigarette from a long, brass-and-black-onyx holder. A curved ash dangled from the cigarette.

"Rutherford Emerson?" Kenney said, walking carefully toward the man.

"Yeah, that's me," the old man replied. "What of it?"

"Oh, so you're a tough guy," Kenney snapped. "Well, very soon you're going to be a real dead guy. What do you say to that?"

"You seem a bit too confident...Kenney, is it?" Emerson replied. "You see, I was whipping young punks like you long before you were a twinkle in your daddy's eye. I'm not scared of dying at the hands of a nobody like you."

"I just want to know what the hell we ever did to you, Emerson," Kenney said. "You feed us bad information, almost make us kill a good man, then you set us up on a hopeless mission to rescue guys who were never in danger in the first place. I want to know why."

"Very simple," Emerson replied. "Profit. The trouble with self-righteous, patriotic assholes like yourself is your lack of vision. You preach a good game, but when it comes right down to it you'd sell out your own mothers for some quick cash."

"Sorry you think so," a voice said behind Kenney. He turned to see Morristown approach. "Because you sold us a bill of goods, our friend is dead. Not *us,* but *you.* You're the bastard who killed him."

"Quit your whining, puppy." Emerson spit. "You think I give a good goddamn about your friends? You get paid to take risks, and we paid you well. What difference does it make? I could make you rich beyond your wildest dreams. Instead of viewing it as acceptable losses and taking the money, you want to bitch on and on about how you've been mistreated. You're just guns-for-hire." He waved his hand at the injured men lying on the ground. "Just like them. You get paid to take risks. Get used to it because nobody's going to treat you differently."

"You're wrong, asshole," Kenney growled. "Somebody already *has* treated us differently. Someone treated us like the professional soldiers we are…Stone. You remember him, right? The guy you sent your goon to try to talk us into killing? Well, the joke's on you now. See you in hell, Emerson."

Kenney started to squeeze the trigger on the M-16 when something hard smacked into his back and sent white-hot lances of pain up his spine. The force of the bullets drove Kenney to his knees and the short burst he triggered went wide of Emerson. He heard a shout of surprise and twisted in time to see a shocked look on Pete Morristown's face just moments before his face exploded under the impact of a more bullets. His friend's headless corpse toppled to the floor next to him, and the impact sprayed Kenney with warm blood.

Kenney's ears began to ring from the weapon fire, almost drowning out Buford Jones's battle cry. A short time later, those screams were cut short by the sound of several autorifles cutting loose. Then all went silent and the only sounds he heard were the call of water birds, the crash of the ocean and the cackling laughter of Rutherford Emerson.

Kenney wanted to jump to his feet and blast a hole through the old bastard's head, but his legs didn't seem to want to respond. He tried to feel his toes, but nothing. The bullets he'd taken in the back had obviously hit his spine. The Kevlar had only protected him from death. Terror washed over Kenney, but he quickly pushed aside the fear. With what semblance of clear thought was left to him, Kenney reached beneath his body and pulled an M-33 HE fragmentation grenade from his harness. He yanked the pin, then laid his hand at his side as he used the other hand to push himself onto his back.

Emerson rolled up to Kenney and leaned forward so he could stare at the soldier. "You see what I mean, Kenney? I've been handling your kind for a long time. It will take more than a few hired guns to bring down an Emerson. A hell of a lot more, in fact."

"You forgot the most important rule on the battle field, Emerson," Kenney said as he released the spoon.

"What's that?"

Kenney held up the primed grenade with a smile and replied, "Never underestimate your enemy."

Houston, Texas

MACK BOLAN SAT on the edge of the U.S. Army OH-58D Kiowa chopper, one foot on the landing skid, a Heckler & Koch PSG-1 sniper rifle resting in his lap. He was secured to the aircraft by special harness specifically designed for door gunners. Grimaldi was at the stick and piloting the chopper, which he'd borrowed from a reconnaissance unit at Fort Sam Houston, toward a TOBA reserve storage facility on the south side of Houston. This was the destination of the shipment that had arrived earlier that day, according to Weygand's information.

It hadn't taken much for Bolan to convince Weygand to cooperate with him after the incident with Samson. Grimaldi had been ready and waiting. The Executioner had planned his visit to the last detail, ready to take down TOBA's empire by whatever means were at his disposal. Bolan had hoped putting pressure on the group would cause any members who were involved with Rivas to get nervous.

A buzz in his ears indicated Grimaldi signaling for attention. The soldier donned the headset hanging near him. "What's up, Jack?"

"I have bad news, Sarge. I didn't want to give it to you now, but the head Fed said you would want to know right away."

"Let's hear it," Bolan told Grimaldi.

"The Quail Group's gone," Grimaldi said. He'd learned long ago how to give Bolan any bad news. Just get it over and done. "Kenney and the others are dead."

The Executioner took a moment to remember them silently. He should have been the one to do that mission. He should never have sent them in to take Emerson on their own. It wasn't their duty, it was his. He'd allowed Stony Man to involve them because he felt he owed Kenney that much; look where it had gotten them. But Kenney and the others wouldn't have preferred it any other way. They had discovered they were fighting on the wrong side, and Bolan could understand why they'd wanted to set the record straight. He admired the living hell out of them and he always would.

"Any word on Emerson?" Bolan asked.

"They got him," Grimaldi said. He could almost hear the grin in the pilot's voice. "Hal said they were picking his smelly hide out of every corner. Guess Kenney got him with a grenade or something before he bid it farewell."

"Okay, Jack," Bolan said. "Let's make it happen."

The chopper tipped steadily as Grimaldi swung the nose around and headed directly south. Bolan watched the city rooftops rush by a few hundred yards below him as his body pressed against the restraint harness. The PSG-1 was a perfect weapon for a job like this. Made from quality materials, the weapon had a superior effective range for a weapon of its caliber, not to mention a smooth action and balance Bolan had come to appreciate over the years. It was also a versatile weapon in a number of climates, and an especially desirable weapon in humid environments such as Houston.

Hoover Weygand had told Bolan that there were security officers armed with side arms at the storage and testing facility, but he didn't have to expect any significant resistance. Bolan believed Weygand, but he also suspected Rivas would put additional men on the job to protect the goods. After all, the guy was probably on the eve of the largest cocaine distribution scheme the U.S. had ever seen, and certainly one of the greatest cons of all time. There was more than keeping drugs off the streets at stake here—there was an entire country that needed reasonably priced oil and had to be able to trust its source.

Bolan knew the only commodity Rivas offered was death. The guy was driven by profit, just as Emerson and Samson had been driven by it. Sometimes greed was the most powerful weapon in the Executioner's arsenal, because he could almost always count on it to consume those who succumbed. The power of gold had overthrown entire empires and laid waste to the great cities under their respective rules.

In either case, Bolan planned to make a very careful reconnaissance of the area before he set to the task of finding and destroying the shipment. He knew it was tainted just because Rivas had bothered to accompany it. What he suspected those drums contained was oil, yet, but smuggled within that oil he believed was pure uncut cocaine. He intended to make absolutely certain it never reached America's homes and schoolyards.

Bolan waited for the signal from Grimaldi that they were less than a minute from ground zero, and began to peer through the scope of the PSG-1. He wouldn't get a second chance to pull this off. If things went south here, it would be difficult to pull back the product.

Surely, Rivas would have different modes of transportation and different routes for it, and there wasn't any way he could have expected to cover all of it.

"We're coming up on the target now, Sarge," Grimaldi said. "In five…four…three…"

At zero Grimaldi took the nose down and skimmed the area, keeping to the borders to give the Executioner a clear view of the entire perimeter. It took only a moment for Bolan's suspicions to be confirmed. He spotted the first two sentries on a roof. These weren't standard security men. They wore dark suits, dark shades and were definitely of Latino origin. They also cradled what looked like shotguns and assault rifles, and that definitely didn't qualify as a standard side arm in Bolan's book.

Bolan studied the rest of the rooftops in the area and noticed there were no other sentries. Okay, so that was probably where the shipment was located. Now he had to consider a way to get in there and destroy it. Well, sometimes the best approach was the most direct one. And in this case, it was the truth. Bolan spotted a pair of open-topped M-998 Humvees rush from what looked like a large, commercial garage and race toward the main building. Some additional hardguys rode in the back of the Humvee, armed in similar fashion to the men on the roof.

Bolan raised the PSG-1 rifle and pressed his eye against the reticle as he ordered Grimaldi to make another pass. He sighted on the first man on the roof, who now realized there was nothing friendly about this chop-

per and suddenly reached for his rifle. Bolan let out half
of his deep breath, adjusted the numbers in the scope
for correct altitude and wind velocity, and squeezed the
trigger.

CHAPTER NINETEEN

♥

Mack Bolan triggered the PSG-1 sniper rifle, the 7.62 mm round smashing into the bridge of the unwary sentry's nose. The bullet exited through the back of his head, leaving a significant hole in its wake. The man's eyes went wide and his knees buckled. His body hit the scorching rooftop less than a second after the bullet blew out the back of his head.

Bolan set his sights on the second sentry as Grimaldi swung the chopper in a wide arc of the storage site. There hadn't been time for a more thorough reconnaissance first, but the Executioner knew he was taking the enemy down and not legitimate security, so it didn't matter at this point. He'd have to eliminate as many of the hostiles as possible before moving in to destroy the shipment.

Bolan sighted on the second man who was now running toward his fallen comrade. The guard wasn't sure what had happened, obviously not having seen or per-

haps even heard the shot, so he had little reason to think
his own life might be in jeopardy. The Executioner settled any question in the man's mind by triggering a
round that struck him in the chest and blew open his
heart. The guard staggered backward and collapsed.

The soldier ordered Grimaldi to land on the rooftop
as he watched the Humvees disappear past the roofline
of the main structure. The Stony Man pilot obediently
descended and the engine turbine revved into high gear.
Dust and small stones were churned in the wake of the
Kiowa's powerful blades as Grimaldi executed a smooth
touchdown on the rooftop.

Bolan disengaged the harness and dropped to the rooftop. He ran toward the entrance door that would take him
below, waving to Grimaldi that he was clear. He reached
the door just as the pilot lifted off. He had fifteen minutes to get inside, locate the shipment and wire it to blow.
He then had to get back to the roof for pickup before time
ran out. The most difficult part would be countering any
resistance that might rise to challenge him.

He found the rooftop access door unlocked, stepped
into the comparative coolness of the air-conditioned interior and began to descend the stairs to the top floor.
The .44 Magnum Desert Eagle and Beretta 93-R rode
in their customary places, along with a full complement
of Diehl DM-51 grenades. A pair of MP-5 K subguns
hung from sling harnesses. Bolan opened the door on the
third-floor landing and peered into the hallway. Mostly
he saw row on row of offices with people occasionally
crossing the hallway to go from one office to another.

Bolan had to keep as many of the innocent civilians working in the building free from harm. He sauntered down the hallway, whistling beneath his breath as he walked. If he received only a cursory inspection, he probably wouldn't stick out, but if someone studied him for any length of time he knew it might create panic.

When he reached the first office, Bolan stuck his head through the door and found himself staring at a pretty brunette.

The soldier smiled. "Hi."

"Hi," she said, half smiling and obviously alarmed at his dress.

"We have a security problem, miss," Bolan said. "I would advise you to leave now and don't come back. Okay?"

The woman nodded slowly, her lips moving although they produced no sound.

"Thanks for your cooperation," Bolan said, then headed to the next office for more of the same. Office by office, cubicle by cubicle, Bolan cleared them out. Soon they were herding down the hallway and taking the stairs to lower levels, bypassing the elevators entirely.

He managed to evacuate the entire floor without running into security. He reached the end of the hallway and turned right. This corridor was much different in that no offices were adjoined to it. Bolan proceeded at a trot now, headed in the direction of the elevators. The numbers were counting down, and he knew this mission would require impeccable timing.

Fourteen minutes remained.

As soon as Adriano Rivas received the call informing him Rutherford Emerson and Benjamin Samson were dead, he picked up the telephone and threw it across the room. The violent gesture caused Prospera and the other four men in the adjoining room to jump to their feet. A couple even reached for their weapons. Prospera held up a hand of restraint and rushed to the makeshift office from the sitting room area of the hotel suite.

Prospera couldn't imagine what might have gone wrong, but he knew it would be serious for Rivas to lose his temper like that. Prospera had only seen this type of behavior a few times in all his years of service to the Colombian drug lord. Of course, it was rare he spent a lot of time around Rivas, since he was usually out doing business dictated by Chico Arauca. Nonetheless, Prospera knew something was up, although he couldn't image what it might be since Carmita had been released to them unharmed.

Prospera hadn't been head of security for long, but he was confident in the training he'd received from Arauca. If all the activities Emerson had planned fell through for some reason, Prospera knew it would be up to them to protect the shipment and insure anyone who meddled in his boss's business got their balls handed to them. Prospera had learned much about Rivas, a man who could be a hard taskmaster. He found some the man's tastes as despicable, but that didn't really matter. He had two jobs: protect Rivas and protect the merchandise.

As soon as the barrels had cleared through American customs officials and all the doctored paperwork was in-

spected and passed, Rivas charged Prospera with getting
the product to a safe location. From there, it would be
distributed to key areas throughout the country. Mostly
this shipment would be for the Southwestern United
States, and the second one—scheduled to come through
in the same fashion a month from now—would go to
those major cities in the Midwest or on the East Coast.

Their storage point was a place on property owned
by Rutherford Emerson outside the town of Coldspring.
The Americans would have called it a one-horse town.
It was located about twenty miles southeast of Huntsville, an internationally famous town for its maximum-
security state penitentiary. Being that close to such an
infamous facility simultaneously bothered and humored
Prospera. Although he didn't like Emerson or trust the
old bastard, he had to admit the man had balls.

"What's wrong, boss?" Prospera asked Rivas.

Rivas looked up, stood and pounded his fists on his
desktop. "That was one of our people in San Lorenzo.
They tell me that Emerson is dead."

"How?"

"Those goddamned mercenaries he hired. They
turned on him and they blew him up!" Rivas punched
the desk again and kicked an open drawer of a nearby
file cabinet. "I'll bet Stone put them up to this."

"You want me to send some people to find this crew
and burn them down?"

"No," Rivas replied, shaking his head. "Emerson
managed to take them to hell with him. He was tough.
But now we must proceed on our own. I will try to

reach our contacts and let them know we're moving up the delivery schedule."

Prospera shrugged. "Boss, we cannot do that. We just got started on the cutting and refining. It's going to take several weeks to get that entire product ready for street-level distribution."

"Forget it," Rivas said. "Our customers will just have to deal with it. And the price went up because they're getting pure product. I'll consider their inconvenience this time in the price, but that's the way it's going to have to be this time around. This venture has already cost me more than I can stand to lose."

"Some of them may not go for that," Prospera said.

"Then fuck them. I'm running the show now!" More quietly, Rivas continued. "I'll get in touch with Emerson's business associates. I'm sure they know by now he's dead, and if they don't they will as soon as I tell them."

"Do you think they'll work directly with you?"

"They have no choice, Antonio," Rivas said matter-of-factly. "I know most of these men personally. I've stood over them to make sure nobody put a bullet in their head while they puked their guts out in fancy toilets because they'd consumed too much liquor. True, they may think I'm still just a punk dope peddler, but then, I don't really care. If I was good enough for Emerson, I will just have to be good enough for them. Otherwise, they can take their business somewhere else."

"I understand," Prospera replied.

The more time he spent with Adriano Rivas, the more Prospera admired him for his genius and tenacity. He was a good boss. Chico had always spoken highly of him. Prospera had never heard Chico criticize anything about Rivas. He knew his master had taken Arauca's death very hard, and he intended to avenge that death in the blood of this Brandon Stone.

"What about Stone?" Prospera asked.

Rivas fired him a look that was half dazed and half surprised. "What?"

Prospera took a deep breath and ventured the thought again. "I asked you about this Stone? You do know that if Emerson's mercenary group was on to him that it's likely Stone knows about our involvement *and* our plans. If he does, he will most certainly come after us."

"What he knows is nothing," Rivas said with a laugh. "He knows about the shipment, but I was careful to ensure we left a decoy. There's a warehouse on the south side of Houston, a refining and storage facility run by TOBA and its chemists. Everyone believes that's where the shipment was transported. If anyone tells Stone about that facility and he believes them, he will be in for a surprise, to be sure."

"What kind of surprise?"

"Well, other than the one hundred barrels transported there this morning containing nothing more than distilled water, I've left more than fifty soldiers there trained here in the U.S. by Emerson's dollar. They should do a good job with this bogus American colonel."

"I thought you wanted him alive," Prospera said. "I thought you wanted revenge."

"And I shall have it," Rivas said. "Stone is as predictable as he is skilled. Why should I do all of this work? Let Emerson's people handle it. You are above that, my friend. Mark my words—this very day, the enigmatic Colonel Stone will meet his destiny."

MACK BOLAN SMELLED a trap.

The soldier had reached the ground floor of the storage facility undetected, and that seemed just a little too easy to him. He took both guards on the roof in plain view of additional crews inside the Humvees, and yet nobody had entered the main floor of the depot and set up a search crew.

Bolan had been playing this game too long to fall for that. His plan to go out through the rooftop wouldn't work. Most likely they already had men filling the holes on the upper floors. The enemy was probably setting the trap as he sat there considering his options, which meant he'd have to change tactics. They would be expecting him to sneak out, take a back way and try to move with minimal to no contact if possible. That had been his plan, but a new tactic was in order.

No, Bolan wasn't going to just plant explosives and steal away. He planned to punch a hole straight through the offensive line. It was time to go into blitz mode and call this game.

The Executioner began the methodical process of planting explosives. He couldn't be absolutely certain, but he figured the barrels were filled with oil and that would work as an accelerant. He did a quick row count and then multiplied to come up with a hundred barrels.

Good. He'd brought enough explosives. They would do the job nicely. The barrels were on pallets about six inches off the floor, and spaced about three feet apart. They were also placed in a staggered formation, which allowed Bolan to remain concealed as he crawled between them on hands and knees.

Bolan interlaced the one-pound blocks of C-4 plastique with detonation cord. He cored a hole in the putty-like C-4, crimped two ends of the explosive cord into the end of the blasting cap, then slid the cap into the stick lengthwise. The total job took about ten minutes, and when he'd finished Bolan had planted a total of twenty pounds of explosive. That would be more than enough to destroy the shipment. The cocaine was probably packed inside the barrels in sealed bags. The oil would heat up quickly, ignited by the gases building inside the barrels, and that would do the rest. Rivas's drugs were as good as destroyed. He checked his flanks as he set the timer for five minutes.

Bolan fisted the MP-5 Ks and crossed the depot at a dead run, hardly surprised when the two Humvees suddenly rounded the corner of the massive open doors of the depot. The soldier stopped, dropped to one knee and triggered his subguns. The weapons chattered, spitting a volley of 9 mm Parabellum rounds with unerring accuracy.

The driver of one Humvee took a blast of glass in the face. His head snapped back with the impact of a single round, then slammed forward into the steering wheel. His body slumped to the side and the passenger reached over and grabbed the steering wheel in an attempt to keep the wide-based vehicle under control. Bolan applied some preventative measures by triggering a burst into the right rear tire as it was exposed to him. The careening vehicle went out of control at that point and spun out. The vehicle came off its two left wheels enough to dump the foursome in back onto the unforgiving concrete floor of the depot.

Bolan had already concentrated his next set of controlled bursts on the other Humvee, which was still very much in commission. The driver got smart and slammed on his brakes. The occupants bailed immediately in the realization they weren't going to take their target as easily as they might have originally planned. The Executioner continued to hammer them with the 9 mm autofire, more to keep heads down than for any other reason. Against that many opponents, he knew he couldn't afford to be picky.

Bolan sprang to his feet and sprinted for the cover of a pair of crates twenty yards to his left. He triggered another burst on the run, but his firing was cut short by a burning sensation in his leg. Bolan slid into a spot that obscured him from the view of the Humvee crews, and as he came to a halt he noticed a streak of blood left from the slide. He looked quickly and saw the source of the injury—a bullet ricochet that had caught him in the left thigh.

Bolan glanced up and to his left, and saw a group of six gunners toting assault rifles emerge from a door on the second floor and traverse a catwalk. They were triggering their weapons on the run, hoping for a shot to bring down their quarry. Bolan intended to make sure he outlived their hopes as he pulled a Diehl DM-51 grenade from his web belt and removed the fragmentation sheath. He yanked the pin and let the bomb fly in an overhand toss, then climbed to his feet and primed a second. The first one hit the back wall bordering the catwalk and exploded as Bolan let go of the second one. The concussive blast of the powerful explosives dumped two of the enemy gunners over the railing.

The soldier sprayed the area in a corkscrew pattern, taking out two more gunners. He emptied the clips, released them, then jammed them against his sides to load two more from spring-loaded clip holders. He let the slides go forward and delivered a fresh volley as the second grenade exploded. The remaining troops fell under the onslaught.

The Executioner returned his attention to the Humvee crews who were now recovering from his assault. Bolan ripped away a Diehl in defensive mode from his harness, yanked the pin and tossed the bomb easily into the clustered group picking themselves off the depot floor. There were shouts of confusion and panic followed immediately by a blast. Superheated shrapnel ripped through the crew, shredding the flesh of some members of the opposition while the concussion dismembered others.

Bolan burst from his cover and half ran, half limped on his wounded leg across the depot. He laid down a fresh volley of autofire from the MP-5 Ks, raking the positions of the survivors from the Humvee crews. A couple had taken positions behind the overturned vehicle. The soldier was halfway for the open door when the upright Humvee caught his eye. It was unattended.

The Executioner grinned at his luck as he changed direction and headed straight for the enemy position. At first the guards weren't certain how to react to the dark specter charging them, but they quickly recovered from the shock and triggered fresh bursts from their smoking SMGs. Bolan continued toward the Humvee in a zigzag run, and soon found cover behind the vehicle. He certainly stood a greater chance of breaking through the enemy offensive using the Humvee than racing across open territory with an injured limb.

Bolan kept his head down as he climbed into the Humvee through the passenger door. He got behind the wheel, pulled the stick into reverse and stomped the wide accelerator pedal. The Humvee's heavy V-8 diesel engine roared as the vehicle lurched backward obediently. The soldier jammed the wheel to a hard right and put some tonnage between him and the gunners still firing on his position. If they were smart, they'd shoot the tires out from under him, in which case he'd go nowhere.

They weren't.

Bolan put the vehicle into drive and pulled away from the depot, racing for open ground. He was almost through the front opening of the building when he spotted two men directly ahead of him. One was kneeling and the other stood over his left shoulder. Balanced atop the kneeler's right shoulder was a grenade launcher, its unmistakable lines glinting in the red-orange light of a setting sun.

The Executioner had only enough time to jerk the wheel just milliseconds after smoke and flame belched from the weapon.

CHAPTER TWENTY

There were moments Mack Bolan couldn't explain the hand fate dealt him. He couldn't count the number of times he'd been on the verge of death and somehow come back, couldn't recount how many missions he'd undertaken that had brought him to the very precipice of Hades and then had the fiery darts of the enemy quenched and victory placed violently and swiftly in hand.

What the Executioner *did* know was this was one of those times...

The blast from the grenade blew just in front of the skidding Humvee and the concussion flipped the vehicle. Bolan braced his hands against the roof, clenching his teeth as the vehicle rolled twice and came to rest on its wheels. Blood streamed from his forehead where an object flying inside the vehicle had struck him. Bright spots danced in front of his eyes and Bolan wanted to succumb to sweet darkness, but he realized his mission wasn't over. As long as Rivas lived, Mack Bolan's mission was incomplete.

He bailed from the vehicle, shoving against the mangled driver's door with all the strength he could muster. The door finally gave way enough, the metal protesting against Bolan's weight, to facilitate his escape. He sought refuge behind the Humvee and drew his Desert Eagle. He pulled back the slide and chambered a round, and then came over the top of the Humvee and took up a two-handed shooter stance.

Bolan acquired his first target, the grenadier, and squeezed the trigger. A 300-grain boattail slug rocketed across the expansive industrial yard and struck the launcher-holder in the chest while he awaited his comrade to load a second shell. The bullet cracked the sternum, splitting ribs and ripping chest muscle, then continued through the trachea and esophagus before shattering the spine and exiting the back in several fragments. The impact lifted the man off his knee and drove him backward. He landed on the pavement and cracked his skull.

The spotter looked in Bolan's direction with surprise as he clawed for a side arm, but the Executioner already had him dead to rights. Bolan unleashed a double tap from the Desert Eagle. Both rounds took his target in the stomach and continued out the lower back, taking entrails and vital organ tissue with them.

A fresh cluster of hardguys broke from an outbuilding less than fifty yards to Bolan's left rear flank. The soldier rushed to the other side of the Humvee for cover as he primed a grenade. He lobbed it in a towering arc so it would come down in the center of the group. The grenade blew on schedule, scattering the crew of gunmen as it peppered them with the scorching 2 mm steel pellets. The blast ignited the clothing of a couple of the enemy personnel while charring others, burning the flesh beneath them in either case.

Bolan traded the Desert Eagle for the Beretta and began to pick off the survivors before they could recover from the blast. One enemy gunner took a 9 mm Parabellum round in the skull. He spun and stiffened for a second before collapsing to pavement. Another managed to get within a few yards from Bolan's position and trigger a short burst that buzzed past the soldier's head. The Executioner shot him twice through the gut and the man doubled over and hit the concrete face-first.

Bolan whirled to see another group of men emerge from another outbuilding and charge his position. The Executioner's assessment he was walking into a trap was confirmed. Perhaps Rivas had hoped to overpower him, but Bolan didn't think so. There was little reason in his mind to continue battling them. Killing these soldiers or mercenaries or whatever the hell they called themselves wasn't accomplishing much. Bolan needed to find the leadership and put them down once and for all.

Bolan kicked up his transceiver. "Eagle One, this is Striker. Come in."

"Eagle One, here."

"Fire mission! I'm in the main yard and I could use some help. *Now.*"

"Well, you're in luck, Striker, because Eagle One's in the speedy delivery business. Stand by and keep your head down."

Bolan acknowledged. When Grimaldi came in he was going to lay down a shit-storm, and no sane human being would want to be even close to *that*. The Executioner knew he'd already be close enough.

The Stony Man pilot hit them hard. There was a whooshing sound as the 70 mm Hydra rockets touched off, putting a quick and neat separation of heated and broken pavement between Bolan and the murderous mob. Grimaldi immediately opened up with 20 mm cannons as soon as the rockets were away. Men screamed and fell under the heavy-caliber bullets.

Bolan watched a head roll away from where he viewed the carnage from the undercarriage of the Humvee. As Grimaldi swept past them, the guns ceased. He swung around for a second pass, strafing the survivors with 20 mm cannonfire. They were running for the cover of the outbuilding from which they had emerged.

Grimaldi's voice reverberated in Bolan's ears. "They're making for that outbuilding, Sarge. Your call."

"Let them go. I think the threat's neutralized. Touch down here for pickup. And make it snappy, Eagle One. We got less than ninety seconds."

"Roger that."

Grimaldi had the chopper on the ground in half that time. Bolan ran to the Kiowa and jumped aboard. He expelled a heavy sigh of relief as his feet lifted away from the pavement a moment later. They were well clear of the main complex when it blew, but even as the explosives went, Mack Bolan knew something was wrong.

The Executioner swung his legs inside, closed the rear doors, then squeezed into the cockpit. As he settled into the cramped seat, he was careful not to accidentally touch or jostle any instrumentation. Once he was settled, he grabbed a headset dangling behind him and gave Grimaldi a thumbs-up.

"Nice job, Jack," Bolan said. "Thanks."

The Stony Man pilot grinned. "Any time, Sarge. What's the plan now?"

"I think we've been had."

"What do you mean?"

"There's no way that was oil I blew up back there, and if that's the case I'd sincerely doubt it was drugs, either."

Grimaldi chewed on his lower lip, thinking hard, and then said, "A decoy."

"Yeah," Bolan said. "Which means that the real shipment was diverted somewhere else. Jack, patch me through to the Farm."

Stony Man Farm, Virginia

HAL BROGNOLA SAT in his office in the Annex and chomped absently at an unlit cigar as he studied the reports on the large screen at the opposite end of the room. He considered their current situation. In part he felt responsible for the deaths of Curtis Kenney and his men, and he could only imagine the Executioner had to have been feeling some of the same. They had turned out to be good men, and America had suffered a loss that day although she might never know it.

After doing thorough checkups on the background of every member in TOBA, Brognola was convinced they had taken out the two bad apples in the group. Provided the machinations of Emerson and Samson didn't plant any seeds, Brognola expected there wouldn't be any further trouble from that group. In fact, once the President explained the situation to Proctor, he called for an immediate suspension of the association as a body, had the IRS freeze all of its assets and ordered a full investigation by the IRS and Justice Department.

None of that would bring back the men of the Quail Group or any of the other numerous innocent people who had died at the hands of Adriano Rivas. He was the main threat now—the *only* threat really—and with any luck Bolan was effectively neutralizing that threat at this very moment.

The intercom buzzed for attention, intruding on Brognola's thoughts. The Stony Man chief pulled himself back into the present before he pulled the cigar from his mouth and keyed the intercom.

"Brognola," he rumbled.

"Hal, it's Barb," came Price's voice. "Striker's calling and needs to talk to you right away."

"Put him through."

A moment later Bolan's voice filled the room, and Brognola could immediately tell he was aboard a chopper somewhere. "Hal, we hit a dead end."

"What happened?"

"I went to the facility Weygand told us about," Bolan said. "I think it was a dud."

"What makes you think so?" Brognola asked as he turned to acknowledge Price, who entered the center and took a seat at the table. "Barb's here with me now."

"Good. For starters, whatever I blew it wasn't a hundred fifty-five-gallon drums of oil. Second, it was in too easy and out too hard. Jack had to level some heavy artillery on the private army Rivas had waiting for me."

"Okay, so we're back to square one," Brognola said with a deep sigh.

"Maybe not," Bolan said. "I have an idea."

"Good ones are always welcome, Striker," Brognola replied.

Bolan chuckled. "I'll bet. Here's the short side. There's almost no chance Rivas had contacts inside the country capable of pulling this off. We already know about his connections with Emerson, who in turn had Samson working the financial angles."

"I think I know where this is going," Price said. "You figure wherever the shipment was diverted it wouldn't be far."

"Correct," Bolan said. "It would have to be close, and it would have to have been under the control of Emerson or Samson. We have a list of assets and property holdings with TOBA. We need to look for something big and remote, someplace they could have taken the shipment for cutting without drawing attention."

"We'll start working on it right away," Price said, giving Brognola a knowing wink. "It shouldn't take long.

Bear will send you the information by secure transmission as soon as possible."

"Good," Brognola said. Directing his voice toward the speaker, he said, "Anything else, Striker?"

"Well, we're going to have to start considering the other fingers in the pie," Bolan replied. "If I don't hit that shipment, then I'm going to have to hit the distributors. Emerson wouldn't have the ability to distribute product of this size and purity on his own. He'd have a whole group of territory czars to handle that. Plus, he wouldn't have done anything that might tie the drugs directly back to him."

"So a list of known associates," Brognola said.

"Yeah, but *especially* business contacts that have mutual ties to Central or South America. These will be our most likely candidates. And with Emerson dead, it's probable Rivas will have to contact them directly. He might even accelerate his schedule. I've been pushing him since this thing started."

"Well, he's managed to keep one step ahead of us through this. It's becoming damn frustrating for us, Striker, and I don't mind saying the Man's getting worried."

"Tell him to tough it out a little bit longer, Hal," Bolan said. "I'm fed up with Rivas. This time his death will be real."

"Works for me," Brognola said. "Be careful out there, Striker. I'll get back as soon as I can with this intelligence."

"Good deal," Bolan replied. "I'll be waiting. In the meantime, I'm heading back to the hangar with Jack so he can refuel, and I'll see if there's anything else useful Weygand might be able to tell me."

"Well, he's there under guard by the U.S. Marshals Service. He's already been told to cooperate fully with you if he wants to keep his ass out of hot water."

"And he's definitely been cooperative," Bolan said. "He's already said he owes me his life, so I won't have any trouble getting his cooperation."

"Good. Take care, Striker. We'll be in touch soon."

"You, too, Hal. Give my best to the crew."

And with that, the transmission ended.

Brognola sat back in his chair and sighed. He had hoped for better news from Bolan, but then if good news were the usual order of the day Brognola would probably be unemployed. When the world was in trouble—and especially when America was in trouble—that's when the President called on Brognola and the Stony Man group's talents. While Bolan pursued missions of his own choosing, he was also willing to accept occasional assignments as long as he could call the shots and work it on his terms. To the surprise of many the relationship had worked out this way, and in some respects Brognola actually liked it better. He secretly wished Bolan would reconcile with his government, but he also knew that aside from the fact the Executioner was a consummate soldier, he was also a patriot of the highest order. He loved his country, and he did what he did out of a sense of duty and loyalty.

Brognola would do everything he could to get the information to Bolan. What the Executioner did with it from there was up to him. But one thing was certain: Adriano Rivas had every reason to fear.

The Executioner was coming to deliver justice.

LESS THAN AN HOUR after he'd placed the call to Stony Man Farm, Mack Bolan had his information.

The list of names associated with Emerson was interesting, to say the least. "Some pretty heavy hitters in this crowd, Jack," he told Grimaldi. Some of the names Bolan recognized, but the majority were either vaguely familiar or names he'd simply never heard before. Ten in all. It appeared Emerson had kept pretty chummy with South and Central American businessmen of questionable character.

The other information centered on two prominent holdings of Emerson and Samson. One was a beach house in Corpus Christi, a kind of timeshare deal that Emerson had going with Samson, but considering the distance, Bolan wasn't going to bite. There would have been no way to transport that much oil to such a location and moreover to be inconspicuous about it.

The second property was of much greater interest to the Executioner. It was about thirty-three acres located near Huntsville just off the border of the Huntsville State Forest Preserve. That wasn't too far from the Huntsville State Correctional Facility. Bolan wondered out loud if he could make a deposit there at the conclusion of the evening, a remark met by Grimaldi with a wry grin.

The pilot was prepared for action. They had returned

to Fort Sam Houston for refueling and as Bolan questioned Weygand further, Grimaldi had the aircraft maintenance crews change out the rocket pods on one side with a pair of AGM-114 Hellfire rockets and install twin FIM-92 Air-to-Air Stingers on the other side. The laser-guided, air-to-ground Hellfires would come in handy if Grimaldi had to take down any structures, and based on their intelligence Bolan believed it was a strong possibility.

The plan was simple: they were going to hit this compound with everything they had. Grimaldi would provide air support when and where the Executioner called for it, and Bolan would storm the compound on foot. What they couldn't allow to happen was Rivas to escape. More importantly, they couldn't allow the drug lord to get his product out for distribution.

"If that much uncut cocaine hits the streets at one time," Bolan said, "it'll have devastating results."

Grimaldi knew no truer words had been spoken. It would not only prove horrific for them, but every single person who tried that junk would have reason to worry. It was bad enough when cut product, which could be laced with anything, got into the hands of Americans, but this was ten times worse. Uncut product was the most dangerous because of its purity. A junkie, even one who used heavily, injected or smoked pure product would die almost instantaneously.

"It seems obvious to me Rivas doesn't care what effect this has on this country," Bolan said. "He's the worse kind of scum. He profits on peddling his death to others. I'm going to shut him down for good. I'm going to burn his operation to the ground, Jack. I swear it."

"I believe you, Sarge," Grimaldi said. "I believe you. Are you ready to move out?"

"Yeah," Bolan replied. "Let's do it."

CHAPTER TWENTY-ONE

Mack Bolan watched the treetops rush past just yards below his feet. He was strapped into the safety harness and ready for the drop. He felt somewhat more comfortable with this operation, because he had the correct intelligence. Aaron Kurtzman had managed to pull architectural blueprints for the estate and outbuildings, and satellite imagery of the entire layout of the grounds. This time Bolan knew what he faced, and it had allowed him to formulate a much stronger and viable battle plan while still remaining flexible enough to change his needs as required.

One thing that had Bolan concerned was that the satellite report showed the grounds were regularly patrolled by a chopper. This bothered the Executioner because he had no idea what kind of helicopter they were dealing with, or if it had any armament. When he'd run it by Jack Grimaldi, the pilot indicated he wasn't concerned.

"Most likely it's a private security company that patrols the area, probably checking for solicitors or hunters trespassing. It's pretty unlikely they would have an armed chopper with military-grade weapons buzzing the area."

Bolan was skeptical but he trusted Grimaldi's intuition. Besides, if they did encounter any trouble he knew the Stony Man pilot would handle it. Grimaldi was a skilled flyer and veteran combatant, and the Executioner wouldn't want to be the one to go against his friend in the air—that would definitely be getting the short end of the stick, not to mention the losing end.

The soldier leaned out of the chopper enough to see the expansive property coming up on their right. Grimaldi had confirmed he would circle in on a northwest trajectory and then swing around so they could approach that same corner of the house, which Bolan suspected would be a blind side since it pointed out toward a copse of trees. As the tail started to swing, he quickly inspected his M-16/M-203 combo he'd traded for the twin MP-5 Ks. The Beretta and Desert Eagle rode in their usual places, and Bolan had changed into camouflage battle dress fatigues in the event he had to escape into the woods on foot.

Bolan and Grimaldi had already settled on an alternate LZ if things went south for any reason.

The Executioner popped a 40 mm high-velocity HE grenade into the breech of the M-203 and slammed the slide into position. He checked the satchel to insure he had a sufficient load of the grenades, along with some blocks of C-4, and then flipped the launcher's sight into position. As they came around for a direct approach, Bolan leveled the M-203 and squeezed the trigger. He was rewarded with the familiar sound of the launcher's report, and a few seconds later a section of the rooftop erupted into an explosive blast.

As they drew near to the roof, Bolan could see the scorched, smoldering hole left in the wake of the blast. The Executioner loaded another grenade, slung the over-and-under and disengaged from the safety harness before swinging a winch into position. Grimaldi brought the chopper in and came to a hover six feet above the rooftop. He was fighting some significant updraft because Bolan could feel the entire craft shimmy, but the Stony Man pilot held the aircraft steady. The warrior clamped his harness to the rope he'd played out from the winch, attached the twin lines to a carabiner, then stepped into nothingness.

Bolan descended quickly through the hole and landed on top of a bed, which significantly cushioned the speed of the drop. He disconnected within two seconds from the rope, then keyed the signaler on his transceiver that would tell Grimaldi he could move up and away. A moment later the rope whipped upward and disappeared through the opening, the sound of the Kiowa's blades quickly dissipating.

Bolan heard the sound of clattering boots on the floor. He snapped a DM-51 grenade clear of his harness, removed the defensive sleeve, primed it, then jumped off the bed and got behind the mattress for cover. Bolan waited until the footfalls got close, then lobbed the grenade toward the door. It opened, and the Executioner's split-second timing put the bomb directly in the center of a cluster of four surprised sentries. Bodies sailed in every direction as the superheated gases instantly burned skin and tissue away from bone.

Plaster dust and wood chips were still falling as the Executioner proceeded through the jagged doorway and into the hall, dealing a pair of mercy rounds to the screaming men before proceeding. A quick inspection revealed the other three were dead. Bolan moved down the hallway, pressing toward his goal. He had to find Rivas; he couldn't afford to let the drug lord escape from the United States.

The soldier probed the west wing of the house, sweeping the muzzle of his assault rifle in every direction. A door opened and two women, their bare skin wet and covered only with towels, emerged from the room and looked at Bolan with surprise. The soldier gestured for them to get back in the room. They didn't have to be told twice.

Resistance arrived a moment later in the form of two more guards toting Uzi SMGs. They burst through a door that led into another wing of the house, and drew a bead on him. Bolan threw himself against a wall, the M-16 barking with fury as he laid down an unerring field of fire. The 5.56 mm ball ammo took the first man high in the chest and spun him into the door frame. Bolan tracked down and to the left for his second target and triggered another volley. This one ripped open his enemy's guts and continued through. Blood sprayed the man's shirt. He let out a scream of pain before collapsing to the floor and bleeding out.

Bolan moved forward cautiously but quickly, keeping the weapon high and level. He reached the two guards, looked down to confirm they were dead, then proceeded through the door that opened onto a sitting room. Bolan didn't meet any resistance so he continued toward a door on the far side, which he suspected led to the home's east wing.

The Executioner came through the door in time to see another battery of guards pour from a number of different rooms. Bolan dropped to a prone position, tucked the stock of the over-and-under tightly against his biceps, and triggered the M-203. The 40 mm HE grenade hit the back wall and blew on impact, driving debris and explosive gases into the rear of his would-be assailants. Those farthest from him took the majority of it, but those in forward positions were disoriented somewhat.

Bolan raised the M-16 and began picking off those guards still standing. When the area was clear and the echoes of autofire died away, the Executioner gave himself a thirty-second respite. He was surprised at what little resistance he'd encountered, and he couldn't keep it out of his mind that he'd been duped once more. Well, he would find out soon enough. The warrior got to his feet.

It was time to find Rivas.

JACK GRIMALDI SAW the chopper approaching and realized he had trouble before it got within range. As it drew nearer, the initial readings coming from his own avionics told him it was more than just an ordinary security aircraft. His first clue was the unmistakable warning hoot that signaled that the other aircraft had some type of missile lock on him. Grimaldi looked up in time to see a flash from the approaching chopper. He immediately veered up, taking the Kiowa straight into the air. The helicopter's powerful engine whined in protest as Grimaldi pushed the OH-58D to its maximum potential. Within seconds the Stony Man pilot knew he'd underestimated the capabilities of Emerson's connections.

As the chopper got closer, Grimaldi could see he was up against a variant of an AH-64. The Apache-style chopper raced beneath him, following in the smoking trail of the 2.75-inch antiaircraft rocket Grimaldi had barely avoided. He heard the chang-chang-chang of the 30 mm chain gun. He knew that weapon well, knew its capabilities and its range, because he'd used it many times himself.

Grimaldi swung the chopper 180-degrees and engaged the HUD weapons system. He studied all sides of the chopper to insure he was clear of any wires—as well as to verify he only had one enemy helicopter to deal with—and then scanned for the Apache. It was starting to swing about and try for a second pass on him. Grimaldi took his gunship down, getting it as low as possible. This tactic would force his opponent to do the same. Air combat had never been about who had the best weapons; it had always been about who was the most skilled at the stick. This was as true today as it had been during the aerial dogfights of World War I. Grimaldi could immediately tell he had that advantage, so it was important he took full control in this game of cat-and-mouse if he expected to survive.

Sure, the Apache was smaller and more maneuverable, and certainly it had him equally matched in the armament department. The question would come down to whether Grimaldi's opponent knew how to use those to the greatest combined tactical advantage. He was guessing the guy didn't, and in just a few moments he'd know for certain.

Grimaldi sailed across the tops of the trees, watching the infrared display while remaining ever cognizant of the Apache's 30 mm tracer rounds skimming all around him. Grimaldi reached a peak speed of 110 knots, then flipped and climbed a hundred feet rapidly before flipping the chopper on its side. The Apache zipped past and suddenly its pilot found himself the hunted and not the hunter.

The Stony Man pilot settled behind the chopper and triggered the 20 mm cannons in concert with a 7.62 mm minigun attached to the underside of the nose, a standard addition to the XM-27 armament kit he'd had the crew at Sam Houston install before their departure. Grimaldi was rewarded with sparks that signaled he'd hit his target, but the Apache didn't pull out or descend into the trees. The initial volley from Grimaldi had struck the opposition but not crippled it.

The Apache swung left, then right, its pilot implementing a standard zigzag to avoid taking further hits while he considered his next move. Grimaldi decided to plan his own strategy. The pilot slowed and then took the chopper up, climbing higher and higher as he rapidly approached maximum hovering ceiling. Grimaldi knew his underbelly would provide a tempting target, and all he had to do now was to wait for his opposition to take the bait.

He didn't have to wait long.

Grimaldi could hear the hooting once more while a buzzer sounded simultaneously to warn him any higher would cause a stall. He waited until the hooting went to a high-pitched tone, then he tipped the nose and headed directly for his target. As he descended, Grimaldi set the arming switch on the twin Stingers. He watched for the flash of the Apache's rocket pods, and as soon as he saw it, the Stony Man flier increased to maximum speed and dropped elevation so that his rate of descent was shallower than the enemy's climb angle.

The 2.75-inch rockets zipped just inches past his rotors.

Grimaldi waited it out a few seconds longer and when the HUD's infrared indicator went green he triggered both FIM-92 ATAS homing missiles. The Stingers roared away from the firing mounts and in the milliseconds that followed, Grimaldi realized he was holding his breath. A second went by, then two, and suddenly the night was lit by a brilliant flash of light as both missiles took the Apache in the belly. The chopper disintegrated under the power of the heavy ordinance and flaming wreckage rained toward the ground in a colorful display of Grimaldi's piloting skills.

The Stony Man ace let out deep sigh of relief, then pointed his chopper in the direction of the house. He could relish in the glory of his exploits later, but right now Mack Bolan could be in desperate need for help. Yeah, there would time to celebrate this victory later.

For now it was back to business as usual.

IT DIDN'T TAKE Mack Bolan long to clear the upper floors.

Outside of the two young girls he'd encountered, there hadn't been any further evidence of civilians. That pair had probably been special-order entertainment for the complement of male soldiers retained here under security. The pair had a look that told him they hadn't been in the business long. They should have been in some freshman college dorm, hitting the books and studying to improve their minds, instead of whoring it out with this kind. Bolan pushed such thoughts from his mind and concentrated on the mission at hand. He could only hope the grim sight he'd presented to them was enough of a wakeup call that they'd get out of their line of work and find safer and more socially productive occupations.

Bolan reached the first-floor landing and probed the main area of the house. He was about halfway across a large sitting room when a pair of guards came through a doorway and trained their weapons on him. The first and closer of the two leveled a shotgun in Bolan's direction, and the second jacked the charging handle on another AR-15 carbine.

The shotgun boomed in the bigger man's hands as

Bolan hit the floor and rolled behind cover. The buckshot buzzed over his head and peppered a nearby wall, a few striking a vase and shattering it. The pieces of jagged pottery fell off the table and left only an ugly base in their wake. Bolan heard rounds from the AR-15 smack the thick sofa he'd hidden behind, and a few even managed to penetrate the back and come dangerously close.

The Executioner yanked a DM-51 grenade from his harness, pulled the pin and lobbed the bomb over the couch. The AR-15 went silent and there were shouts of warning between the two men. A second later the grenade exploded and Bolan heard one of the men scream. The soldier rolled away and got to one knee about four feet from the edge of the sofa. He peered over an antique table and saw the shotgunner writhing on the ground, yelling at the top of his lungs, his body covered in blood.

The guy with the carbine was no longer visible, and Bolan suspected he was hiding behind the cover of an overstuffed chair on the opposite side of the room. The Executioner reached to the satchel at the small of his back and withdrew a 40 mm TH3 grenade. He popped it into the M-203, aimed toward a far corner of the room and stroked the launcher's trigger.

The incendiary bomb exploded on impact and showered the immediate area of impact with the oxygen-fed thermite mixture. Bolan could hear the shout of surprise followed by pain. He looked over the table once more and saw that his opponent had jumped up from where he'd been hiding. Flames engulfed his shirt and were quickly spreading. The skin on his face was charred in sections and his hair was awash in flame. His shouts of surprise turned to screams as he raced across the room while trying to beat out the flames. He got three-quarters of the way before Bolan cut him down with a 3-round burst from the M-16.

The flaming body hit the ground with a thump as a cloud of smoke rose, and with the acrid stench of burning human flesh. The Executioner fired another 3-round burst in the target to make sure he was dead. There was nothing ethical about letting someone suffer through that kind of horror. It was inhumane.

The enemy neutralized in that area, Bolan continued his search for Rivas.

CHAPTER TWENTY-TWO

Adriano Rivas had learned to survive in his business because he listened to the experts.

So was the case when Antonio Prospera entered the office and announced it was time to vacate the premises. It seemed an unidentified aircraft was approaching the house, and Prospera suspected it might be Stone. Only minutes before that, Rivas had been told of Stone's attack on the decoy facility and also of the air support he'd received. The ambush had turned into a miserable failure and, according to the reports, Stone was alive and well.

Rivas had made his phone calls and a meeting was scheduled at a retreat on the fringes of Huntsville.

"Is it possible to save any of the product?" he asked Prospera as he gathered his papers from the desk.

"I ordered the men to extract all the bags from the drums as soon as we arrived. They did as instructed and everything's accounted for. It's being loaded into vehicles as we speak. I'll save as much as I can of it. Right now, the most important thing is to get you to your meeting."

"What about Stone?"

"I'm leaving enough men behind to keep him busy for a while," Prospera replied. "Stone won't pose any problem, Adriano. Now please, it's time to go."

Rivas finished packing the papers into his briefcase and the pair descended to the basement in a hidden elevator. A reinforced tunnel led from a bunker in the basement of the house to a lift beneath a six-car garage. Two of the spots in the garage were reserved for armored Humvees that included extended bodies to support additional cargo, along with mounted Heckler & Koch HK-23E machine guns. When the lift had fully ascended into the dimly lit garage, Rivas took a minute to check the back of the Humvees and confirm the presence of the cocaine packages extracted from the barrels of oil. True to Prospera's words, they were stacked there neatly, and each Humvee was guarded by a quartet of Prospera's handpicked soldiers armed with full-auto assault rifles.

Once Rivas was satisfied, Prospera directed him to another spot in the garage where a specially equipped, black Mercedes-Benz awaited. Rivas climbed in back and was immediately flanked by two of the largest and most muscular bodyguards. Once they were situated, Prospera leaned his head through an open window and flashed his boss a reassuring grin.

"I'll be in the lead car," Prospera said. He tapped the top of the hood to demonstrate the solidity of the Mercedes-Benz. "This thing is lined with two inches of Kevlar. You'll be safe as long as you stay inside."

Prospera looked at his men in turn. "If anything happens, you stay in this car with the boss. Either of you leave him and I'll shoot you myself. Understand?"

The men nodded and then Prospera indicated they should roll up the window. Within a minute, the convoy moved out of the garage and onto the main road. Prospera occupied a silver Mustang GT that took point position in the convoy. Next was one of the Humvees, then Rivas's Mercedes, and finally the other Humvee bringing up the rear. The journey would be short, a ten-mile jaunt to the northern neighboring town of Pointblank.

The town boasted a small, obscure resort that catered to small groups of tourists who happened to stop along the way. Most of the resort's business stemmed from a tour bus group that made Pointblank a regular stop along its scenic route. For the most part, the place was deserted in the off season, and Rivas had used Emerson's influence to schedule a meeting with his associates. Surprisingly, none of them had heard of Emerson's death, and they were suspicious but accommodating when Rivas requested a meeting.

The drug lord considered the situation, and it didn't look good. He would give each of his new associates one chance to accept the uncut product, and if they refused then Rivas figured he could scratch that individual for any future business. Right now, more than anything else, Rivas needed men who would scratch his back. He could understand the inconvenience this placed on them, but he'd invested a lot of time and money in the deal, and he couldn't afford to watch it fall apart because others didn't want to participate.

Adriano Rivas was a man of vision and he always had been. He'd tried to treat all of his associates with the kind of respect he sought in return, but there were those who simply considered themselves above everyone else. Rivas didn't have time for men like that, because it usually meant those men didn't have vision. What Rivas wanted more than anything was to establish himself once more as the ultimate supplier in Colombia. The other small-time dealers would pay a piece of their action to Rivas to keep in business. That was the way of things in his business—the way of a survivor.

It was the only way for a visionary and survivor like Rivas.

Very shortly, Rivas would restore his empire and once more wield ultimate control on the drug supply into the United States. It had been vitally important for him to establish that foothold prior to execution of the Proctor Initiative. His plan to stall the Americans had worked; well, it had actually been Emerson's plan, but that hardly mattered now. The important thing was to consummate this transaction. Once he demonstrated his ability to provide good product, Rivas could squeeze out any competition. He couldn't remember any time where there was more riding on a purchase than now.

Adriano Rivas could literally taste the power that would soon be his. Soon. So very, very soon.

THE RECEIVER in Mack Bolan's ear buzzed for attention and Jack Grimaldi's voice filled his head. "Eagle One to Striker."

"Go, Eagle One," Bolan replied as he continued to search the ground floor.

"Ran into a bit of trouble, Sarge. Looks like we've got some ground bogeys that got away from us. I think it may be our target. Instructions?"

"I think you're right. I'm coming up empty-handed here," Bolan said. "Meet me out front in two minutes."

"Roger that."

The Executioner finished his sweep of the house and then headed for the front lawn. He waited at the edge of the portico on one knee as Grimaldi set the OH-58D down on the grass. Once the chopper was grounded, Bolan rushed to it and jumped aboard. As soon as he'd confirmed he was secure, Grimaldi lifted off and headed in a northerly direction. Bolan donned the headset that allowed him to communicate over the secure internal linkup.

"What's the story, Jack?" Bolan asked.

"Four vehicles left one of those outbuildings and headed north," Grimaldi said. "I guess it was a garage. I spotted them leaving on my way back."

"From where?" the Executioner asked.

"Let's just say I underrated my assessment of that security chopper," Grimaldi said. "He kept me busy for a bit."

"Glad you're still here with me," Bolan said with a chuckle.

"You and me both, Sarge," Grimaldi replied.

Bolan heard the Kiowa's powerful turbine engine noise increase and felt the chopper accelerate. The wind was relatively cooler here than it had been in Colombia and Ecuador, but the Executioner shook off the chill. The numbers were running down and he was thankful Grimaldi had been watchful of the surroundings in Coldspring. They were taking a chance following the convoy, perhaps it was another decoy, but they didn't have any other leads and it seemed unlikely that Rivas's men would turn and run. Once more he'd left crews behind to keep the Executioner busy while he made his escape. Well, there was nowhere to run now. Bolan was hot on his trail.

REG HUCKLEBERRY Wheaton cursed as he banged his knuckles against the engine of the rundown bus parked outside Pointblank Bed & Breakfast. The old scrap heap should have been retired a decade ago, but Ella Jean Shaker—owner of the PB & B and the most stubborn woman Wheaton had ever known—insisted on its regular upkeep and repair.

"Before too much longer I ain't going to be able to find no parts for it," Wheaton had told her one day.

"That don't matter," Shaker'd replied. "You just go on and fix it like I asked ya to. I always pay you whatever you ask me, don't I?"

Well, there was no way Wheaton could argue with her about that. So here he was, nine-thirty at night, tinkering with the dang thing when he felt like taking the wrench he was holding and beating the thing to scrap metal. Not that it wasn't too far from that now, although he couldn't have probably sold off the salvage to anybody if he'd wanted to. Instead he was forced to continue with the maintenance as if the hopeless junk-heap held some sentimental value for old widow Shaker.

Wheaton scraped his knuckles again and, letting out a curse, threw down the wrench, slammed the hood—not remembering that he hadn't replaced the radiator cap—and stomped toward the main meeting hall. Shaker had some important VIP types that were arriving soon for a business meeting, and by God he was going to tell her how he felt before she got too busy with that. He had feelings for her that he'd denied, but now the time was right. He'd waited long enough to get her notice, and he wasn't about to just stand around and keep taking all she'd dished out these past few years. After all, he wasn't no spry chicken anymore and neither was she.

Wheaton pushed through the side door and let his eyes rove over the meeting hall. There was a burnished table in the center dressed with a white linen tablecloth and fine china and silver. A cozy fire crackled in the large, stone fireplace against the back wall. The smell of fried chicken and cornbread wafted through the place, and for just a moment Wheaton thought he'd died and gone to heaven. Mixed into those smells was the undeniably sweet odor of freshly baked apple pie.

"Miss Ella!" Wheaton called, clomping across the old wooden floor in his work boots. Big feet ran in his family of big men. "Miss Ella, I'm needing to talk to you!"

There was no answer so Wheaton headed for the

kitchen, which was actually closed off by a heavy oak door that let very little sound through. That coupled with Shaker's difficulty hearing would have explained why she didn't answer him. He was halfway across the massive dining room when lights suddenly flashed through the row of casement windows lining the wall facing the parking lot.

Wheaton paused and let his eyes roam toward those lights. One vehicle pulled into the lot, then a second, then two more after that. Wheaton couldn't see any details, but he knew the company of business yokels was arriving in force now, and that meant he wouldn't have the time to say what he'd come to say if he didn't find the widow Shaker right damn quick.

Wheaton turned on his heel and marched the remaining distance to the oak door of the kitchen. He shoved it open and poked his head through, but he didn't see Shaker.

Where in tarnation did that woman sneak off to now? Wheaton thought.

The burly mechanic turned at the sound of the front entrance doors opening. Some big, well-dressed men came through the door followed by a tall man with dark hair and skin. Despite the fact it was nighttime, the man wore sunglasses. He was dressed in a pretty dapper suit, and Wheaton shook his head at the sight. Those big-city fellers certainly did like to show off.

"Evening, gents," Wheaton greeted them with a smile, his errand to find Shaker forgotten for the moment. Wheaton walked toward them and looked the nicely attired one up and down. "Those are some might fine duds you got on there, pal. You from Houston, or you visiting from out of town?"

"Out of town," the man replied gruffly.

The visitor's accent sounded Spanish, although Wheaton couldn't really be sure. He was only going by looks. "Well, why don't you come in and put your feet up. Ella Jean's going to be your hostess—" Wheaton scratched his head absently "—although I can't imagine where the heck she's gotten off to. I'll find her though, don't you never fear."

Wheaton turned and headed for the kitchen once more. Shaker had probably been taking out the garbage, or run to the outside storage shack for something. That woman never slowed down; where she got her energy was a complete mystery to Wheaton, and it was also an item of interest for him. Most gals her age would have slowed down quite a bit right now, settled for just sitting on their backsides and doing little else, but not Ella Jean Shaker. Nope, she just kept on a plugging along like that damn bus she insisted Wheaton keep up.

"Hold it!" a voice called behind Wheaton.

The old mechanic turned and saw that a new man had come through the front door. This one carried a briefcase. He was dressed as well as the first one, but he was darker and smaller. From his looks, Wheaton was now pretty sure they were Mexicans or those Puerto Rican fellers that occasionally found there way into town.

"What you say there, young feller?" Wheaton said.

"Who are you?" the man demanded.

"Well, my name's Reg if it's really important to you, but I don't see as how that's much of your concern. You here for some big business meeting?"

The man's gruff manner seemed to subside and he showed Wheaton twin rows of white, perfect teeth. "Yes… yes, of course. My apologies for being so abrupt."

The accent was so heavy that Wheaton could barely understand the guy. Yeah, definitely one of them Puerto Rican fellers.

The man continued. "I'm just tired. I've come a very long way and could use something to eat."

Wheaton delivered a perfunctory, two-finger salute and said, "Well, as I told your buddy there, I'd come in and put my feet up until I can find Mrs. Shaker. She'll be happy to tend to you."

Before anyone else spoke, more headlights flashed through the windows to signal additional vehicles were arriving. Now Wheaton knew the party would be in full swing in just a short time, and if he didn't find Ella Jean pretty quick he was going to have a whole handful of these city guys to deal with. That would put him up a crick without a paddle, since he didn't know the first thing about entertaining big mucky-mucks like them.

Wheaton nodded, turned, and walked toward the kitchen with added haste. As he pushed through the doors, there was a thunderclap followed by sudden warmth against his back. Wheaton spun on his heel in time to see every front window shatter as a bright flash lit the parking lot. In that brief moment where night became day, Wheaton saw the shadowy outlines of a dozen armed men clustered around the military-style vehicles, and it became immediately apparent this was no ordinary meeting.

The men inside reached beneath their suit coats and withdrew pistols, and the taller man in the suit pushed his counterpart in Wheaton's direction as he drew his own pistol. The old mechanic didn't need to see any more to know he shouldn't stick around. He took a few uncertain steps back and almost fell through the heavy oak door. He staggered beyond the doorway, then jumped forward and threw the small bolt to lock the door.

Wheaton turned to see Shaker coming indoors from outside.

"That won't hold them," he announced.

"What won't hold them?" she said. "What's going on?"

"I don't know, Ella Jean," Wheaton replied, "but I think we got ourselves a whole mess of trouble. I think we better get out of here and real quicklike."

As she moved closer to him and her face was illuminated by the lights of the kitchen, Wheaton could see Shaker's skin had paled and her lips had discolored. She was muttering something, but Wheaton couldn't understand a word of it.

"Well, quit spouting that gibberish and speak up!"

"There…there are men outside with guns," she said. "And there sounds like there might be some kind of helicopter coming toward us. What's happening, Reg?"

"You know as much as I do," he snapped. "Why for the love of Pete would you be asking *me* what's going on?"

To Wheaton's surprise, Shaker rushed to him and

threw her arms around his neck. He could feel her entire body trembling, and it was now apparent something had gone terribly wrong out there. Well, he'd wanted to be closer to her, although he couldn't imagine it would be quite this way. For a moment he wasn't sure what to do. Then he wrapped his arms around her and gently led her to a back door in the kitchen that would take them to the cellar. It ran the entire length of the meeting hall and at the far end there was a trapdoor that would take them up and out by the bus.

With any luck, that path would lead them to safety.

JACK GRIMALDI BROUGHT the chopper in low and under orders from Bolan fired an illumination flare to burst just above the low-slung building.

The flare effectively cast light on the situation at hand, giving both men a clear look at the picture. A sports car and luxury sedan were parked in the front lot along with a pair of Humvees. A cluster of well-armed men stood outside the vehicles in a ring, obviously ready to die where they stood to protect the cargo.

Just as the flare reached maximum intensity, Bolan saw two new vehicles pull off the access road and crunch to a halt on the gravel parking lot with pine logs used to mark the individual spots. The place was some type of meeting lodge with a second building lined with doors. It was obviously a bed-and-breakfast of some kind, which meant there might be civilians to consider. Bolan would have to execute a surgical strike.

Grimaldi accelerated out of his temporary hover and

headed for the rooftop as men climbed into the back of the twin Humvees and manned the mounted machine guns. Bolan could hear the intensity of autofire as Grimaldi cleared the roof line and took them out of immediate danger. The wood-shingle roof had about a twelve-degree slope, and its coarse surface would give the Executioner enough grip to keep from tumbling off.

"Jack, get close to the roof!" he commanded.

Grimaldi acknowledged the order even as he swung the Kiowa into position, maneuvering the chopper within five yards of the roof. Bolan slung his M-16/M-203 combo, and then jumped from the skid onto the angled roof. The chopper lifted away as he scrambled up the roof and studied the scene over its peak. The Executioner saw that the gunners had abandoned their weapons and were now positioning the vehicles farther from the building to increase their field of fire. Luckily, they were bringing themselves right into Bolan's sights.

The warrior drew his Desert Eagle and braced the .44 Magnum pistol on the downslope of the roof in a Weaver's grip. As the first Humvee rolled into view, Bolan leveled his gaze down the slide and centered the three-dot sight picture on the driver's windshield.

Bolan squeezed the trigger.

CHAPTER TWENTY-THREE

The Humvee's windshield exploded under the impact of the Executioner's first .44 Magnum round. The resulting decimation of the driver's skull beyond that windshield was visible to Bolan even in the pair of weak overhead lights illuminating the parking lot. Blood and gray matter splattered throughout the interior.

The vehicle continued backward and bounced over a massive log bordering the parking lot. The rear tires continued into a culvert separating the log from the street, and the vehicle ground to a halt. Bolan saw movement inside the Humvee and waited for the opportune moment. It came a short time later when a pair of Rivas's guards pried and pushed their way through a side window.

Bolan shot the first one through the neck, the blood visibly spurting from his carotid artery. The gunman spun and clutched at his throat, and the look of surprise was evident on his comrade's face even from that distance. The soldier unleashed another .44 Magnum round. The 300-grain bullet smashed through the second target's side and tore a massive gully in his abdomen. The man's intestines spilled through the opening and he dropped to his knees, his screams audible even above the echo of the big Desert Eagle's booming reports. Bolan finished the job with a head shot.

The Executioner's attention was now drawn to the second Humvee that hove into view. He quickly holstered the Desert Eagle and switched to the M-16/M-203. Bolan didn't bother to engage the leaf sight, since the vehicle was relatively close. With muzzle trained just above the vehicle, Bolan triggered the grenade launcher. It kicked like a shotgun against his shoulder and a moment later he was rewarded with an explosive blast that tore through the Humvee. The diesel tank caught and the gel-like fuel splashed across the hood.

Bolan could see some large, brown-paper packages bounce out of the vehicle. The Humvees had obviously been the transport vehicles for Rivas's shipment. The Executioner locked a fresh 40 mm HE round into the breech and slammed it home. Ten seconds later, the mangled Humvee was little more than a charred, flaming shell.

The Executioner loaded another grenade and was prepared to destroy the ditched Humvee when he was distracted by a burst of autofire that doused him with wood chips from the roof shingles. Bolan rolled away from the fire, then slid down the roof until he'd reached the edge. He glanced in both directions to make sure he was clear, then dropped to the sandy ground at the rear of the lodge hall.

Two gunmen rounded the corner as Bolan regained his feet. He leveled the M-16 and triggered a full-auto burn that cut a figure eight across the pair, nearly cutting both of them in two. Blood and bits of wet tissue exploded outward in a gory spray and they collapsed to the ground at nearly the same moment. A third man peaked around the corner and tried to draw a bead on Bolan, but the Executioner was already in motion. He shoulder-rolled away from the short burst triggered by his opponent and came to one knee. He returned the fire with a burst of his own, then followed with the 40 mm grenade originally intended for the other Humvee.

A fiery explosion engulfed the enemy gunner along with two more of his comrades who had rushed to help him. The blast lifted the men and tossed them several feet downrange. Body parts rained down in every direction along with large chunks of earth.

Bolan jumped to his feet and whirled in time to see one of the sedans that had arrived shortly after the show started. The Executioner raised the M-16/M-203 to his shoulder as he flipped the selector to 3-shot bursts. He triggered a trio of 5.56 mm rounds, followed by a second 3-round burst and a third. He was rewarded with sparks from the gasoline tank, which ignited fumes. The trunk erupted into the air and the sudden introduction of intense heat melted the rear tires into bubbling mush. The vehicle's back end dropped as the transaxle and differential dropped free and skidded to a halt. Passengers jumped from the vehicle, human torches that lit the night, their clothing and hair awash with bright orange flames.

A new storm of automatic rifle fire buzzed around Bolan, and the warrior grabbed the cover of thick tree. He crouched with his back to the tree, dropped the magazine from the M-16 and replaced it with a fresh one. He also loaded the M-203 with another HE grenade and then considered his options. He had undoubtedly surprised his enemy—they hadn't expected such a swift and sudden assault.

Rivas would have to make his stand here and now, and if he stood any chance of coming out of it alive, Bolan knew Rivas would have to find innocent hostages. He couldn't hope to escape intact by any other means—the Executioner had just demonstrated that with the sedan that probably belonged to one of Rivas's associates. So all Bolan could do now was to keep the enemy's head down and wait for Rivas to make his move.

THE MINUTE THE NIGHT lit up and the sound of chopper blades reached his ears, Prospera and his men formed around Adriano Rivas and ushered him toward the door through which the old man had disappeared.

A pair of Prospera's men led the way, and another pair took up the rear, sandwiching their boss and Rivas between them. When they reached the oak door, they found it secured. One of the men turned to look at Prospera, who only waved at the door with an impa-

tient expression. The big thug turned, shrugged and
cleared the solid but ineffective barricade with a well-
placed kick.

The group moved inside, the bodyguards fanning out
with their weapons tracking the long, narrow kitchen.
The old man was nowhere to be seen, and the back door
looked as if it was shut securely. The man wouldn't have
gone out that way, not with all the shooting and explosions happening. Prospera squeezed past the pair on
point and walked quickly the entire length of the kitchen.
He found a door with an old-fashioned wooden latch in
the wall perpendicular to the kitchen door leading to the
exterior. He noticed the exterior door had a bolt slid in
place, which confirmed nobody had left that way.

Prospera gestured with his pistol for the others to follow, and when they'd reached him he opened the door
and jerked his head to indicate the point men should retake their original positions. They followed orders silently and Prospera returned to Rivas's side. No matter
what happened, he would make sure his boss got
through this in one piece. Anybody that stood in their
way would get killed.

Beyond the door were narrow concrete steps leading
into a low-hanging cellar. The six men squeezed their
way through a narrow walkway, the area to their right
crammed with shelves of canned goods and other food-
stuffs wherever they could be fit between thick, concrete
piers supporting 2×8 floor joists. Ahead of them, Prospera could hear the sound of hushed voices echoing in
the cramped confines of the cellar.

The Colombian enforcer grinned as an idea crept from the shadowy recesses of his mind and began to take form.

REG WHEATON BEGAN to feel the well of hope spring eternal as his weakened eyes spotted steps at the end of the dark, dank cellar. Those steps signified more than a way out of these creepy surroundings; they signified freedom. Even within the relative safety offered by the cellar, Wheaton could think of other places he'd rather be. The noise outside hadn't subsided; in fact, it sounded as if it was getting worse above them. Explosions sounded more frequently, and there was no mistaking the sound of automatic weapons fire.

Wheaton knew that sound all too well. He'd served as a U.S. Marine during the Korean War, and he'd known his own share of situations not too dissimilar from the one in which he presently found himself. The difference between then and now was that he'd been armed, and had a buddy along with him, not a scared woman who was too damn obstinate for her own good at times.

"For heaven's sake, Reg, slow down! I'm not twenty anymore, you know."

"Miss Ella, you won't live to see your golden years, either, if you don't keep up with me," Wheaton replied.

"I'm doing the best I can."

"You'd best do better and quit worrying about arguing with me. Take the lead out, woman!"

"Now you listen here, I won't have you—"

Wheaton whirled on her and stuck a finger in her face, something he wouldn't have dared do prior to that moment. If there was one thing he didn't have time for it was stopping to argue with an overly contentious woman like Ella Shaker.

"Now you listen good, missus. I have no intention of standing here to debate with you. We can argue later where it's safe. Right now let's just figure out a way to get out of here with our skins intact, okay?"

Wheaton turned and continued to the stairs. He climbed a few steps until he could reach the doors, prayed the groundskeepers had forgotten to put the lock on it again and pulled on the rope. With some effort, he managed to push one door up and outward. It landed on the ground outside with a dull thud. Wheaton cocked an ear and listened—it sounded as though most of the shooting had stopped, and what occasional gunfire he did hear was distant.

He didn't bother to open the other door. He reached down and grabbed Shaker's hand, nearly pulling her off her feet as she scampered up the steps upon his urging. Once they were above ground, Wheaton slammed the doors closed. He searched frantically for the lock but was unable to find it in the darkness. Well, there was no time to look for it. Holding tightly to Shaker's hand, Wheaton hustled toward the bus. They could hide inside until the sheriff came, which probably wouldn't be long with all the racket going on.

Wheaton helped Shaker aboard and then climbed into the bus, holding on to the faded chrome railing that lined the steps. He closed the single folding door and urged Shaker to move to the back. The two took a rear seat and hunkered down.

MACK BOLAN WAITED only long enough behind the cover of the tree to catch his breath, then sprinted across the narrow side of the meeting lodge and headed for the front. The tactic was risky, but under the circumstances it made the most sense. The last thing the enemy would expect him to do was head back into the thick of things, and maybe with luck he could reach the other Humvee. While the vehicle was out of commission, Bolan figured the machine gun he'd spotted couldn't hurt any.

The Executioner reached the front of the hall unscathed and took cover behind one of the sedans. Armed men were moving in and out of the front entrance while others moved from vehicle to vehicle and waited anxiously for some sort of target to present itself. It was going to get crowded fast.

Bolan keyed the microphone on his transceiver. "Striker to Eagle One."

"Go, Striker," Grimaldi replied immediately.

"Where are you?"

"Circling in the north, heading back your way."

"I need a diversion and a loud one, Eagle One. Got any help?"

"What's your position?"

Bolan gave it to him.

"I'm coming in on you now, Striker," Grimaldi replied. "Get clear."

"Roger and out here," Bolan said.

The sound of the Kiowa's rotors reverberated through Bolan's ears swiftly and suddenly. He burst from cover and sprinted for the Humvee as the chopper whined to a hover exactly a hundred yards to the west of the front-side crew's position. They swung their weapons in Grimaldi's direction, totally oblivious to the Execution-er's movements.

Hardly a shot was fired before the Stony Man pilot opened up with a concert of his own. He began with a fanfare, triggering one of the Hellfire missiles for effect. The high-powered ordnance struck a point thirty meters forward of the front entrance. Flame and superheated gas washed over the area, cooking the flesh of those within its deadly reach. The concussion shattered the windows on the vehicles, and a Mercedes-Benz blew apart at the seams given its proximity to the blast.

Those that managed to escape the fury of Grimaldi's opening salvo found themselves pinned between 20 mm cannon fire and the incessant chattering of the HK-23E machine gun now under the Executioner's skillful tute-lage. Bolan and Grimaldi decimated the survivors with a cross fire of high-velocity slugs that tore flesh from bone and cut the remnant of Rivas's army to ribbons.

As the last of the heavy resistance fell, Bolan clicked the mike to signal Grimaldi he could back off. The pilot obeyed instantly, lifting up and away and moving into a circular pattern while shining a spotlight on the area. Bolan continued to hammer the few survivors with au-tofire. The German-made machine gun spit 5.56 mm

NATO slugs at a cyclic rate of 750 rounds per minute and a muzzle velocity of 950 meters per second. The enemy felt the wrath of the Bolan blitz, and in that minute the Executioner sent them an agonizing message. In that brief span of time, Bolan poured out vengeance for men like Curtis Kenney and the others of the Quail Group, and that unyielding punishment was clearly a reminder of what happened to those who preyed on the helpless.

When the belt-fed gun went dry, Bolan dropped to the ground and moved away from the Humvee at an unhurried pace. When he was fifty yards distant, Bolan turned, leveled the over-and-under and triggered the M-203 grenade launcher. The bomb sailed in a graceful arc and landed dead center on the Humvee. The vehicle's tires left the ground as white-hot flames licked hungrily at its exposed interior. Within that fiery furnace burned the last of Adriano Rivas's white death. There would be no cocaine distributed to Americans this night.

The Executioner had made certain of that.

THE TWO POINT GUARDS pushed against the cellar doors and quickly broke through to the surface.

Prospera followed after the pair and tracked the area with his pistol. They had heard the massive explosions coming from the front of the lodge hall. None of them had to perform an inspection to know what carnage they would find there. The flames were reaching higher into the sky as gas tanks on the vehicles heated up and triggered secondary explosions. The night was lit with a bonfire of destruction, and the smell of death in the form of burning flesh and oily fumes consumed by an unquenchable fire lingered in the air.

Prospera helped Rivas up the cellar stairs and the men formed a human gauntlet around him. A bus immediately ahead of them called for attention, and Prospera ordered his men to inspect it. He didn't see the old man, but if he was close by Prospera figured he would be hiding. The man couldn't have gone far very quickly, and the bus seemed the most likely hiding place.

Prospera's men forced open the bus door and scrambled up the steps. The kept low as their training dictated, pistols out and ready to meet any opposition. Less than a minute elapsed before the two men shouted for their boss to come aboard. In the flickering light cast by flames through the bus windows Prospera watched his men pull the old man from where he hid in the rearmost seat. The Colombian enforcer smiled when he discovered there was a woman hiding along with the old man.

The old man's eyes suddenly registered anger. Prospera shouted in an attempt to warn the old man not to resist, but it was too late. The man turned and slugged one of Prospera's bodyguards. The blow didn't really affect the heavyweight soldier that much, but it caused enough confusion to set off the man's partner. Prospera shouted a second time but again it wasn't in time.

The second guard triggered his pistol and in the scuffle his hand was jarred. The bullet missed the old man by an inch and instead struck the old woman in the right upper chest. Shock filled the elderly woman's features as she staggered backward and landed hard on the seat. The old man turned with a surprised cry and bent over to help her.

Prospera stepped forward and grabbed the man by the collar. "You are a stupid man! You can drive this bus?"

The old man turned to look in Prospera's eyes. It was an expression of pure hatred, but it was coupled with fatigue and defeat. He had no fight left in him, and no longer any reason to resist. He knew that to continue to struggle would do nothing but result in his death and perhaps the death of the woman, as well.

He turned on the man who fired the gun and slapped him across the face. "You think there's any skill in killing old women?" He waved at the woman and said, "She isn't even armed, you fool! Get up front and protect Mr. Rivas." He looked at the man's partner and said, "You, too! Before I shoot you myself!"

The men obeyed, although the one Prospera had slapped was visibly red even in the dim interior of the bus. He didn't give a damn. The man deserved to be embarrassed in front of his peers. Chico Arauca wouldn't have dared tolerate such unprofessional conduct, and Prospera wasn't about to put up with it, either. He grabbed the old man by the collar and shoved him up the aisle of the bus.

"Drive!" he said, pushing the man roughly into the driver's seat.

The old man complied, although he hesitated as he reached for the ignition switch. "I don't know if it's going to start, mister."

Prospera put the barrel of the pistol the old man's head and replied, "You should pray to whatever god you choose that it *does*."

The old man nodded with perfect understanding as he engaged the switch to power the batteries, depressed the squeaky clutch and pressed the starter button. The engine sputtered and coughed twice, started, then died. The man glanced at Prospera who disengaged the safety on his pistol to reinforce his earlier point. The man pushed the starter a second time and breathed a sigh of relief when the engine started and remained running.

Prospera smiled as his prisoner struggled to force the gearshift into gear. The transmission ground against the maneuver, but after a few pumps of the clutch it clanked into first. The bus lurched into motion and nearly threw Prospera off his feet. He checked to his right to insure Rivas was already seated and then took the seat immediately behind the old man.

"Miss Ella needs a hospital," the man told Prospera.

"You will worry about driving," Prospera said. "Once we are away from here, we will leave you alive. Now don't speak again, or I will simply kill you here and drive myself. Do you understand?"

"Yes," the old man whispered. "I understand."

As they jerked into second gear, Prospera looked out the window to his right and saw a shadowy wraith of a figure firing a grenade launcher at one of the Humvees. Rivas saw the spectral vision simultaneously and both men inhaled noisily. It was Colonel Stone! Prospera began to curse under his breath, angry that he'd been robbed of the opportunity to deal with the American bastard once and for all.

CHAPTER TWENTY-FOUR

As the wreckage rained upon the Humvee's smoldering shell, the receiver in Bolan's ear buzzed for attention.

"Striker, here."

"Striker, Eagle One. I've got a single ground bogey departing off your six, civilian make and very old. The enemy might be trying to escape."

"Hold off, Eagle One," Bolan said as he whirled to inspect the taillights rapidly dwindling with sound of the vehicle's engine. "There may be innocents on board. Come down on this locale and we'll pursue by air."

"Acknowledged."

Bolan shielded his eyes from the dust, ignoring the gravelly sand that pelted his exposed skin. He rushed to the Kiowa as soon as it touched down and a moment later Grimaldi was lifting off once more. Bolan tried not to let exhaustion creep over him. What he wanted to do more than anything was just lie back and succumb to the fog threatening to overtake his sleep-deprived mind and body, but he disciplined himself to remain alert. For all he knew the lives of innocent people hung in the balance.

As they lifted over the treetops, Bolan reached for the headset and confirmed with Grimaldi he was on the air.

"Infrared shows a total of eight heat signatures," Grimaldi reported. "It looks like some of them are packing firearms. There's one in the very back that's giving off quite a bit of external heat, but internal body heat is abnormal. If I had to venture a guess, I'd say it's someone bleeding, Sarge."

The Executioner considered the news. Okay, so one or more hard cases had taken a hostage and were now attempting to escape. He trusted the pilot's assessment regarding a bleeder. It would make sense. Bolan had known this might turn into a real possibility when he opted for a blitz play on the lodge hall, but he'd hoped to confine any danger to the enemy.

The warrior keyed the switch on his headset. "Jack, we got any open road ahead?"

There was a brief pause, then, "Got about a mile stretch coming up in less than a minute with nothing but field on either side. Then it gets thick enough there's a chance they could lose us."

"As soon as we've made that clearing, take me down as close as you can."

"What are you going to do?"

"Hitch a ride," the Executioner said with a grin, then pulled off the headset and hooked up to the winch.

Bolan swung into open air and took a deep breath. He kept his hand on the brake pressed to the small of his back. A mile at that speed wasn't much time. He'd have approximately seventy-five seconds, maybe ninety tops, to get down to the level of the bus and touch down on the roof. He'd also have to give Grimaldi enough time to lift away with the winch line to avoid catching it on a telephone line or bridge.

No, that wouldn't do. He'd have to rely solely on the freefall and manual brake to do the work. He couldn't risk endangering Grimaldi or the chopper. He thought about telling the pilot his plan, but he decided against it. Wouldn't make much difference anyway, since Grimaldi would pull up when he had to, and he wouldn't have anyway of gauging Bolan's position or even doing anything about it if he could.

The chopper made a rapid descent. Bolan focused on a point just forward of the bus's taillights and timed his descent. Fifteen seconds elapsed and the Executioner gauged he was halfway to the rooftop.

Thirty-five seconds: the roof of the bus was now visible to him.

Fifty seconds: the roar of the bus engine reached his ears, protesting against the speed being coaxed from the ancient engine.

Sixty seconds: Bolan's feet brushed the roof of the bus and he disengaged the quick connects.

The chopper lifted away and the soldier expelled a breath as he realized he was lying upright on the roof of the bus.

Bolan took just a moment to thank whatever deity might be listening he had survived the maneuver, then dropped into a crouch. Wind and a passel of bugs pelted Bolan's face. He turned his back to the assault and considered the best way to make entry. A frontal attack would be the least likely but the most suicidal since any opposition aboard the bus would be facing that direction. Entry through a side window would be impossible.

That left the rear door.

Bolan knelt and checked the action on the Desert Eagle, then holstered it and performed a similar inspection of the Beretta 93-R. He then got to his belly and crawled to the rear. Keeping his body flat, he pivoted on his stomach and swung his legs over and down, dropping quickly onto the rear bumper while keeping a vise-like grip on the roof.

Bolan reached for the rear door handle, yanked downward and pulled it open with a single motion. He quickly swung his legs inside and propelled the rest of his body after them with the impetus. A gunner seated two seats forward turned with surprise but the Executioner already had a fistful of the Colombian thug's shirt. Bolan yanked him out of the seat and pulled him close, which took the man off center. The soldier then reversed direction with a backward shove that sent the unbalanced man tumbling to the aisle floor. His weight did the rest as he performed an involuntarily backward roll and continued through the open door. Bolan never heard his body hit the pavement, but the visual was enough to tell the story.

A second guard clawed for hardware and produced the pistol in time to get off a single, wild shot that missed the Executioner by nearly a foot. Bolan grabbed the gunner's extended arm at the wrist and shoved it away from him while bringing his palm in the opposing direction. There was an audible pop as the move displaced the man's elbow. The gunman wailed with pain, but Bolan stopped it short with a karate chop to his windpipe. The rigid bone crushed the man's larynx. Blood bubbled at the corners of his mouth as he dropped to his knees.

Bolan whipped the Beretta into play and shot a third bodyguard at point-blank range in the forehead. Blood and brain matter splattered the face and neck of the man behind him. Beneath that gory mask the soldier recognized the grim features of Adriano Rivas. The Executioner readjusted his aim and was leaning back on the trigger when something jarred his arm. The shot missed Rivas and instead spiderwebbed the left side of the windshield.

The Executioner suddenly found himself being shoved into the seat by a massive Colombian. The man tried to pistol whip the Executioner, but Bolan moved his head to one side and the butt of the thug's pistol smashed the metal of the window frame instead of its intended target. The soldier brought up a knee and connected with his opponent's groin. A sharp exhale and muffled cry escaped his enemy's lips. He followed with a double-elbow strike to the chin. The thug's lower jaw cracked and dislocated. Blood sprayed down the front of Bolan's fatigues, but he ignored it as he reached for the Desert Eagle. He jammed the pistol against the enemy's abdomen and squeezed the trigger twice. The heavy-caliber slugs punched through vital organs and exited through the spine. Bolan swung his legs back and propelled his body weight forward to toss the heavy corpse aside.

The bus suddenly lurched to a crawl and everyone aboard was thrown to the floor. The Executioner scraped his chin on the cracked linoleum of the aisle as the bus swerved and started to jounce and bounce on a downward course of uncertain doom. Seconds seemed like minutes as the bus continued along that roughshod trail, but finally the ride ended at the bottom of a shallow gully with a tremendous splash.

Bolan shook the cobwebs from his head, his blurred vision looking ahead to see water filling the forward area of the bus. The vehicle was canted at greater than fifty degrees. He turned to see that they'd somehow lost the rear door.

The Executioner pulled himself into an upright position and realized in that moment he'd dropped the Desert Eagle. Before he could search for it, something metallic flashed in front of his face. Bolan reacted with instincts born from years of training.

It saved his life.

He deflected the hand holding a knife with his left palm and caught the wrist with his right. A struggle ensued as the Executioner fought to clear the fogginess from his head. The hot breath of his opponent seemed to Bolan like the fiery breath of a Satanic dragon dispatched straight from Hell, and he did everything he could not to fall victim to its influences.

As his vision cleared and a surge of adrenaline restored his strength, Bolan realized he was battling against a skilled knife fighter. Neither of them had the advantage of environment, but the Executioner realized he had innocents to consider. That took precedence above all else, and the thought they might be compromised by this precarious situation gave Bolan the additional edge he needed to gather his wits and fight for not only his survival but theirs, as well.

Bolan twisted sideways to increase leverage and pulled the arm wielding the knife past him. He then curled his other arm under his opponent's left armpit and slid the flat of his hand against the man's right cheek. The soldier continued the twisting motion until he'd stretched his adversary's head in the opposite direction to the knife. Bolan then rocked forward on his heel and slid onto his buttocks, letting his feet slide down the aisle until they rested against the front dash. The move dropped the head of Bolan's opponent below the waterline, which was continuing to rise.

His enemy began to struggle, but Bolan held firm against the resistance. He had gravity and weight going for him. Slowly but steadily the movements of his adversary began to weaken and became less frantic. Finally they stilled.

The Executioner released his hold and shoved the corpse away from him. He slipped and scrambled to the driver's compartment and reached beneath the water to pull the limp form of the old man he'd seen driving from behind the wheel. The Executioner pulled the man to the surface and began to administer mouth-to-mouth rescue breathing. Twenty seconds elapsed, then thirty, and then Bolan was rewarded with a cough and gasp as the man regurgitated water.

Bolan put his ear to the man's chest, nodded with satisfaction at the rapid but steady heartbeat in his ears, then dragged the unconscious man to the rear opening and hauled him through. The warrior then turned his attention to the elderly woman lying on the floor, her frail body wedged between the uprights of the seats. He put two fingers against her neck and searched for pulse.

He didn't find any. Bolan experienced a sinking feeling. He was about to pull the woman's body from the seats when she suddenly opened her eyes and stared at him, demonstrating just how very much alive she was.

"What the heck you going to do there, young man, let us both drown? Die of exposure to this chill, I suppose?"

Bolan couldn't resist a grin. "I thought you were dead."

"It'll take more than some young upstarts to kill me."

"I don't doubt it," the Executioner replied with a chuckle.

Bolan noticed the wound in the woman's shoulder and yanked a compress from the medical pouch attached to his web belt. He quickly dressed the wound and then carefully extracted the woman from the seats. Bolan climbed through the rear and hauled her far enough up the gully to insure she was out of danger, then returned for the elderly man. As Bolan placed the old guy next to the woman and nodded to reassure her he was alive, the Executioner detected the unmistakable snap of twig.

Bolan whirled to see a figure moving hurriedly away from his position. He couldn't tell who it was but a quick look at the bus told him he hadn't accounted for the final status of one occupant: Adriano Rivas. It had to be him.

The soldier scrambled to his feet and headed in pursuit. He called for Grimaldi to put out some illumination, but the pilot didn't respond. Most likely the transmitter had become waterlogged and failed. Bolan pushed himself, his leg muscles screaming that they had reached the end of their endurance. But the Executioner had come too far and seen too many sacrifices to let Rivas escape now. He had a duty to end this once and for all, and that's just what he was going to do.

Bolan's feet crunched on the dried foliage and leaves, and he quickly saw he was gaining ground. Rivas was slipping and sliding, trying to outdistance Bolan, but the Executioner had the scent of his quarry and there was no way he'd allow himself to be thrown off the trail.

Rivas suddenly dropped from sight. It wasn't until Bolan was almost on top of the hole that he stopped short and realized what had happened. He looked down and saw that the Colombian had fallen through a set of boards into a pit about twelve feet deep.

Bolan watched as Rivas climbed about halfway up before the soft dirt around the sides of the hole gave way and he descended to the bottom. The Colombian drug lord looked up and stared into Bolan's eyes, but the warrior kept his expression impassive. It looked like this time fate had truly dealt a hand in Bolan's favor.

"We have a score to settle, Rivas," the Executioner stated.

"It would seem any score we have is already settled, Stone," Rivas muttered.

"Hardly," Bolan replied. "I've had my fill with your kind, Rivas. You pollute everything you touch. You have the stink of greed and filth on you. Every dollar you've touched was blood money. You're just another scum-sucking lowlife who cares for nothing and nobody."

Rivas laughed mockingly. "Who the fuck are you, Stone? I mean…who are you, really?"

"It's not who I am that's important, Rivas. It's *what* I am."

"Huh?"

"I'm your judgment. I'm the one appointed to make sure you account for all the pain and grief you've caused. It's my job to make sure the American people no longer have to worry about you filling their veins with that junk you deal. It's over. And now it's atone-ment time."

"Go ahead and kill me," Rivas said. "I'm not afraid to die."

"Glad to hear it," Bolan replied with an icy smile. He reached to his web belt and detached the last DM-51 grenade in his arsenal. "Of course, there are lots of ways to die. And at the moment, this just happens to be the most convenient."

Bolan wrapped his teeth around the pin and yanked it free, watching as Rivas's eyes grew wide. The man began to plead with the Executioner, but the soldier wouldn't hear it. His senses were dulled by his belief no deal could settle such a bloody score. There had been too much loss and depravity doled out through this man's hands. Men like Rivas couldn't be rehabilitated. He'd gone too far to change his ways now, and he didn't deserve to live out the remainder of his days in a cushy American prison. The Colombians wouldn't want him back, and Ecuador's people would simply dump it in America's lap to handle.

And with the simple relaxing of his hand, Bolan delivered the judgment Rivas so richly deserved.

EPILOGUE

Stony Man Farm, Virginia

Mack Bolan stared out the window of the farmhouse onto the vast and peaceful grounds arrayed in front of him.

A week had been ample time to give his injured leg a chance to mend some, not to mention a respite from sheer exhaustion. In just under eighty hours, Bolan had put an end to the empire of Adriano Rivas and his associates, as well as averted multiple disasters for America. The export of oil had begun immediately and gas prices were already dropping at a remarkable rate.

"The President says we'll be at the lowest prices we've seen in two years by the end of the month," Brognola reported.

The fact he could do something to take the pressure off the American people was enough reward for the Executioner, because they sure as hell weren't going to pin a medal on him. His activities had drawn quite a bit of attention both at the civilian and political level, although Bolan wasn't sure how it could have been avoided.

Fortunately, the battle in Coldspring had been too remote to attract attention. The helicopter explosion over the Huntsville State Forest Preserve was explained away as a faulty fuel tank, and the activities in the neighboring town of Pointblank were attributed to a militia going hog-wild during a drinking binge.

Bolan took a sip of coffee and focused on the peace and solitude. He didn't often get the chance to watch the stars sparkle against a sky of deep amethyst. The fringe of a blue line bordered the irregular treetops scattered across the Blue Ridge Mountain range, a signal that dawn approached.

He enjoyed these brief respites from the hellgrounds, as few and far between as they were. Tomorrow was another day. For now he'd just relax and smell the roses. He figured it was as close to heaven as he'd ever get.

JAMES AXLER

DEATH LANDS

Shatter Zone

In this raw, brutal world ruled by the strongest and the most vicious, an unseen player is manipulating Ryan and his band, luring him across an unseen battle line drawn in the dust outside Tucson, Arizona. Here a local barony becomes the staging ground for a battle unlike any other, against a foe whose ties to preDark society present a new and incalculable threat to a fragile world. Ryan Cawdor is the only man living who stands between this adversary's glory…and the prize he seeks.

Available September 2006 wherever you buy books.

James Axler
Outlanders®

**An ancient Chinese emperor
stakes his own dark claim to Earth…**

HYDRA'S RING

A sacred pyramid in China is invaded by what appears to be a ruthless
Tong crime lord and his army. But a stunning artifact and a desperate
summons for the Cerberus exiles put the true nature of the looming battle
into horrifying perspective. Kane and his rebels must confront a four-
thousand-year-old emperor, an evil entity as powerful as any nightmare
now threatening humankind's future….

Available November 2006 wherever you buy books.

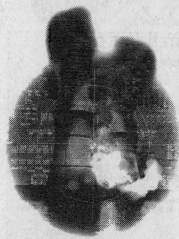

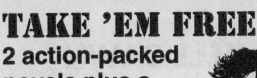

TAKE 'EM FREE

2 action-packed novels plus a mystery bonus

NO RISK
NO OBLIGATION TO BUY